Rave Review SMITTEN

"Crush is an unforgettable, stimulating romance that will have you reeling in astonishment when the unthinkable strikes in Cami's world! Which of these characters will come out of this deceitful web carefully designed by this wonderfully talented author, Lacey Weatherford! I give this book my thumbs up!" ~*Jessica Johnson, Book End 2 Book End*

"Ms. Weatherford has done what I thought impossible and given us a sequel that is just as enjoyable, if not *more* enjoyable than the first book. With *Smitten,* Lacey Weatherford has cemented her place among my favorite authors. I can't wait to see what she comes up with next!" ~*Melissa Simmons, Girls Heart Books*

"Lacey Weatherford keeps the surprises coming. Just when you think the story ended at SMITTEN, she hits us with a semi truck, POW, with another fantastic and explosive storyline. Makes you fall in #LOVE with the characters all over again!" ~*Lisa Markson, The Paranormal Bookworm*

"Dylan and Cami have done it again! They made me laugh, cry, and turned my heart into a puddle of goo! "LOVE" is the best book in this series yet, and I have enjoyed every step of the journey this series took me on*!"* ~ *Christina Racich, Pretty Lil Page Turners*

"You thought you had a #CRUSH. You thought you were #SMITTEN. Prepare your heart for full blown #LOVE as Dylan swoons his way to the top of your book boyfriend list!" *~Belinda Boring, Bestselling Author of the Mystic Wolves Series*

OTHER BOOKS BY LACEY WEATHERFORD

Of Witches and Warlocks series:
The Trouble with Spells
The Demon Kiss
Blood of the White Witch
The Dark Rising
Possession of Souls
Book of Shadows series:
Fire & Ice
Chasing Nikki series:
Chasing Nikki
Finding Chase
Crush Series:
Crush
Smitten
Love
A Fringe Novel:
Tell Me Why
Anthology:
A Midsummer Night's Fling
Faery Kissed
Novellas:
Over the River and Through the Woods

Sequel to #1 Bestsellers,
CRUSH & SMITTEN!

Dylan,
I Love You!
Cami

USA TODAY Bestselling Author

LOVE

Lacey Weatherford

LOVE Copyright © 2014 Moonstruck Media and Lacey Weatherford

Edited by Kim Swain, Red Line Editing

ALL RIGHTS RESERVED

Published by

Moonstruck Media

Arizona

Without limiting the rights under copyright reserved above, no part of this publication may be reproduced, stored in or introduced into a retrieval system, or transmitted, in any form, or by any means (electronic, mechanical, photocopying, recording, or otherwise) without the prior written permission of both the copyright owner and the above publisher of this book.

ISBN-13: 978-1499103427 ISBN-10: 1499103425

This is a work of fiction. Names, characters, places, brands, media, and incidents are either the product of the author's imagination or are used fictitiously. The author acknowledges the trademarked status and trademark owners of various products referenced in this work of fiction, which have been used without permission. The publication/use of these trademarks is not authorized, associated with, or sponsored by the trademark owners.

This book is also available in ebook format.

ACKNOWLEDGMENTS

This book. Man. Where do I start?

Well, first off, due to massive health issues, it released two months later than it's original date. So I think it's appropriate to thank my doctor, Elizabeth Bierer, for all her help to get me up and running again.

Second, I'd like to thank my "cheerleaders," James Weatherford (my hubby), Kamery Solomon (my daughter), and Belinda Boring (my soul sister and BFF). You encouraged me to keep plugging along even when I didn't feel like it.

Also, I give a very special thanks to Belinda for being my beta reader while she was dying in agony over her own health issues. Girl, you are a rock star! Also, I send special love to the ladies of The Beta Readers Elite x 2. You all amazing!

And thank you to Kim from Red Line Editing, for squeezing my edits in on her flight to Ireland. You are awesome!

Last, but definitely not least, thank you to all my amazing readers around the world for loving the Crush series so much and making it such a huge bestseller! Without you, I am nothing.

I send you all my LOVE!

Lacey

DEDICATION

For my fabulous cover model and muse,
Aleksandar (Sasha) Petrovic.
It's always wonderful to find new friends like you!

DYLAN LOVE

PROLOGUE
Dylan-

I hadn't expected to come home to a heart attack. Literally. Unable to stop my grin from spreading, I couldn't believe how long this must've taken her. Paper hearts were strewn across the floor, stuck to the wall, and even some that appeared to have writing on them hanging on strings from the ceiling. Shifting the bouquet of roses under my arm, I moved closer so I could read them.

Follow the hearts.

Wondering what surprises Cami had in store for me, I followed the paper trail through the kitchen, down the hall, to the French doors leading out onto the backyard patio. Twine was strung back and forth like clothesline with more of the paper hearts pinned to it. In the center of the patio, the outdoor table had been draped in a red and white-checkered tablecloth with lit white taper candles next to white place settings and glasses. An empty vase stood in the middle, filled with a small amount of water.

Chuckling, I realized she'd anticipated my Valentine's Day flowers. I removed them from the plastic wrap and placed them in the vase, carefully hiding the small box with the diamond earrings I'd purchased for her amongst the blooms.

"Cami?" I called.

Seeing no sign of her anywhere, I glanced around the yard noting there were even rose petals in the pool. She had really gone all out.

Soft music suddenly clicked on over the speaker system and I turned to see her standing in the doorway. She never ceased to take my breath away. I couldn't believe how much my love for her had grown in the time we'd been together—every day more than the last—something I'd assumed would never be possible. I loved her with every single part of me.

Her hair was pulled up in a loose knot with several tendrils escaping to brush the creamy skin of her neck. The white slip of a dress clung to her, hugging every one of her luscious curves. Suddenly I had the urge to skip the fancy dinner and sweep her off to the bedroom.

"Don't you even think about it," she said with a light laugh.

"What?" I asked, instantly defending myself.

She stepped through the door and I noticed, for the first time, a small rectangular black box with a bow in her hands. "I recognize that look. Heaven knows I've seen it often enough before you drag me off to bed."

"Drag you?" I folded my arms. "I can't think of one time that you haven't been a perfectly willing partner. In fact, there have been plenty of times when you've done the dragging."

Setting the small gift on the table next to one of the plates, she turned to me with a smile. "And I intend to drag you again tonight, but later. Dinner first."

Moving closer, I wrapped my arms around her and pulled her tight against me. "Happy Valentine's Day, Goody."

"To you, too." Her eyes were twinkling.

Bending to kiss her, I gave myself over to the shock that always zinged through my lips whenever we touched, instantly igniting a fire inside me. Her arms wrapped around my neck, holding me closer as she opened her mouth to accept my invasion. Kissing her was like drowning, but in a good way. This was my favorite—coming home and letting her kiss me into oblivion, a place where only she and I existed and we were all that mattered. My hands drifted down over the silky fabric to her hips, anchoring them to mine as she moaned.

"You sure we have to eat first?" I asked softly, continuing to nibble at her.

"Yes," she answered breathlessly. "Besides, the anticipation will only make things more fun later on." Flattening her hands against my chest, she pushed at me slightly and I reluctantly released her. "Have a seat while I get the food, but no peeking at your present."

"Okay." I was perplexed by her gift. It looked like a jewelry box, but I couldn't imagine what kind of jewelry she would've bought me. "What's for dinner?" I called as she disappeared back into the house.

Reappearing a few moments later, she was holding a pizza box. "Well, I hope you'll forgive me. The hearts took a little longer than expected and I ran out of time. But, I think you will still enjoy this." She opened the box, revealing a heart-shaped pizza with pepperoni spelling out the word LOVE.

I chuckled. "This is awesome! They made it this way for you?"

She nodded. "Yep. They actually had a Valentine's Day special going on. Heart shaped pizza and garlic bread. I thought it looked cute, so I ordered both and made a salad to go with it. If you want to dish us up a piece, I'll go get the other stuff."

Taking the box from her, I proceeded to do as she asked. She returned shortly with the bread, salad, and a bottle of sparkling cider.

"What's the matter?" I teased. "Valentine's Day not worthy of wine?"

Smiling sweetly, she shook her head as she handed me the bottle to open and began to serve the rest of our food. "Actually, I figured this would settle a little better on my queasy stomach."

Instantly, I felt like an idiot. "Are you still not feeling well? Here, sit down and let me take care of this."

She laughed. "You're always so chivalrous. I love it." Bending down, she lightly kissed my forehead, straightening up before I could grab her, and moved to sit in her chair. "I'm fine, really. I just want to enjoy tonight with you. And technically, as you so often point out, I'm not old enough to drink."

Scanning her features for any sign of distress, I watched as she sat. "But you're twenty now, so only one more year. Sorry. It's that whole former "cop blood" running through me. It's a hard habit to break."

"I don't want you to break it." She smiled lovingly at me. "There's nothing wrong with being a law abiding citizen."

I couldn't stop staring at her. "I feel way underdressed," I piped up suddenly. "You look ready for a night out on the town and I'm still in my fire uniform. That dress looks fabulous on you, by the way."

"Dylan, it's not a dress. It's lingerie." She laughed, heartily, reaching across to take me by the hand. "Don't you know the difference by now?"

I shook my head. "Not really. Fashion is all over the place these days; and I never really pay attention to the lingerie you wear, except to take it off you."

Rolling her eyes, she lifted her fork and stabbed at her salad. "Well, that I believe. It's usually a waste to wear. As soon as I put it on, it's off again thirty seconds later."

Smiling, I shrugged. "What can I say? I like getting to the pretty package underneath."

"Whatever. By the way, thank you for the roses. I knew you would bring me some."

"You're welcome. I know how much you like

them. But you didn't stop and smell them like you usually do."

Standing, she leaned over to sniff the fragrant aroma, her eyes suddenly noticing the small box nestled inside. "Oh! You got me something else, too!" Opening the box, she smiled widely at the small diamond studs.

"I know you don't like things that are big and flashy, so I got them small."

"They're perfect."

Getting up, I leaned over the table and gave her a kiss. "Not as perfect as you are. Nothing I could buy will ever match you. You're the real gem."

Her eyes watered and I stepped back. "What's wrong?"

"Nothing." She waved her hand and gestured for us to sit again. "I'm just happy. Really happy."

I sat down, not really sure what was going on, but had the feeling she was up to something. "I'm glad you are. I am, too."

"Open your present. I can't wait any longer." She slid the box closer to me and I took it.

"I've been trying to figure out what it is," I admitted. "It looks like a jewelry box and I thought maybe a fancy watch, but you gave me one for Christmas. Can I shake it? Or is it something expensive?"

She smiled. "It's up to you, but I promise it's the most expensive thing I've ever given you."

"Well, now I'm really intrigued. I know you're not one to throw money around." I popped open the box and stared, perplexed, at the white stick inside. Then I noticed the little windows and the blue streaks in them. "Holy hell!" I shouted, jumping up from the table so quickly I knocked my chair over. I stared at her. "Is this for real? Are you pregnant?"

Cami laughed and nodded her head. "I guess that's why I've been sick."

Unable to stop the whoop of glee that escaped me, I snatched her up and twirled her around. "This is amazing news!" My mouth dropped to hers, all thoughts of dinner quickly flying out the window as I devoured her lips, my tongue sliding smoothly in between them to taste her sweetness. Kissing wasn't enough to convey my emotions to her though, I simply wanted to melt into her and become one.

She broke away and stared at me. "You're not upset at all, are you? I know we weren't planning this; and in the past, you said you wanted to keep me to yourself for a while before we had kids."

"Honey, I'm not even the slightest upset. I've had you all to myself for almost two and a half years. I guess I never realized what this would actually mean to me." My hands drifted slowly down to her flat stomach and I imagined it growing rounder with my child. "How far along are you?"

"Well, if I calculated everything right, about five weeks. The due date the website gave me was October fifteenth."

I couldn't stop staring at her, feeling both elated and amazed.

"Are you sure you're okay with all this?" she

asked, concern evident in her eyes. "I know you wanted me to be finished with school before we had a baby."

I continued to stroke her belly. "You and me together. That's what is growing inside you. How could I be upset about that?" I kissed her again, sweeping her off her feet and carrying her into the house.

"What about dinner?" she asked with a smile.

"It'll be there later."

"At least blow out the candles!"

Turning, I hurried back, not bothering to put her down, and extinguished them before going back inside. Entering the bedroom, I immediately noticed the rose petals all over the bed. "You have been busy today," I commented as I gently laid her on top them. She looked like a goddess spread out before me. Suddenly, I was worried. "Are you sure it's okay for you to do this?"

"Lay on rose petals?" she asked, confused.

"Have sex," I replied, pulling my shirt over my head before kicking my boots off.

She laughed. "Yeah, I'm sure. Pregnant women do it all the time."

"How are you feeling, though? Are you still sick?"

"I'm fine, Dylan. Now shut up and let's finish what you started."

Grinning, I dropped my pants and crawled onto the bed, stroking my hand over her curves through the thin, silk fabric. Her eyes never left mine as she arched into my palm with a soft moan. My hands slid down to her stomach again, in wonder. I was still in shock, barely able to process this new development. "Cami, you're going to be the most beautiful mother anyone has ever seen. I hope our children will know how lucky they are."

"Children? Do you know something I don't?"

I chuckled and leaned over, bending to kiss her neck before sliding lower. "Only that I can't seem to keep my hands off you; so our odds of having more than one seem pretty good."

She giggled, and the sound was music to my ears. "You do know it's not your hands that did this to me, right?"

"You're such a tease." My fingers slid underneath her slip. "Sit up so I can take this dang thing off."

"Just wanted to make sure you actually know what you're doing."

Leaning back, I stared at her. "Are you questioning my skills?"

"You have skill?" She bit her lip trying to hide her smile. "I didn't realize it was so difficult—insert part A into part B and move."

"Ha, ha, ha," I said dryly. "You're so funny. The skill comes from being able to make you writhe with pleasure during said insertions."

"Oh, well, if that's the case, then yes. You are very skilled."

"I'm glad you think so; but since you've questioned my abilities, I'm going to have to demonstrate them to you, again."

She laughed outright. "Sorry to make things so hard on you."

"Cami, you always make things hard on me. And that's a compliment."

Laughter burst through her lips and she grabbed my face, pulling me to her. "I love you, Dylan," she whispered before pressing her lips to mine. "Thank you for loving me back."

"I couldn't breathe without you," I said against her skin, wondering if she really knew she was my whole world. Then I set out to show her.

CAMI LOVE

CHAPTER ONE
Cami-
Five months later

"Oh, that's simply precious! We must get that one, too!"

Watching my mom tear through the racks of baby clothes was almost comical. Glancing at my overloaded cart, I suddenly realized she was a grandmother gone wild. "Mom, I think we've got plenty of things here for Peanut. There's no way he could possibly wear all this stuff before he outgrows it."

"Sweetheart, babies soil their clothes multiple times a day. Between diaper changes and spitting up, you can never have enough things for your little one to wear. Besides, half the stuff in that cart is bedding. It looks way worse than it is." She continued to browse through the baby aisle. "Oh! Look at these cute diaper bags! Let's get you some of those."

"I still have three and a half months until I deliver. I think we have plenty of time to get

Peanut's room ready; and really, one diaper bag should be plenty." I couldn't help smiling at her, though. Dylan and I could easily afford all this stuff, but my mom insisted that it was her right, and duty, to help out. She was so extremely excited there was no possible way I could tell her no. Besides, I didn't get to spend time with her nearly as often as I would have liked, and I missed her.

"That's another thing. Have you and Dylan come any closer to picking out a name for the baby? You can't call him Peanut forever."

I sighed. "We are trying to find something we both like. So far we are leaning toward Brandt or Weston as the middle names. We thought it would be nice to pay tribute to one of our dads."

"I'm sure either of them would absolutely love that." My mom smiled. "Maybe someday we'll get a sweet Cecily or Connie after us moms."

"I'm sure there's a very good possibility of that happening." Slipping my arm around her shoulders, I gave her a squeeze.

"Have you and Dylan decided how many kids you want to have?"

"No, not really. I think we'll play it by ear. We're both from small families though, so that's what we are used to. I could easily see us having two. Of course, if my birth control doesn't work right, like this time, we could end up with a whole lot more than that!"

Mom laughed heartily and even blushed a bit. "I don't think it's escaped anyone's notice that Dylan can't keep his hands off you. I don't think I've ever seen a man so in love before."

"Not even Dad?" I asked, surprised by her comment.

"Oh, your dad thinks the world of me, and he loves me a lot, but Dylan, well, he just burns with a fire you just don't see in most men. He's pretty romantic, too. I thought some of that might fade after your first year of marriage, but I was wrong. If anything, he seems even more crazy about you."

"I guess I got lucky; but I feel the same about him. I love him so much." I smiled, letting my mind drift to memories of romantic moments Dylan and I shared together– long evening walks hand in hand, water skiing and picnicking together at the lake, driving over the border into Mexico for a day of shopping, laying in each other's arms after making love. It was hard to believe we'd already been married over two years, now. My pulse still accelerated every time he walked into the room.

"You're both lucky. Just a couple of great kids." Mom's voice broke into my thoughts and I realized she was leaving me behind as I'd daydreamed about Hunter. Tears welled in my eyes when I realized I'd called him by his alias. He was truly Dylan to me now, but Hunter was the name of the man I'd fallen in love with—the undercover cop who'd posed as a student at my high school. It just fit him so naturally. Sometimes I missed calling him that.

"Maybe I should name the baby Hunter," I said softly, feeling the tears streak down my cheeks.

My mom turned to stare at me, shocked. "Are you *crying*? In the middle of Baby Town?"

I started laughing and I walked toward her. "I can't help it. It's these dang hormones. I swear they're going to kill me. I cry about everything, commercials, books, television shows, the State of the Union address."

"Oh, sweetie. All of America was crying over that!" She pursed her lips together and waved a hand to dismiss the subject. I laughed harder over the symbolic gesture indicative of her conservative nature.

"How about forgetfulness?" I asked, contemplating all the crazy changes I'd experienced so far. "Does pregnancy cause that?"

She chuckled. "It can. Some people call it "Momnesia." They attribute it to a surge of hormones, lack of sleep, and multitasking. Have you been getting enough rest?"

Shrugging, I fingered a cute baseball outfit. "I thought I was. I'm taking some online summer courses and working at transposing songs for the music department, so it's not like I do anything to physically get tired. But lately it seems like I keep misplacing and forgetting things."

"Like what?"

"My car keys. I always hang them on a hook by the door to the garage, but lately they're never there and I find them all over the place, even though I swear I made a special point to hang them up. And the other day, Dylan came home from work and asked why I'd parked out on the street. I never park on the street. I'd gone to the grocery store earlier, but I don't remember parking there. He says I move things of his around, too." I laughed, feeling like an idiot. "I guess I've finally gone nuts. It was bound to happen someday."

Giving me a quick hug around the shoulders, she leaned her head against mine. "I don't think you're nuts, at all. I think you're excited for this baby to get here and he is preoccupying most of your thoughts. That's a good thing."

Running a hand over my baby bump, I smiled. "I never thought it was possible to love someone so much. I mean, I haven't even met him and already he's such a part of me. I can't wait to hold him and nuzzle all his tiny features." Immediately, I started tearing up, again. "But then it all seems so unreal at other times, as if he will never really get here."

"Spoken like a true expectant mother. Be patient and enjoy your pregnancy– and the rest you're getting now. After this little guy is born, neither Dylan nor you will be getting much sleep."

"Great. Now I'll have two boys keeping me awake at night," I grumbled, jokingly.

Mom laughed and shook her head. "I'm afraid you're right. I don't think that husband of yours will leave you alone much, kids or not— not that it's a bad thing. Shall we check out now?"

Smiling, I nodded. "Yes, I think we have enough for three nurseries in our cart now, and that's not counting the baby furniture being delivered."

"Well, let's go put this all together and then you'll have something to surprise my son-in-law with."

"Sounds like a plan." I hooked my arm in hers, happy for the time we'd been able to spend together, as the two of us made our way to the front of the store.

***

"Surprise!" I threw the door to the nursery open and watched Dylan's face light up. "Didn't it turn out great?"

"Honey! This is awesome! I can't believe you and your mom got all this done today. I hope you didn't wear yourself out."

"I'm tired, but I love this room. I don't want to leave it." I slid my hand across the pale yellow walls. "I think you painted it the perfect color. It'll work well for a boy, and any girls we might have in the future."

"Your idea of the having the zoo animals fits perfectly in here."

"It does. You have to sit in the nursing rocker/recliner we bought. It's so comfy, and it's in easy reach of the changing table or anything I might need on the shelves." I ushered him over to the chair and pushed him into it.

He laughed, but looked pleasantly surprised. "Oh, that *is* nice." Smiling, he sank further into the chair, laying his head back.

"But that's not the best thing. Look at this!" I opened the closet and drawers to show him the full wardrobe of clothes, baby blankets, teething toys and other paraphernalia.

"Good grief! Did you go a little crazy with the shopping today?"

"Mom bought it all! She was like a kid in a candy store, going berserk over everything. I think it's pretty safe to say this baby is going to be spoiled rotten."

Dylan stood and moved behind me, reaching around to place his hands on my belly. Instantly, I felt the baby flutter inside me.

"He moved! Did you feel it?"

"I did," he replied with a smile as he kissed my neck. Turning me to face him, he knelt in front of me lifting my shirt so he could continue stroking my bare stomach. "Hey, Peanut. Daddy's home, now." He kissed my belly and was rewarded with another kick. Soft laughter erupted from him. "I hope that means you're happy I'm here." He kissed the spot again. "I sure love you and your mommy."

"Of course he's happy. He always moves more when you're around. I think he gets excited to hear your voice."

Dylan stood and pulled me against him. "Then he must be like his daddy. I get excited when I hear your voice."

Gently, his mouth descended to mine, and I sighed. My fingers naturally threaded their way into his dark silky hair and I moaned as his tongue slid inside my mouth. Kissing Dylan was the best experience ever, his full lips pressing firmly against mine as he held me. Everything about him made me feel safe—the flexing muscles of his arms, the hardness of his chest and abdomen, and his height towering over me. He seemed so strong, so invincible, so able to protect both our baby and me. I loved the way he cared for me, both in the past and in the present. There was no doubt in my mind that he would be a wonderful father.

"What about Hunter?" I asked when we broke apart, staring into his warm brown eyes flecked with caramel.

"Hunter?" he questioned, clearly not following.

"For the baby. I thought maybe Hunter Weston, after you and your dad. Of course Russ will think we chose Weston after his last name and not for your father."

A smile creased his lips and he chuckled, continuing to stare at me as his hands stroked me softly. "Good ole Russ. What would we do without him?"

"He's been a great friend."

"Yes, he has. As far as the name Hunter, I don't know, maybe. I know how much you love that name. There for a while, I thought I was going to have to start using it permanently."

Tears floated in my eyes. "I'm sorry. I love your name, Dylan. It was just so hard to make the mental switch after calling you Hunter for so long. If you don't like it for the baby, we can try something else. I just thought since it's your middle name, that it would be a good way to pay tribute to you and your dad, also."

"I love the name. And I love hearing it on your lips, so don't ever feel bad for when you slip up and call me that. I also think it would be a nice tribute, but what about your dad?"

I shrugged, glancing down as I traced my finger over the large bicep peeking out from under his sleeve. "There will be other babies."

He chuckled. "Just how many kids are you planning to have? Do we need to get a bigger house?"

Rolling my eyes, I stared at him. "We could easily have seven kids in this house right now and still have plenty of space. So, if you think we need a bigger place, we've got problems."

A wicked gleam appeared in eyes. "Well, I did say I couldn't keep my hands off you. And you never know; we could have several sets of twins or triplets in our future."

"Bite your tongue," I said, playfully slapping at his shoulder.

"How about you bite it for me?" Sweeping me into his arms he gave me a wink as he carried me out of the room.

DYLAN LOVE

CHAPTER TWO
Dylan-

"I have a present for you."

"You do?" Cami got up from where she was reading on the couch and came to give me a kiss. "Welcome home. Where is this present you speak of?"

I shook my head, wrapping my arms around her. "I don't know. I think you might have to find it. Maybe a strip search is in order."

Laughing heartily, she shoved at me. "You'd like that too much and then we'd never make it to dinner. The baby and I are starving!"

"You think you know me so well." I grabbed her, pulling her back against me. This was my favorite part of the day—coming home and having her in my arms, again. Even though I loved my job as a firefighter/paramedic, I hated every minute I was away from her. Working with Russ was a good perk, though. Even though he was still considered a "newbie" on the team, it was nice having my best bud around with me.

"Look at me, Dylan." Cami said waving a hand over her body. "I do know you very well. *This* is what happens when you come home from work and have sex with your wife nearly *every day* for two years."

I grinned. "I haven't heard you complaining."

"Nor will you." She smiled. "I enjoy being with you."

Damn. I swear she made me burn hotter for her every single moment we were together. I had to force my mind back to the subject at hand. "If you know me so well, then tell me what the present is that I got for you today."

"Flowers?"

I shook my head. "Nope."

"Did you bring take out home?"

"Wrong again."

"Hmmm." She pressed her lips together. "Did you get a raise at work?"

"Maybe you should give up. I don't think you know me well enough to guess it."

"Whatever. You're such a dork. Just tell me what it is."

"How about you follow me to the garage? I left it out there."

"Oh my gosh! You did not buy that motorcycle you've been talking about, did you? I swear those things scare me to death! You have to take it back, Dylan. I'd die if something happened to you on one of those things." She was quickly working herself into hysterics, so I hurried to the door and flung it open. A small yelp filled the air and a tiny Dalmatian puppy flopped its way happily across the floor to Cami's feet.

"You got a puppy?" Cami said, staring in shock.

"He's the perfect dog for us, don't you think? He goes right along with the whole firefighter image."

Sinking down, she crooned as she stroked him and I wondered if she'd even heard a word I said.

"Hi, pretty baby. Look at you and how sweet you are?" There was some serious nuzzling going on. I could tell already that these two were going to get along famously.

"His name is Oreo."

"Oh! I love that! It's totally fitting for him!" she squealed with delight. "Isn't that right, boy? Such a cute Oreo and sweet like cookies, too." The dog was clearly eating up the attention. "Where'd you get him?" she asked. I chuckled; surprised she still remembered I was in the room. It looked like I was going to have some serious competition. *Maybe I didn't think this out very well.*

"The Chief's dog had puppies and he was trying to find good homes for them. I always hate leaving you here alone, so I thought this little guy might be a good companion for you. Plus, when he gets bigger he'll be a good guard dog."

"He's adorable, though I've never potty trained a puppy before. I think cleaning up after him might make my pregnant tummy a bit queasy."

"No worries there. He's paper-trained. I'll go to the store for some supplies to put in a doggy door that goes out into the backyard so he can learn to go out there and also get outside to run. And, just for you, I'll clean up after him. He'll need to be walked every day, though. This breed is pretty energetic." Concerned, I stared at her, second-guessing. "Do you think you can handle this? I don't want you to be overwhelmed. I know you get tired easily outside in this summer heat. I don't want you to be uncomfortable."

"Don't worry. We can walk him together in the evenings you aren't doing your night shift rotation. It's cooler then. That way his paws won't get burned on the concrete. We can take him to play in the park down the street. I think he'll be a great addition to our family. I love him already." She picked up the squirming puppy and turned toward me. "He's definitely not a purse puppy, is he?"

Laughter escaped me. "No, he's not; but he still looks good on you." I took the wriggling dog from her and set him on the ground. Straightening, I pulled her into my arms. "I love you. If the dog is too much, I can take him back. I just worry about you being lonely."

"You don't need to. I'm not just sitting around twiddling my thumbs, you know. True, I'm not putting out fires and saving people's lives, but between the music gig, homework, and keeping this place clean, I'm staying pretty busy."

"I'm glad you've been able to work from

home. I know you haven't always felt well with this pregnancy." I kissed the top of her head. "I simply want you to be happy and not overworked."

"I am happy. I couldn't have a better life." She grinned. "I'm exactly where I want to be."

"Good, because I can't imagine a life any better than this, either. I love you, Cami."

"I love you, too." She popped up on her toes to kiss me and I squeezed her tightly to me. We both started chuckling. "That baby is really starting to come between us, you know what I mean?" I asked as she slid my hands down to her stomach.

"I'm getting pretty fat, aren't I?" She frowned a bit.

I snorted and dragged her back to me. "There's not an ounce of fat on you. And you're beautiful. I love knowing that part of me is growing inside you."

She snickered. "Does that make you feel manly?"

Grinning, I nodded. "You bet. I'm thinking of having you wear a sign that says, "My husband did this," just so everyone knows how awesome I am."

Rolling her eyes, she giggled. "You're hardly the first man to get his wife pregnant."

"True. But how many can say they did it while their wife was on birth control?"

"Probably way more than you know. Besides, that doesn't bode well for our future birth control needs."

I shrugged. "We can try something else, or

just have a bunch of kids. I'm okay with either, really."

"Seriously?" She seemed surprised by that comment. "As long as it's with you, I don't care what size family we have. I simply want us to be happy—just like we are right now." I bent to kiss her again, only to be interrupted by loud yapping from Oreo. Glancing down to where he was hopping about at our feet, I sighed. "That's it. The dog has to go."

"What? Why?" Cami cried out.

"He interrupted our kissing time. That's a no-no."

Laughing hard, Cami playfully slapped my arm and bent to pet the dog. "I guess you'll simply have to train him."

"I've been ditched for a dog," I grumbled. "I'm making a new rule right now. He's not allowed to sleep in our bed. That's *my* playground."

Cami shook her head. "You're incorrigible, but that's fine with me. And thank you for the gift."

"Anything for you."

***

Attempting to snuggle closer to Cami, I cursed at the puppy curled up between us, sound asleep. How'd the damn dog get in here? I sighed, noticing Cami's hand was sweetly curled around the offending creature, in the dim light from the window. I couldn't separate them now, she looked so peaceful.

Our peace was shattered in that moment as a series of tones came through the hand held radio sitting on my bedside table. "Shit," I muttered to myself, reaching for it as the dispatcher began speaking.

"General page, general page, all engines and crew from firehouse nine. We have reports of a five alarm warehouse structure fire . . . ."

"Cami, sweetheart, I've got to go." Sitting up, I leaned over and kissed her forehead.

"Be careful," she muttered in her sleep-laden voice. "Hurry home."

"I'll do my best." Jumping up, I threw on the spare uniform that I kept beside the bed every night for precisely this reason. I didn't turn on the light, not wanting to disturb Cami anymore. The dog gave a whimper as I stepped out of the room and I turned to glance at both of them lying there one last time before shutting the door behind me.

Hurrying out to my Camaro, I jumped in and headed to the station a few blocks away. The bay doors stood wide open, indicating the departure of the on-duty crew in the first two trucks already. Several other men were pulling up in their vehicles to man the third truck.

I ran to the wall where my turnouts were hanging with my boots just below them and quickly suited up. Jumping into the driver's seat, I fired up the engine. Russ jumped in the passenger seat beside me, and as soon as the rest of the crew was on board, I picked up the radio.

"Dispatch, Engine nine dash three is en route to the five alarm, code 3."

"Copy, Engine nine dash three. En route time

is zero one forty hours."

Leaning over, Russ clicked on the lights and siren and a loud wail filled the night air. The adrenaline rushed through me, just like it did in my old police days, as a sense of urgency filled us all. There was no doubt where we were headed, the orange flames and billowing black smoke was shooting high into the air above our destination.

"This one looks like a doozy," Russ said dryly, fastening his helmet.

"It sure does," I replied, surveying things as we got closer. "And we have other buildings close by. If the fire spreads to them, things will get even crazier."

"Looks like they have a flare and an officer down the street signaling you."

Slowing the massive truck considerably, I worked my way up to the officer and rolled the window down.

"Incident Command is set up over there at the end of the parking lot. Go there for your orders." He pointed to where several emergency vehicles were staging.

Giving him a nod, I turned into the lot and lifted the radio. "Dispatch, Engine nine dash three is on scene. Reporting in to Incident Command."

A voice crackled back through the receiver. "Copy, Engine nine dash three, arrival time, zero one forty-six. Incident Command requests you change to channel four for instructions."

"Copy, dispatch. Switching to channel four." I clicked the radio to the new station. "You got times noted in the chart?" I asked Russ.

"Got them." He waved the clipboard.

"Incident Command to Engine nine dash three." The captain's voice came through the speaker.

"Engine nine dash three," I replied.

"We need you to stage near the hydrant on the back side of the building. Right now we are trying to attack the fire from the outside only and prevent spreading to the nearby buildings. Repeat, outside attack only."

"Copy Incident Command, stage on the backside of the building and attack with no entry. En route to new location."

"I'm glad they aren't sending us inside that mess," Charlie, one of the seasoned firefighters, muttered from the back seat.

"Me, too. No point risking anyone. That particular building is beyond saving."

Carefully maneuvering the truck behind some of the non-burning structures, we dropped hose at the hydrant and pulled forward until we were as far as we could safely go. By the time the truck was parked and the pump on and ready to go, Russ had the truck stabilized and the ladder ready to extend toward the building. Already, I could feel the heat through my turnouts. The fire was much heavier back here.

"You climbing up first?" I shouted to Russ and he nodded, pulling a small Velcro name tag with the large letters of his last name, WESTON, off his uniform and handing it to me. Taking our command board out from behind the seat, I placed his name in the spot marked Ladder.

Being the highest-ranking officer on this side of the building, command for this crew would fall to me. It was imperative I know where all my guys were at all times. As the rest of the crew continued to set up hoses, I moved to the controls that would boost Russ into the air on the ladder. "You ready?" I called, watching as he secured his position and then gave me the thumbs up. Carefully, I pushed the lever, watching as he slowly rose higher, awaiting his signal and directions.

"Engine nine dash three, up about another two feet and to the left a little." His voice came over my radio.

"Copy," I replied, doing as he asked. A few seconds later a giant stream of water arced out of the giant hose toward the raging inferno. Despite the massive gallons of water hitting it, there wasn't much of a noticeable difference right away. Turning back toward the truck, I started shouting orders. "Maxwell and Houston, you guys attack from the front of the truck. Charlie, start spraying this building next door down to keep it from getting too hot. There's not much space between these two and we've got to keep it from spreading."

"Got it!" he yelled back, opening his line and letting the water loose.

Glancing around to make sure my crew was all where they were supposed to be, I adjusted their names on my board and picked up my radio. "Incident Command, Engine nine dash three is in place. We are attacking the fire from the rear and implementing neighboring building protection."

"Incident Command copies Engine nine dash three. Continue attack as needed; notify us of any pertinent changes."

"Copy." Sticking near the pump on the truck, I surveyed operations, sighing heavily. We were in for a very long battle.

CHAPTER THREE
Cami-

Big fires were always the worst. They made me so nervous. I knew there were massive dangers involved with firefighting in general, but big fires happened so rarely and I knew Dylan was responsible and wouldn't do anything stupid. I just preferred it when he spent the majority of his time responding to medical emergencies. But, I couldn't really complain, seeing that I'd agreed to this trade off with him. It was way better than having him work undercover for the police department. I'd seen, first hand, the dangers that type of assignment involved. I couldn't sleep knowing that every day someone could find out his identity and he'd end up with another bullet in him. I was thankful when his strength and perseverance allowed him to work his way quickly up the ranks of the fire crew. Having command of his particular unit also meant he was directly out of the line of fire, literally.

Several hours later, I pulled into the parking lot of the structure fire and drove toward the command center, parking in the designated area I'd been directed to.

"We're setting up over here, Cami," Charlotte's voice called to me as I stepped from the vehicle. Glancing around, I saw her waving toward a small white tent that had been set up.

"Thanks. Let me grab my stuff and I'll be right over." Turning back to the car, I stared down at the wriggly, excited pup on my seat. "You need to stay in here, buddy; but I'll roll the windows down a bit and check on you in a few minutes. Okay?"

Hurrying to the trunk, I tried to ignore the tender whining from Oreo as I opened it and quickly gathered up several boxes of doughnuts. It had become tradition for the spouses of department members to bring food and drink to large fires, helping to ensure the first responders stayed properly hydrated and fed. We made up quick finger foods like sandwiches and bought doughnuts—things they could easily scarf down before returning to work. Water and sport drinks were their drink of choice, and I could already see the ground was littered with containers that had been gulped and discarded. Several women were behind the long table setting out the items they had brought, and I made my way toward them. I quickly scanned the firefighters in the tent, hoping to see Dylan; but he wasn't there.

Setting my boxes down, I turned to Charlotte, Chief Daniels' wife. "How's it going with the fire?" Glancing toward the burning building, I could see places where the heavy black smoke was curling up, suggesting there were still some pretty good hot spots going.

"They managed to keep it from spreading to the buildings on the side and they've knocked it down enough that some of the teams have moved in for the interior attack. But I think they still have a long fight ahead of them to get it down completely. It'll be a while before they can start investigating the cause. The fire inspector is here waiting, though."

"I hope they'll get it taken care of quickly." I hated the idea of anyone being inside that building. Even if the fire wasn't as bad, the structure could still be a danger and weak areas could fall in. I knew the crews were careful to shore up any unstable areas they were working in, but it still made me nervous.

"Dylan should be in here any time. They just relieved Engine nine dash three so they could take a break."

As if on cue, I saw my husband come through the tent flap. His hair was wet and matted thickly to his head, and dark streaks of black had run over his cheeks. Even with his darker complexion, it was obvious his skin was flushed and he looked worn out. Six hours had passed since the initial call had gone out, and I could tell he'd worked every minute of that. Shrugging out of his turnout coat, he tossed it over a chair and headed straight for me. Reaching out, I quickly grabbed a water bottle and handed it to him. "Sit and drink," I commanded, pointing to the chair next to me. He didn't argue, plopping down into it while cracking the bottle open and chugging it heavily.

Hurrying back to the table, I grabbed a doughnut and a couple of the sandwiches, placing them on a small paper plate and taking it over to him.

"Thanks," he said, accepting them and tearing into the food without saying anything further. Seeing more of his crew come in, I left to help them get proper refreshment, too. As soon as everyone was happily situated, I got a sports drink and took it over to Dylan.

"Thanks, honey," he said, eyeing me with concern. "Now, tell me, what are you doing here?"

His comment caught me by surprise. "What do you mean? I'm here helping, like I always do when there's a big fire like this."

"Cami, you're pregnant now. Who knows what was in that warehouse. I don't want you here breathing in all this smoke or any other chemicals that could harm you or the baby."

Slumping my shoulders dejectedly, I sat in the chair beside him. "I'm sorry. That thought didn't even cross my mind. I wanted to help out. It makes me rest easier when I can see for myself that you're okay, especially after the stories all over the news and how dangerous this is for the crews fighting it."

He smiled and gave me a wink. "I know you worry, but the worst of it is past. I promise to be careful." I wondered if he was sick of constantly having to reassure me when he was out on dangerous jobs. "Why don't you go ahead and go over to my mom and dad's house? Who knows when I'll be finished here, but I can meet you there for dinner. I'm sure Sheridan is probably already over there. You can play with your niece."

"That sounds doable." A smile floated dreamily across my mouth as I thought of little Christianna, whom we had affectionately nicknamed Chrissy, since she looked so much like her dad, Chris. She was the cutest two-year old I'd ever seen, and she made me so excited for my own baby to arrive.

"I'm sure my parents would love spending extra time with you before they leave on their cruise."

Smiling at him, I nodded. "I have to say, I'm slightly jealous of them. Sailing off for two weeks of water, beaches and fun in the Caribbean." I sighed dreamily. "It must be nice."

Dylan leaned forward, lightly stroking my face with his dirty thumb. "I promise I'll take you someday." His gaze drifted over me. "When you're less pregnant."

"Oh, so never," I teased back and he smiled.

"Kiss me and get out of here."

I shook my head slowly as I moved closer. "So demanding."

"You love it and you know it." He grinned, our faces close as we stared at each other. I could see the love shining from his eyes, even through all the grime that covered him.

"I know I love you," I replied softly, our breath mingling together.

"And that couldn't make me happier." Without glancing down, I felt his fingers toying with the bottom of my hair, rubbing it between his fingers like it was fine silk. It was something he always did when we talked like this.

"Oh, for heaven's sake, either kiss her or sign out and get a room!" Russ's voice burst into our bubble, shattering the sweet cocoon we had been in. Dylan sighed, heavily, and leaned in for a quick kiss before standing and offering me a hand.

"Get out of here, sweetheart."

"Yes, sir." I stood and glared at Russ.

"I sure will be glad when you find a girl and I can torment you the way you do me." Dylan laughed as he clapped Russ on the shoulder.

"That is never going to happen." Russ shook his head before guzzling down more of his Gatorade.

"And why is that? You've decided to play for the other team, now?"

I giggled, watching their banter.

Russ choked a bit on his drink. "Hell no," he responded, spraying drops of liquid.

"What's wrong with men, Weston?" We all turned to see Wilson, an out, loud and proud gay man in the department looking at Russ with raised eyebrows.

My "gaydar" would've never pegged him. He was tall, muscular, extremely good looking, and one of the nicest, well-mannered men in the whole department in my opinion. Nothing about his appearance gave anything away about his sexual preference—sporting zero flamboyancy that society so often associates with gay men. I'd grown quite fond of him. He was a great guy with a big heart. "We'd happily welcome you to the team," he added.

Russ faltered a bit. "Umm, thanks for the invite, but I've got one serious problem before I can hook up with you."

"Really? What's that?" Wilson's eyes traveled over Russ with interest before returning to his face.

"I like women." Russ raised his shoulders and gave a crooked tight-lipped grin before taking another swig from his bottle.

Wilson shrugged. "Sex change is always an option, I guess."

Russ sprayed his drink through his lips and Dylan and I burst out laughing.

"Take it easy, Weston. I'm just messing with you a bit." Wilson winked.

"Aw, that's too bad," Dylan broke in and both men glanced at him. "You two would look amazing together as a couple."

"We would, wouldn't we?" Wilson said, moving closer and wrapping one of his thickly muscled arms around Russ's back. Russ was glaring daggers at Dylan.

"Look, Cami," Dylan spoke again, drawing me into the conversation. "Don't you think they make a cute couple?"

I felt bad, but I couldn't resist the opportunity to razz Russ up a bit. He was always dishing it out; it didn't hurt for him to receive it. "They're absolutely adorable together. I wonder why I never noticed it before. It's like they were made for each other. And it totally explains why Russ hasn't been dating much. How did we never see it?"

Russ's face flooded as he stared slack jawed between the two of us. "Hey, um, I need to go ask the Chief something real quick." He scurried from the packed tent as fast as he could without glancing back.

Dylan burst out laughing. "That was priceless, man." He held his hand up to Wilson who returned his high five with a big grin.

"I predict he'll be flaunting a new girlfriend by the end of the week," Wilson added.

Dylan nodded. "I think you're absolutely right. Maybe we should place bets on how fast."

"I'm in." One of the guys standing nearby piped up, and soon the bets were flying.

I scooted closer to Wilson. "Maybe we should just start calling you Mr. Matchmaker."

He laughed and draped his arm around my shoulders. "I think that would be fun. Too bad you aren't my type or I'd steal you from Wilcock for myself."

"Like hell," Dylan said with a grin. "You'd die trying. No one is taking that girl away from me. She is all mine and I intend it to stay that way as long as there is breath in my body."

"Oh, he's a little possessive, isn't he?" Wilson said, giving me a squeeze.

"He is, but I like it that way. It makes me feel special." I smiled at Dylan as he continued to take bets.

"Honey, you are special. Everyone knows it." Wilson squeezed me tighter. "If you two ever want to come and hang out, or have dinner, give me a call. I'd love to have you over to my place sometime."

"Thanks, Wilson. That sounds wonderful. We'll be sure to take you up on it."

"I mean it. Anytime. You have my number."

"Thanks. I have to go now, though. Stay safe and keep my guy safe, too."

"Don't worry, doll. We've all got his back."

"Thank you." It made me teary to see how much the other men respected my husband.

Dylan moved closer to me. "I'll meet you at Mom and Dad's as soon as I can. Tell them not to wait for me, though."

"Okay. Do you think it would be all right with them if I bring Oreo? He's in the car."

"Definitely take him. They will enjoy meeting him. My family loves pets and I'm sure Chrissy will get a kick out of him. The dog's been around all the Chief's grandkids, so he should do fine with her."

"I'll be careful and take him on the leash, just to be sure."

He leaned down and placed a soft kiss on my lips.

"See you soon, hopefully," I said, staring into his warm brown eyes.

"Not soon enough." I felt his stare on me all the way out of the tent.

DYLAN LOVE

CHAPTER FOUR
Dylan-

Something felt off. I noticed it the minute I stepped into the house. The small hairs on the back of my neck rose like hackles and all my cop instincts clicked into overdrive. Standing stock still, I did a brief scan of the kitchen, noticing nothing out of the ordinary; but the house seemed way too quiet. Usually Cami, and now the dog, came to greet me. Fear sliced through my heart. Stepping back into the garage, I stealthily made my way over to the shelves on the far side of Cami's car. Sliding a few boxes to the side, a small locked gun case came into view. Quickly dialing out the combination, I lifted the handgun and popped the loaded clip inside, making sure the safety was off before slipping back inside the house.

My heart rate increased as I slowly made my way from room to room, clearing each one as I worked my way toward the bedroom. The doors to the patio were open, and a breeze blew through the house, stirring the curtains and scattering some of Cami's music papers she'd been working on from the table to the floor. It wasn't like her to leave her things unprotected. She was very organized.

Approaching our bedroom, my nerves clicked up a notch. Feathers were blowing around on the tiles in the hallway and the remnants of a severely shredded pillow were clumped in the entry. Creeping to the edge of the doorway, I felt panic squeeze at my chest, imagining all sorts of terrible sights I might be about to walk in on.

Please, let Cami be okay, I prayed silently. I could handle anything as long as she was all right.

I eyed the area I could see before raising my weapon and moving into the room, quickly turning in every direction to check the large space for an intruder. An audible sigh of relief escaped me when I saw Cami and Oreo curled up together on the bed, fast asleep. Still, I made my way into the bathroom, checking it before lowering my weapon and relaxing.

Everything was okay. She must've forgotten to shut the patio doors. But still, that didn't make sense to me. It was July. Why would she have the doors open during the heat of the day? As if confirming my thoughts, I could hear the air-conditioning running constantly, trying to compensate for keeping the house cool. Cami often complained of being overheated and kept the house on the fairly cool side. Nothing else seemed to be wrong, though, and she and the dog were obviously all right.

Carefully, I made my way back through the house and put my gun away. I kept another in my nightstand, so there was no need for this one in the house. After it was unloaded and stored, I went back inside, chiding myself for being so hyper-aware. Clearly the dog must've torn up the pillow after Cami fell asleep.

Following my previous trail of progress, I went back and closed the doors and locked them, and then I busied myself picking up Cami's music and organizing it by page numbers, before placing them in a nice stack in the center of the table. Tugging my phone out, I dialed the nearest Chinese restaurant and order some of our favorite dishes. I knew she'd feel bad that she didn't make my dinner before I arrived home—she always tried to have something good waiting for me. It was my turn to take care of her for a change.

Grabbing a broom and a dustpan, along with a trash bag, I began cleaning up the pillow mess. I allowed my thoughts to wander back over the warehouse fire we'd fought two days ago. The fire investigator had ruled the blaze as arson, started by Molotov cocktails thrown through several windows. Whoever started it made sure that particular building was ignited. Investigators were leaning toward it being a targeted crime. Any leads surrounding the owners of the warehouse were being pursued to see if any kind of connections could be made. We'd been advised to keep our eyes open for suspicious behavior and to notify the cops if we came across something. I felt that itch to be in the middle of everything going on with the police force right now as they tried to solve the case. I loved my job and the department, but I'd definitely left a piece of myself behind on the police force. I knew I'd made the right choice to switch jobs—there was no way I wanted Cami to live everyday in fear of what might happen to me.

Lifting the damaged pillow, I examined the fabric, feeling my nerves skyrocket, again. This didn't look chewed up. It looked sliced. And it was one of the pillows from my side of the bed. Getting a garbage bag, I carefully put it inside and made my way into the kitchen. Pausing to stare at the block of sharp cutting knives on the counter, I noticed they all seemed to be in the right place. Grabbing a plastic baggie, I slid my hand inside and carefully began removing each knife from its slot one at a time and examining it. I stopped with a small paring knife, immediately noticing a tiny clump of black strings clinging near the base, an exact match to the color of my pillowcase.

My heart was pounding. Unless Cami was pissed at me and had gone a little crazy, someone had been in my house—our house—with her.

Carefully, I slid the plastic off my hand and over the knife, placing it in the bag of pillow remnants. Hurrying to my car, I put the items in the trunk and removed my gun from the shelf, reinserting the clip once again. I placed it into the waistband at the back of my pants and pulled my shirt out to loosely cover it.

"Hey, Dylan. I didn't hear you come home."

I had to force myself not to jump a mile. She caught me completely off guard. Oreo ran up and wiggled, squirming at my feet. For only living here a couple of days, he certainly seemed attached.

"Sorry I don't have dinner ready. I over slept."

"Don't apologize. You need your rest. Besides, I already ordered your favorite, Walnut Shrimp. It should be here soon. I hope that's all right with you."

She smiled and placed a hand on her rounded belly. "It sounds great. I'm starving. What are you doing out here?" she asked, looking around the garage.

Bending down to pet Oreo, who refused to be ignored any longer, I glanced at her with a smile. "Just putting some stuff in my trunk. I need to stop by the police station and drop some things off for Chief Robson. I have another surprise for you," I added before she could question me about anything else.

"Really? What's that?"

"Well, my parents invited us to stay at their house while they're gone on their cruise. It's time for the pest control service to come by again and spray for bugs, and I don't want you exposed to the chemicals. I thought maybe we could take them up on their offer, and then you'd have some of the help there with you while I'm at work. You can take Oreo with you, too. What do you think?"

"Dylan. You know I hate to make anyone wait on me. I'm capable of doing things myself. It just makes me feel awkward."

I needed to convince her. I had to get her out of our house until I knew it was safe for her to be alone here. "I know that, Goody, but come on. It's a great chance for both of us to chill and rest for a few days. I really need to get the exterminator over here. Plus, I've been thinking about getting a better security system installed, just for extra safety. You don't need to be around all the dust and whatnot while they install it. It's perfect timing."

"We already have a security system," she complained, giving me a confused stare. "Why do we need more?"

"The one we have only secures the doors, not the windows, too. Plus, you always forget to arm it. I want to get one that can help you in an emergency, so you could talk to someone, like if the baby came early or something. A live person could coach you through things."

"Isn't that what 911 is for? And what about you? It's not like I live with a paramedic or anything. You're completely capable of delivering a baby." She arched an eyebrow and I knew she had me there.

"Trust me, Cami. I just want to know you're protected. Okay? It'll help me rest easier." At least that was the truth.

She smiled as she approached and I straightened, grasping both her hands in mine so she wouldn't put her arms around me and feel the weapon at my back. "Fine. I'll do it for you; but if you ask me, I think all of this is overkill."

"Really? After what the two of us have been through together in the past, you feel I'm overreacting?"

"Okay, okay. Point taken. But those people who tried to hurt us are either dead or have been sent to prison. I don't want to live my life in constant fear, Dylan. It almost consumed me, before."

"Then that's the perfect reason for you to let me do this, so you don't have to live in fear and we can both have peace of mind." I squeezed her hands and bent to kiss her lips. I loved that the spark between us never seemed to dim, but only grew greater with time. I loved her more with each and every breath I took, and I'd be damned before I'd let even the most minor threat against her go unattended.

"I love you," she whispered, her lips brushing against mine. "Thanks for always being so concerned about my wellbeing."

"Always. Now, why don't you run and start packing us what we need to stay at my parents' house and I'll wait for the delivery guy while I load the dog food and the collapsible kennel. By the way, what happened to my pillow?"

She gave me a perplexed look. "What do you mean?"

"I found it shredded on the floor by the bedroom door."

"You did? That's odd."

"I figured Oreo chewed it up after you fell asleep."

"Hmmm. That's not possible. I put him in his kennel before I laid down so he wouldn't have any accidents in the house. I assumed you had let him out when I found him on the bed with me." That just further confirmed my suspicions.

"You were both asleep together when I got home. His kennel door was wide open."

"Well, I'm sorry. I must not have closed it all the way. We'd been playing out in the backyard earlier, while I took a break. I brought him inside and closed all the doors and shut the doggy door because he kept trying to run out. Then I had to chase him around the house to get him in the kennel because he was so rambunctious. I don't know how he got out because he whined for quite a while and I had to get up and shut the bedroom door so I could sleep.

I had to work hard to suppress my rage from showing. "Don't worry about it. We can easily replace the pillow. I'm just glad you got some rest."

"Me, too. It was nice. I'll go get our stuff ready."

Bending down, I pet the small dog at my feet, watching until she was completely out of earshot. "Oreo, someone was in our house today. Don't let anyone come in the house."

The puppy grew still and sat, staring at me with his wide eyes, as if he knew something bad had happened. The doorbell rang, breaking into my thoughts and I sighed heavily. "Come on, boy." I headed for the front door, listening to the clipping sounds of the dog's toenails hitting the tile floor as he walked, but I couldn't stop the words that kept running through my mind on repeat.

Someone had been in my house. Someone had been in my house with Cami. Someone had been in my house with Cami and had done malicious damage to my pillow. This was no accident. Someone was sending a message and I'd received it loud and clear.

CAMI LOVE

CHAPTER FIVE
Cami-

Looking over the top of my book, I stared at Dylan, watching him curiously as he gazed off at nothing. He'd been sitting this way in his parents' library for almost thirty minutes now, his face grim, lips pursed, his jaw ticking as he clenched his teeth. Something was eating at him, badly, but he hadn't breathed a word about it.

I'd also noticed how overprotective he'd been lately. Whenever he was off work, I could hardly get him to leave my side, not that I was complaining. I loved having him with me, but something was definitely off. The only time he'd left me was to go talk to the police chief about some case they needed his input on, and to check the progress of the new security system that was being installed. Ever since he'd returned from our house, he seemed upset. I kept waiting for him to tell me what was going on, but he didn't say a word, sitting silently in the chair across from me with Oreo curled up asleep at his feet.

I couldn't take it any longer and I lowered my book. "How's Fort Knox coming along?"

He jerked his head to look over at me. "What?" He looked completely confused.

I laughed. "The new security system. That's what I've decided to start calling our house now, Fort Knox."

Giving a half-hearted attempt at a smile, he relaxed a little. "They should be finished tomorrow." I waited, but he didn't offer anything more. Sighing, I put my book down and got up.

His eyes never left me as I crossed to him, but he adjusted his position as I crawled onto him, straddling him. Stroking the sides of his face, I stared deeply into his eyes. "When are you going to tell me what's bothering you?"

His hands slid around behind me, stroking my back soothingly. "What makes you think something is bothering me?" I could totally tell he was trying to evade the question.

I traced my thumb over his lips and he kissed it gently. "Oh, I don't know. Maybe the fact that you've been staring off into space for the last thirty minutes while clenching your jaw so hard that I was worried you might snap it."

"So you've been spying on me, have you?"

"Yep. Just waiting for you to spill it, but it looks like you're going to need a bit of coaxing."

"Coaxing. That sounds fun. What did you have in mind?"

I smiled. "Not what you're thinking of."

"Damn," he muttered, his hands drifting

lower to squeeze my bottom and pull me up snugger against him. "What I was thinking of would be so much fun."

"I'm sure it would, but you need to talk to me first. I've been worried about you."

Lifting his hand, he brushed some of my hair away from my face, pushing it back behind my shoulder. "I love your red hair," he said. "It's so beautiful. Everything about you is beautiful." Drifting to my rounded belly, he brushed his palm over the side of it. "And I love seeing this. You're going to be an amazing mother."

I shook my head. "I know what you're trying to do. Now, quit trying to evade me."

"What? Can't a guy take some time to admire his gorgeous wife?"

"Of course, but not when he's trying to get out of answering her questions."

He sighed heavily. "There's nothing to tell, really. I'm just feeling a bit overprotective of you, lately."

"Why?" I asked, curious as to what brought it on.

"The other day, when the dog got out of his pen and we didn't know how, it made me wonder if maybe someone had been in the house and let him out. All of a sudden, I just felt kind of sick that you're home alone and unprotected all the time. I guess it brought out some of those police officer tendencies in me, again. It made me feel like you were vulnerable and I needed to do more to ensure your safety."

"Oh, sweetheart. Why didn't you just tell me that? I've been going crazy trying to figure out what's wrong. I love you; and I think you do a great job protecting me. I don't think there's a woman out there who has a better husband than you. You're always so thoughtful and considerate."

"You're my life, Goody," he replied, using his favorite nickname for me. I'd finally grown fond of hearing it and how it reminded me of our first days together. "You and this baby," he continued. "I wanted you from the moment I first laid eyes on you. I'd do anything to keep you happy and safe."

"I know that." I stroked his face again. "Trust me, I know that. Just remember, you don't need to hide things from me. I'm a big girl. You can tell me the truth."

Immediately, his eyes shuttered and he glanced away.

"What is it, Dylan? Are you telling me everything?"

Turning back to face me, his expression was grim. "The pillow wasn't chewed up by the dog. It was shredded with a knife, a knife from our kitchen."

I could feel the color draining from my face as he spoke.

"When I came home, the patio doors were open and your music was blown across the floor. The kennel was open and the dog was in bed with you. The pillow was laying shredded in the doorway to the bedroom." He swallowed hard. "The police department confirmed that the fibers on the knife in the kitchen were the same from the pillow, but there were no prints on the knife except for yours, which would be on it since you put it away. So unless you taken up sleep walking and shredding pillows . . . ."

"Someone was in the house with me," I finished for him, my voice sounding weak and soft. He nodded confirming my conclusion.

"I didn't want to tell you. I know you haven't felt the greatest with your pregnancy and I didn't want to worry you with this. And I don't want you to be afraid to be in our home; but it won't be our home anymore if I can't ensure that you're safe in it."

"But who would do this? And why?"

He shook his head. "I have no idea, but the police have been to the house to check things out. They didn't turn anything up, though. They're trying to help, but we don't really have much else to go on as far as leads."

"Well, now I know why you're turning the house into Fort Knox, at least. And thank you for telling me. It'll help me to be more alert about things that might be going on." I didn't want him to see how nervous I was. I felt violated, almost like I'd lost something dear to me. My safe haven had suddenly become a cold, sinister environment.

"If you're uneasy about going back, I know my parents will let us stay here as long as we want."

I laughed wryly. "We can't live here forever. At some point we've got to go home."

"I know. I just want you to feel comfortable there."

"I will," I replied, leaning in to kiss his lips. "I

know I'm safe and protected with you."

***

"This security system is state-of-the-art, yet easy to run, Mr. And Mrs. Wilcock. Let me walk you through it real quick."

I couldn't believe the system Dylan had purchased. When he said he intended for me to be safe, I hadn't realized how literally he meant it. Every door and window in the house had not only been wired, but had laser motion sensors attached, providing double security. Even the slightest movement near them would set off the sensor. Thankfully, they'd all been installed high enough that the dog wouldn't set them off. The system would also tell me whenever a door or window was opened, even the doggie door Dylan had installed for Oreo. I had to admit it, I was nervous about accidentally setting it off, myself.

Thankfully, the system could be easily deactivated with a punch code to the keypad on the wall, if accidentally triggered. Otherwise, the alarm system signal went straight to a control center and an operator would immediately be in communication through the speaker set into the keypad.

"It also has a smoke detector to warn of any possible fire emergencies." The security installer, Tom, according to the name embroidered on his shirt, went on and I rolled my eyes. *I hope I never burn dinner. That's just what I'd need—for Dylan's whole department to show up here. That would be humiliating.* "Do you two have any other questions?"

"I don't think so," I replied.

"Well, then, let's arm your system. You need to choose a pass code and then punch it into the keypad, hit enter, and lock. We recommend you change your pass code every three months. To do that, you just enter your current code and hit the 'Set New' button, then enter the new number and lock it, again. Someone from the security company will call you to verify that you're the one who changed the code." I was never going to remember all of this.

"What do you want to put in for the code?" Dylan asked, turning to me, and the security guy moved away to give us some privacy.

"Something easy. I don't want to be flustered trying to remember a bunch of stuff if I accidentally set this thing off."

"How about our anniversary?"

"That's fine with me."

"Excuse me," Tom broke in. "I forgot to mention we usually recommend you don't use anything like birthdays or special dates as your code, just in case those are things someone else could easily figure out."

"Oh, okay. Thank you. That makes sense," Dylan replied, glancing back at me.

"Well, there goes that idea."

Dylan's gaze traveled to my stomach and he smiled. "I know the perfect code." Lifting his hand he pressed the number '1' button. "One for me, one for you, one for the baby makes three. 1113. Does that work for you?"

I smiled widely. "I think that's perfect."

"Awesome," he replied and hit enter and

lock.

Immediately, a set of double beeps emanated from the keypad and the small digital screen flashed the word 'ARMED.' Tom helped Dylan finalize things with the company and set up security passwords to prove we were who we said we were for verification reasons, and then gathered his things and left.

Turning to me, Dylan smiled and held his arms out toward me. "Welcome to Fort Knox."

I laughed and stepped inside them, relishing the warmth and strength I found there. "Well, I certainly feel protected, that's for sure."

"Dog door, open," a computerized voice spoke from the keypad and I jumped.

"That might take some getting used to, though," I added.

"I know, but it makes me feel better. And now you'll know if the dog is inside or outside, so you won't have to go searching for him."

"You're going to keep spouting off how great this system is until I love it, aren't you?" I snickered against his chest.

"Probably." He chuckled and it resonated through him. He squeezed me tighter. "I simply want to know that you are safe and happy."

"I've always been happy," I responded, glancing up at him. "And I think you have more than taken care of the safe part."

"Nothing's too good for my girl." Bending down, his lips captured me and I opened my mouth so his tongue could tangle with mine. My hands slid up around his neck as I kissed him back. It was crazy how much I loved this man.

I'd heard people say that love would continue to grow, but I didn't really believe it. I thought I had always loved him to capacity, but that capacity continued to constantly expand.

"Thank you for everything you do, and for being concerned about me," I whispered against his lips.

"Always," he replied. "I love you."

DYLAN LOVE

CHAPTER SIX
Dylan-

"You've got to be kidding me," I mumbled into Cami's ear.

"Do it or she's going to kick you out," she replied softly, elbowing me in the stomach. "Besides, this was your idea."

"I didn't know it was going to be taught by one of Satan's minions."

"Whatever. Just do it." I could tell Cami was trying not to laugh.

"Maybe you should've brought the dog with you instead. He'd be a natural at this."

She snorted, catching the attention of the She-Devil across the room. Immediately, the instructor locked her gaze on me, eyes narrowing, as she made her way toward us.

"Do it now!" Cami practically growled.

"Hee, hee, hoo. Hee, hee, hoo." I began making the ridiculously exaggerated Lamaze breathing sounds.

The instructor stood before me and it really

wasn't a far stretch for me to imagine her with horns and a forked tail, holding a whip. "You shouldn't be staring at me, sir, but at your wife, who is having *your* baby."

Not wanting to cause any conflict, I obediently stared back at Cami and resumed coaching her breathing. As soon as the woman was out of earshot, I spoke softly. "Sorry. I'm a trained police officer. My eyes tend to go toward the biggest threat in the room." Cami elbowed me and I started my breathing, again. The instructor continued to move about the room, shouting out directions.

"What's wrong?" Cami asked between breaths.

"Nothing. I'm still just a little scarred from the birthing video. It was not pretty."

She giggled softly. "You've seen birthing videos before. Hello, Mr. Paramedic, remember?"

"Our training videos were not that gory. Besides, I practiced deliveries on a rubber pelvis with a fake baby covered in gel. Messy yes, gory no."

Cami's eyes flicked to make sure the instructor was still occupied elsewhere. "You're a paramedic, Dylan. You've seen lots of gore."

"True, but I've never imagined any of that gore coming out of my wife, and I'd like to keep it that way. The way that woman in the video was screaming, I kept expecting her to give birth to an elephant or something."

She giggled softly. "If it scared you, imagine how I feel. That's what's going to happen to me!"

Giving her a gentle hug, I kissed her forehead. "I promise I'll do whatever I can to help you, Goody,—even if it means panting like a dog."

She smiled. "It's only fair. After all, it was all your panting that got us here in the first place."

My eyes widened. "Now that is not fair, at all. You were panting just as much as I was."

"Are you sure about that?" she asked, continuing to goad me.

"Positive. I always make sure you're panting. I consider it part of my job description."

A laugh escaped her and she tried to muffle it with a cough. Quickly, I searched the room for the drill sergeant. "Don't worry. Cruella DeVil is emasculating another poor man right now. She didn't hear you enjoying yourself over here."

"Thank goodness. She is kind of a tyrant, isn't she?"

"That's putting it mildly. The lady could send armies running in retreat. How many more of these classes do we have left?" I wasn't sure I could take much more of this.

"Four."

"How do you feel about natural childbirth? With a midwife, perhaps?"

"You don't want to come anymore, do you?"

"Not one bit. There has to be something better than this."

"The classes aren't mandatory, Dylan. It's just to help the hospital get ready for us, so our check in will be easier, and to give me some help with getting through the delivery."

"I'll buy you every Lamaze and birthing video on the planet if you'll tell me we don't ever have to come here again." A woman who was moaning loudly across the room interrupted my thoughts. Her husband was by her side, visibly coaching her to breathe with exaggerated breaths. "Um, they do realize this is just practice, not the real deal, right?" I asked. A quick glance around the room showed I wasn't the only one feeling uncomfortable.

"That's the couple I was telling you about. Remember? The actors that run the community theater?" Cami's eyes widened as the woman got louder. "Apparently they're really getting into their role."

"That's it. I can't take it anymore." Standing, I pulled Cami to her feet, grabbing her yoga mat and dragging her to the door.

"Where are you going?" the instructor spewed out angrily, her eyes narrowing as she turned on us.

"Sorry, family emergency. Got to go!" We hurried through the door, practically running down the hall.

"Dylan, slow down. I can't keep up." Immediately, I slowed my pace, feeling bad for dragging her along that way.

"Cami, I'm so sorry. I just had to get out of there. I think all those people are crazy."

She snickered. "They were pretty funny."

"Maybe you can visit with your mom, or mine, and let them give you some tips. That lady tonight was way too into her job."

Cami laughed again. "Yeah, she kind of was.

I guess we lucked out that she's retired from nursing."

"I wouldn't let her anywhere around you while you were having a baby."

"Oh, so you're going to be one of those dads."

"Yes, I am. Only the best for you."

She shook her head. "I'm glad you care."

"Of course I do."

***

"You doing okay?" I asked Cami as I handed her a plastic cup full of ice and punch. She was fanning herself with a paper plate and her cheeks looked flushed.

"Yeah, I'm managing, thanks," she replied, accepting it and taking a large swallow. "Are you having a good time?"

"Yep. I just won a bunch of money." I gave her a wink and she stared at me perplexed.

"What do you mean?"

"Look." I nodded toward the right and she followed the direction indicated, hiding a snicker behind her cup when she saw Russ approaching with a very curvy girl on his arm.

"He has a date!" Sounding amazed, she giggled again.

"I knew he wouldn't show up to the Annual Fireman's Barbecue without one, not after we all razzed him at the fire."

"I wonder where he found her? I don't recognize her, but she's very pretty."

"She seems a bit on the young side to me, but your right. She's a looker," I agreed.

"Hey, now!" Her leg flashed out, kicking me

softly in the shins. "Keep your eyes where they belong."

Bending over, I kissed her cheek and whispered, "Goody, if you were in a line up with every other girl in the world, I'd still pick you out first."

A rosy flush spread across her cheeks, causing them to flame even brighter, and she stared up at me. "You still have that sweet talking thing going for you."

"And you still have that luminescent glow that attracted me from the first moment I saw you—though I'd say you're glowing much more than usual lately." Allowing my gaze to drift briefly at her rounded belly, I slid my hand down to rub it. "You're so beautiful."

She laughed. "I'm glad you like fat women."

"You aren't fat. You're perfect."

"Hey, Dylan, Cami," Russ's voice interrupted us. "I'd like to introduce you to someone."

Turning toward him, I saw he was nervous. "Hey, man. How's it going?" Extending my hand, he slapped it and followed it with a fist bump, as was our ritual greeting.

"Good, good. I wanted to introduce you to my friend, Daphne Fuentes."

Cami piped right up. "Hello, Daphne. It's so nice to meet you."

"Nice to meet you, too," she replied as they shook hands before she shook mine. "Russ talks about you a lot."

"He does, does he?" I asked. "I hate to say it, but he's failed to mention you before now. Why is that, Russ?" I thoroughly enjoyed making him squirm, after all, what were best friends for?

"Actually, we only met last night," Daphne rushed to rescue him. "So he hasn't really had time. We were out late, and then here, today."

"Two dates in a row?" I nodded, glancing at Russ. "You usually don't even make it through the first one. I'm impressed." Glancing back at Daphne, I added. "He must really like you."

Cami rushed to Russ's aide, ruining my fun. "How'd the two of you meet?"

"Blind date. Her mom knows my mom. They kept hounding us both; so we finally agreed to go out, just to get them off our backs." Russ glanced at Daphne and grinned sheepishly.

"And I kind of liked him. So I said yes when he asked me to come, today."

"Just kind of, huh?" Russ said, still smiling at her.

She shrugged. "Yeah."

I slipped my arm around Russ's shoulders. "Convenient how you picked this weekend to finally call her up. How many weeks has your mom been suggesting this, now? I know I've heard you grumbling about it for a while."

"You were grumbling about me?" Daphne said, arching her eye at him.

"Hey, in my defense, I didn't know you, yet. And I'm sure you had your share of grumbles, too."

She eyed him before laughing. "Okay, you got me. But I think it's working out nicely so far."

"Oh, you won't hear any complaints from

me," I piped up. "I think this weekend was perfect timing, though others on the department might not agree."

Daphne and Russ both looked confused. After a moment, Russ began shaking his head. "Please tell me you guys haven't been betting on me."

"Ah, it's okay." I scrubbed my hand through his hair. "A little side betting never hurt anyone."

"When?" he asked.

"At the warehouse fire."

"Damn, I knew you wouldn't let that go."

"What are friends for?"

"You suck, man."

"Yeah, but you still love me."

"Don't worry, Daphne," Cami broke in. "They're like this all the time. Why don't you come with me and I'll introduce you to some of the other girls."

"Is that okay with you?" Daphne asked Russ.

"Sure. I'll join you in a minute," he replied.

I waited until they were out of earshot. "You did good, bro."

"She is hot, isn't she?"

"A little young, maybe, but she is. Is she a keeper?"

Russ snorted. "Some of us aren't lucky enough to find love at first sight like you, dude. And don't be pointing the finger at me, Mr. I-fell-in-love-with-a-high-school-student-while-I-was-working-undercover."

I laughed. "I guess you've got me there, huh? It may have been love at first sight for me, but I had to work to convince Cami."

"No. You just had to convince her to give in to what she already wanted. Everyone saw the way you two looked at each other. It was no secret."

"We were that obvious, huh?"

"Pretty much." He looked seriously at me. "Hopefully someday I'll be that lucky."

I smiled. "Then why are you still standing here talking to me? Go get the girl!" Shoving him in the direction of where Cami and Daphne were standing in a circle of several other women, he stumbled forward.

"Russ, say what?" Wilson's voice floated through the air as he approached. "You brought a girl? I thought you were my date for this afternoon."

Russ's face reddened and he shook his head, grinning. "Like hell, man."

"I'm just messing with ya, bro." Wilson slapped him on the back. "But dang that girl has style. Come on, I think I should be introduced to your pretty lady. We can go shopping together."

Moving slowly behind them, I watched as they joined the group and several of the other firefighters came to meet Daphne. Russ had to like her more than a little to risk bringing her to this event. He was setting himself up to be teased unmercifully by everyone. Nothing escaped the notice of these guys, and they were always looking for someone to give some hell to. They would for sure tease him about robbing the cradle. Secretly, I hoped it would last. I often worried he was lonely. Hanging around with

Cami and me all the time couldn't be that exciting.

However, my cop blood still ran strong and you could bet money on the fact I'd be checking this girl out and making sure everything was on the up and up with her. Russ was my closest buddy, and that made him family. And I always watched out for my family.

CAMI LOVE

CHAPTER SEVEN
Cami-

Dylan approached, gently taking me by the elbow and leading me away from the group I was visiting with, his face grim. I knew something was wrong, immediately.

"What is it?" I asked, fear gripping my heart.

"Chris just called. The alarms are going off at the house. The police are en route. I'm going to meet them."

"I'm coming with you."

"I'd rather you stay here where I know you're safe."

"The house will be crawling with police officers. How much safer can I be?" I argued. "I'm going and that's final."

"What's going on?" Russ asked, appearing at our side.

"We have an emergency at the house and need to leave early," Dylan replied. "Can you make our excuses to the Chief? I don't think we'll be able to make it back."

"I'll take care of it. Are you sure everything is okay?"

"I don't know what is going on. Chris called to tell me the alarms had gone off and the police were on their way over. It could be nothing."

"Okay. Let me know if you need me."

"Will do. Thanks, man."

Dylan and I hurried to the car. "Do you think it's a false alarm?" I asked as we slid into the Camaro.

"Normally, I'd say yes." Firing up the engine, he quickly pulled away from the curb, gunning it until he was up to the speed limit and then slightly over. I knew he was anxious. "But I know someone was in the house with you in the middle of the day before. I wouldn't put it past them to try again."

"I don't understand it, though. If someone wanted to hurt me, why not do it while they were in the house with me the first time? They obviously had the opportunity."

"I think whoever it is, is playing a game with us. They want us to feel terrorized. I'm just worried about the incidents escalating."

"So you think someone is stalking us? Who? Why?"

He kept his eyes glued to the road as he weaved in and out of traffic. "I have no idea. It could be anybody. I don't know if someone has picked us out randomly, or if maybe someone from my police days is targeting me. Whoever it is, we need to catch them."

"Maybe the police will right now."

"I hope so. They'll approach the house in

stealth mode, but I worry the alarm will have scared whoever it is away."

He turned down our street, and I saw two cop cars with lights on parked outside the house with the doors wide open. Chris's personal vehicle was parked across the street and he was leaning against it, radio in hand.

I had very fond feelings for my brother-in-law. He'd put his own life on the line to save both Dylan and me when my best friend at the time, Clay, had attacked me in high school. I knew Dylan had looked up to him, too, ever since Chris had married Sheridan. I didn't know if it was because Chris had always been there to help us in high-pressure situations, but I always felt safer when he was around.

"Cami, please, if you love me at all, stay in the car until I tell you it's clear." Dylan glanced over and I nodded, knowing he wanted to keep me safe.

"Please be careful."

"I won't leave you behind. I promise. I'll be where you can see me the whole time." He parked next to Chris's Jeep Wrangler and hopped out immediately. "What's the word?" he asked and I rolled down the window so I could hear them. Chris waved at me and I waved back.

"There's four officers who just went inside. If the house is open anywhere, they'll go in to clear it. If not, they may need you to let them in."

"The yard is clear," a voice crackled over the radio. "The house doesn't appear to be open anywhere that we can see."

"Officer Wilcock is on the premises, now. He can let you in." I smiled internally at Chris's use of Dylan's old moniker. It was no secret that Chris had never wanted Dylan to leave the force. Apparently he still thought of him that way. It made me a little sad because I was sure Dylan missed it a lot, too. I knew he'd only given it up for me.

Dylan produced his keys and went to the front door, unlocking it. Two officers appeared, weapons drawn, and he backed away as they entered the house, staying true to his word and keeping where I could see him. I knew he was just as capable of clearing the house, but he wasn't wearing a bulletproof vest and he didn't have either of his weapons on him. I didn't want him anywhere that he could get shot. We'd already been down that road and the scar, just below his collarbone, attested to how close he'd come to losing his life. Chills ran through me at the memory, causing goose bumps to pop up on my skin. I had to refrain from the urge to jump out of the car and run to hug him. I couldn't imagine my life without him.

Chris approached my window. "How you doing, Cami?" Reaching in, he patted me on the shoulder.

"Good, if we can catch whoever is doing this. It's a bit unnerving."

"I agree. We definitely need to figure out what's going on. Piss anyone off lately?" He chuckled.

"Not that I'm aware of. Unless you count the

Lamaze instructor we ran out on the other night."

He laughed harder. "Yeah. Dylan told me about her. She sounds crazy."

"She kind of was," I agreed. "But all this started before our Lamaze class."

He sighed, staring over at Dylan. "I know he is more worried than he lets on."

I stared at him, too. "I'm aware of that. I think it's pretty obvious now that he's turned our house into Fort Knox. He also sticks to me like glue, lately. I can hardly leave the room for a glass of water without him following me."

"I don't blame him. I'd do the same for Sheridan and Chrissy if I felt they were in danger."

"How's Chrissy feeling, by the way? Sheridan told me she had the flu."

"She's been better since yesterday. Sheridan took her to the doctor and they prescribed something to help settle her stomach so she can keep food down."

"I'm glad to hear it. I know you both were worried. I can't wait for our kids to play together."

Chris smiled. "The family is growing bigger. I don't think I've ever seen Dylan's mom happier."

"Connie sure loves getting grandkids," I agreed. I knew exactly what he was doing. He was trying to keep me calm with normal talk. Dylan had done it to me enough for me to recognize the strategy. It was working though, and I appreciated it.

The radio crackled. "The house is clear."

"You can go in. It's all clear," Chris called to Dylan, opening the door for me, and extending a hand to help me out.

Dylan disappeared inside the front door and I heard the alarm turn off as we approached. He was speaking with an operator through the keypad as we entered, verifying his identity and confirming the arrival of the police and that everything was okay. Two more officers came in the door behind us, immediately going over to the two who had cleared the house. I could hear Oreo yapping wildly from his kennel in the other room. He must be terrified.

"What's the verdict?" Dylan asked.

"We didn't find anyone, but there are some scratches around a handle on one of the patio doors, suggesting someone, perhaps, tried to get in that way," one of the officers said.

Dylan nodded. "The patio doors were open last time, too, so that makes sense."

"We'll call someone to dust the door for prints. Maybe we can pick up something that way," Chris said, and Dylan nodded, again.

"I'm going to get the dog," I said. "He sounds terrified." Hurrying from the room, I rushed to Oreo's kennel in the kitchen. His barking grew louder when he saw me. "Hey, boy, hey." I opened the door and he waggled up to me. "Oh, poor baby. I bet that loud noise was horrible to your sweet doggy ears, wasn't it?" I sat on the floor, letting him crawl into my lap, he jumped up, licking my face as I scratched under his chin and petted him. "Oh, yes, poor,

poor baby. It's going to be okay now, I promise. Mommy and daddy are home, now. I'm sorry you were scared."

"I wish I had a video camera." I glanced over to where Dylan was leaning in the doorway staring at me, his eyes shuttered.

I laughed. "How come?"

"I think this is the first time I've heard you do so much puppy talk. I think it's cute."

"Then why are you scowling at me?"

Pushing away from the wall he came toward me and Oreo ran over to him, wagging his tail. He lifted Oreo, stroking him. "Because someone tried to break in here, again. And alarm system or not, I can't leave you alone in this house knowing someone is trying to get in."

"Well, you're going to have to. You have a life and a job. You can't put everything on hold to babysit me every second of the day. Plus, I wouldn't want you to."

He put the dog on the floor and came closer, pulling me up and into his arms. "I can't risk you, Goody. I can't risk our baby. What if someone made it in the house and harmed you before help could get here? Yes, the alarm will notify the police, but precious minutes would be lost, first."

"What makes you so sure this person is after me? As you pointed out before, they were in the house before and didn't harm me. Plus, it was your pillow that was shredded."

"True, but the attacks also seem to come during the times when you're most likely to be home alone."

"And what better way to get to you, than to mess with me?" I added. Despite being in his warm embrace, I shivered, feeling like ice was creeping through my veins.

"Anyone who knows me at all, knows my family is the best way to get to me. And they'd also know my wife would be number one on that list."

"That's why I'm going to have the department run your past collars," Chris said from behind us. "Maybe we can find something there."

"I don't think Cami should stay here anymore until we figure it out." Dylan squeezed me tighter, as if he was afraid he might lose me.

"So where should we go? Back to your parents' house?"

"No." Chris shook his head. "If this person is targeting Dylan, Connie and Weston's house won't be safe, either."

"You need to go home," Dylan said. "Stay with your parents in Copper City. That'll get you out of the area and I can rest easier knowing that you're taken care of."

"And what about you? I don't want you left here in the middle of danger. How is that fair?"

"If I'm here, I can still be bait. And I know how to take care of an intruder. It'll be easier for me if you aren't here to get hurt in the crossfire."

"I can stay with him, too, if that would make you rest easier," Chris suggested.

"No." Dylan looked at him sharply. "You need to stay with Sheridan. If someone is targeting my family, she and Chrissy could be a target, too. It could be any of us."

Chris sighed heavily. "You're right."

"And what if this intruder has been scared off?" I asked. "How do you know they'll come back, again? I can't live with my parents indefinitely."

"What would you have me do, Cami?" The frustration ran heavily through his voice.

"Let me stay here with you."

"It would kill me when I had to go to work. I can't do that."

I stared aimlessly at the microwave, wondering what to do. I wanted to make Dylan happy and feel safe, too; but I didn't want to leave him, either. "The microwave isn't working," I said suddenly, noticing the digital clock wasn't on.

"What?" Dylan asked, obviously confused by the change in subject.

"The microwave. The clock isn't on."

Releasing me he went and opened the door, closing it again before trying to push some of the buttons. Chris stepped to the light switch and flipped it, staring at the ceiling. Nothing happened. Lifting his radio, he spoke. "Hey, check and see if the neighbors have any power."

"Copy," a voice came back.

"Where's your fuse box?"

"Outside," Dylan replied. "Let's go look."

I followed the two of them and watched as they checked the box. "The main breaker is on and nothing has flipped," Dylan said, checking everything.

"Detective, the neighbors have power," the voice over the radio came again.

"Copy," Chris replied.

"Let's call the power company and see of there's another way the power could've been cut," I suggested.

"Okay," Dylan agreed. I quickly looked up the number for the service provider on one of our bills and Dylan dialed it. After waiting on hold for a few moments, an operator answered his call. He quickly gave our account number and asked if there was any reason we didn't have power. A perplexed look crossed his face. "That can't be right." He stared at me.

"What is it?" I asked.

"They said the service was scheduled for termination today, that the account had been cancelled . . .by my wife, Cami Wilcock."

I felt the color drain from my face. "I never called them."

"What if someone thought cutting the power would disable the alarm, not knowing there's a back up battery?" Chris asked.

"I'll call you back," Dylan said, ending the call immediately. "Cami, get packing. You're going to your parents' right now."

This time I didn't argue.

DYLAN LOVE

CHAPTER EIGHT
Dylan-

The sound of the garage door opening immediately caught my attention. Grabbing my gun from the end table where I'd laid it, I made my way toward the kitchen. The sound of a car pulling in made me set it back down. I knew exactly who it was. Sighing, I opened the door, watching as she climbed out of her car. "What are you doing home?" I tried to sound upset, but truth be told, she was a sight for sore eyes.

The dog ran happily toward me as she turned, tossing her gorgeous red hair behind her shoulder. She folded her arms across her chest, clearly prepared for an argument. "It's been a week, Dylan; and while I did enjoy the visit with my parents, I can't stay there forever. You said yourself, not one thing has happened while I've been gone, yet you keep refusing to let me come home. I decided to take matters into my own hands. I think whoever was here before was probably scared away by the alarm system.

They know they can't get in now. Besides, I missed you. I hate sleeping without you, and the baby has been moving so much this week and you're missing out on all of it. There's only so much a girl can share with her parents before she needs to be with her husband, again." She was rambling and I loved it. Clearly, she'd been having this argument with me in her head for the last two hours while she drove home. "Besides, every time I go into Copper City I have to pass Clay's old street. I'm always afraid I'm going to run into his parents. He's dead because of me, and facing them was one of the hardest things I ever had to do. It's just so awkward now and I can't do all this alone anymore. I miss being—."

"Cami." I cut her off as tears started dripping over the rims of her eyes. "I'm happy you're here. Welcome home." Stepping from the doorway, I hit the button to close the garage and moved toward her, grabbing her around the waist and pressing her against the side of the car. Glancing down, I chuckled. "You're belly's gotten bigger since you've been gone. This doesn't work quite as well as it used to."

"No, it really doesn't." A corner of her mouth perked up in a half smile and she sighed heavily. "Promise you aren't mad?"

Slipping to the side of her stomach, I leaned in close, staring at her lips. "I promise. While I love video chatting with you on the phone, it's got nothing on holding you in my arms." Pressing my lips against hers, I slid my hands over her shoulders and down her arms until my fingers linked with hers. "I missed you. A lot."

"I missed you, too."

"I kind of got that already." Grinning, I kissed her again. "How are you feeling?" She looked so tired and suddenly I felt bad for sending her away. It appeared to have taken a toll on her. I knew it had on me.

"Honestly? Like a beached whale. Nothing fits right, I'm exhausted all the time, and it seems like the more I try to do, the deeper I bury myself in the sand."

Squealing as I swept her off her feet, she threw her arms around my neck. "What are you doing?"

"Taking care of my wife. Let's get you all comfy in bed, okay?" Moving to go back inside, I paused at the door. "Turn that knob, will you?" She did and I pushed it open, allowing Oreo to come inside before letting it close. "You'll feel better if you can rest in your own bed. We'll get you in your favorite robe and I'll prop you up with pillows, rent you some movies, order in dinner, and maybe massage your feet for you, if you'd like. We can snuggle together for the rest of the night. How does that sound?"

"As long as I get to be with you, it sounds like heaven. The dog has been cooped up most of the week, too. He might enjoy running around out in the backyard. My parents' yard had a space between the gate and the wall, so I had to keep him inside except for taking him out on the leash to go potty. Plus, I only walked him once a day. I was too tired to take him more often."

"Don't worry. I'll let him outside and set some food and water on the patio. He can play out there for the rest of the day."

She snickered. "Yeah, you sound all noble, but I know you just want to keep him from lying between us on the bed."

I laughed. "Okay, you caught me; but is wanting you all to myself really a bad thing?"

"Not at all. I want that, too."

Setting her back on her feet in our bedroom, she moved to sit on the bed while I went to the closet and removed her robe, taking it to her. "Here you go. Get changed. I'll go put the dog out and order some food. Anything in particular that you would like?"

"Pizza. A thin crust veggie pizza sounds divine. I've been craving one all week, but my mom was so happy we could cook meals together, again, I couldn't bear to ask if we could order one. I didn't want to offend her." She slipped her blouse over her head, tossing it in the nearby chair before unhooking her bra. I couldn't help but watch, my eyes drifting over her beautiful figure. She still looked the same as the day I first saw her, except for the perfectly rounded belly that jutted out in front of her, and her breasts were a little heavier and fuller, a perk of pregnancy I happened to greatly enjoy, especially when she wore lower cut shirts. Immediately, my body reacted to the sight of hers and I felt like a jerk for wanting to forget everything else and spend the night making love to her over and over again. To say we had a healthy physical relationship was a bit of an understatement. The two of us enjoyed our alone time together and frequently spent hours relishing in the pleasure we found in each other's arms. Having her gone for a week hadn't been an ideal situation at all, for either of us, but she seemed too tired for any of that at the moment.

She slipped her arms into her robe, sighing heavily. "Thanks for your help. I'm sorry to be a burden," she said, snapping me out of my lustful musings.

"No problem. I got it taken care of. You get comfortable. I'll be back in a couple of minutes." Herding Oreo from the room, I shut the door. "Come on, boy. Let's let you go play." He happily ran outside when I opened the patio door and I grabbed his food and water from inside and placed them outside, watching for a moment as he happily ran alongside the pool, sniffing the ground. Hopefully, he would enjoy the rest of the afternoon and evening out there. I'd let him in after Cami went to sleep. Checking to make sure the doggie entrance was closed, I went into the kitchen to order pizza and reset the alarm system.

I hadn't told Cami, but I'd purposely kept the alarm system off while I was at home, hoping to catch whoever had been terrorizing us in the act. But there hadn't even been so much as a nibble. That, of course, made me rest a little easier at having her back. Maybe she was right. Maybe the intruder had been scared off already. I could only hope that was the case.

**

Shrill screams shattered the air, making me jump straight out of bed. "Cami?" I hollered, instantly worried when I noticed she wasn't in the room.

"Dylan!" her terrified voiced echoed through the halls. "Help me!"

Reaching in the drawer, I grabbed my gun and ran down the hall, not even caring that I was naked. "Where are you?" I called out.

"On the patio!" Her loud sobs were audible as I rounded the corner and saw blood everywhere. A second jolt of fear bolted through me as my eyes raced over her, seeking an explanation. "Holy shit! Are you okay?"

"I'm fine," she replied, her voice trembling heavily. Moving she pointed. "It . . . it's Oreo."

My gaze drifted to where our little puppy lay mutilated in a puddle of blood and I noticed right away there were words written in sticky liquid on the sidewalk.

STILL HERE.

Rage punched me in the gut and I raised my weapon, my eyes darting to the darkened corners of the yard, worried that someone was still out there. "Cami, come back inside, now, and lock the doors behind you." I kept my gun trained on the yard as she came inside. As soon as I heard the lock click, I lowered my weapon, immediately noticing the bloody footprints she left on the tile floors as she walked. She sank into the nearest chair, hiding her hands in her face as she sobbed. "Who would do this?"

I didn't answer, hurrying to rearm the system while pressing the panic button.

"Security Plus, how can I help you?" a female voice came through the speaker.

"We've had another intruder at this residence. Our dog has been slaughtered and a threat is written on the patio in blood. Please send officers immediately. I'm not sure if anyone is still out in the yard, but we are locked in the house."

"Yes, sir, Mr. Wilcock. I'm alerting the police right now. Please stay on the line with me until the police can confirm arrival."

"Okay." I could hear her talking on another line, presumably to the dispatcher.

"Mr. Wilcock?"

"Yes?"

"For the police, how many people are currently in the residence with you at this time?"

"Just my wife and me are here."

"All right. Let me relay this information." Again we could hear the once sided conversation.

Kneeling next to Cami, I wrapped my arms around her. "What happened, honey?"

"I . . . I got up to go to the bathroom and realized we'd both fallen asleep and hadn't let the dog back in. I . . . I put on my robe and came in here to open the doggy door, expecting him to rush right in, but he didn't, so I opened the patio door and called s . . . softly for him." She was so upset she was stuttering. "W . . . when he didn't come, I got worried that he got out of the yard somehow, so I flipped on the light. Th . . . that was when I saw him lying there. I rushed over to him, but there was n . . .

nothing, I could do."

"Okay, honey, okay. Don't worry. We'll get to the bottom of this. I promise." I stroked my hands over her back in a soothing manner trying to calm her down while my own anger rose to near boiling temperatures. Someone was definitely targeting her, or me, and after what I'd seen tonight, I was sure it was one very sick bastard. I needed to get Cami away from here. "Honey, I need to go get some clothes on real quick before the police get here. Will you be okay for a minute?"

She nodded.

"Listen for the dispatcher," I reminded her before running through the house to our room. Flipping the light switch on, I didn't bother with any underwear, instead grabbing the sweat pants and t-shirt I'd been wearing earlier and slipping them on as I moved back toward Cami. I didn't want to leave her alone.

"Mr. Wilcock?" the woman's voice came through the keypad as I entered the room, again.

"Yes?"

"There should be a squad car pulling up in front of your house right now. I'll stay on the line while you confirm it's them at the door." A hard knock sounded at the front door almost as soon as she spoke the words.

"I'm going to let them in, Cami. Are you okay here?" She nodded, still hiccupping, and I hated to leave her for one more second. Hurrying to the front entryway, I opened the door to find two officers on the step and recognized them as former colleagues, Nicklaus and McMahon. I was surprised to see Chris pull up right behind their squad car. "Down the hall, guys," I said, motioning the way for them to go. "Cami is back there." They hurried off. "The police have arrived," I confirmed to the security woman from the keypad by the front door. "Thanks for your help."

"Any time, Mr. Wilcock, good luck and good night. Let us know if you need anything else."

"Thank you, I will."

Chris entered, closing the door behind him. "I heard the call over my scanner and recognized your address. What's going on?"

"Back here."

I led him into the family room where the back door had been opened, revealing the grizzly site to them. Officer Nicklaus put his hand on his weapon and flipped on his mag light, stepping carefully around the blood as he searched the dark recesses of the yard. His light bobbed around, revealing nothing out of the ordinary that I could see.

"I don't see anyone out here now. There are some partial bloody footprints out here, but it looks like those might belong to your wife."

"Well, this looks like an obvious crime to me," Chris said. "I say we get a team out here and see if they can lift anything that will give us something to go on."

"I'll get right on it," Officer McMahon said. "Nicklaus can get the official statement."

I knelt down by Cami, who was still sniffling with a blank stare on her face. "Why don't we go into the other room, Goody? Let these guys do their job. I don't want you to be in the thick of things."

"Who would kill my dog?" she asked in a tiny voice, wringing her hands. There was blood on them, too. "I don't understand. He was just a puppy. He would never hurt anyone."

"Honey, whoever is doing this is sick. They aren't thinking rationally. This is why I don't want to leave you unprotected." I hoped it was finally sinking in for her. My instincts had been dead on. Taking her by the elbow, I guided her into the other room, getting her seated comfortably. "Would you like something to drink? Some warm tea or something to help calm your nerves?"

"No, I'm good. Thank you." She straightened her spine and began retelling her experience to Officer Nicklaus, who carefully wrote things down in his notebook. I went into the bathroom and wet a washcloth with warm water, before going to wash the blood off her hands and feet. Before long, more people were entering the house and Chris was heading up a full-fledged investigation.

Glancing at Cami, who still sat with her hands clenched in her lap, I brushed her hair to the side. "Honey, why don't you try getting some sleep? There's going to be cops in and out of this place for hours. Get some rest while things are safe and we can discuss what we want to do in the morning. You look worn out."

The fact that she slipped her hand into mine without argument spoke volumes. Once she was safely tucked back into bed, I turned on some soft relaxing music, hoping it would soothe her. She closed her eyes and I turned out the light.

"Call for me if you need anything." I went back into the family room, silently watching the team at work. I needed to make some sort of plan, and I needed to do it fast.

CHAPTER NINE
Cami-

I'd been awake for hours now, simply lying there, listening to the silence in the house. Dylan was sound asleep next to me and I didn't want to wake him up. I had no idea when he had finally come to bed, but I knew he was supposed to start his night shift rotation this evening. I wasn't sure what he had planned for me, but I knew for certain I would not be staying here alone.

My eyes drifted to the nightstand where his gun lay loaded, so he could easily reach it and it my heart hurt. I kept hoping that last night was just some kind of terrible nightmare, but I knew it was true. I was afraid to get up and go into the family room, again. I didn't want to look outside.

Had they removed my puppy? Were things cleaned up now? I didn't think I'd ever be able to go into the backyard, again; and being here, in this house, felt scary to me, now. Just the thought of going into the kitchen for some food unnerved me. I knew the alarm system was on, but I still had a fear of someone jumping out at me. I felt traumatized and terrorized. Whoever was doing this to us, if that was their plan, then they were succeeding.

Closing my eyes, I tried, unsuccessfully, to stop the tears that were leaking. I needed to be brave, be angry, stand up to this person and not let them ruin my life. Something had to give, though. There was no way I could bring a baby home to this. I protectively rubbed my hand over my belly. I wanted my little boy to be safe, to feel loved. How was I supposed to be a good mother if we were constantly running in fear?

I hated living that way. I'd been there before and it was an extremely unpleasant experience—one that ate its way into every facet of my life. I was angry at whoever this was for taking me back to that place.

Dylan's hand snaked over where mine rested and he linked fingers with me. Glancing at his face, I saw the unfettered concern there. Immediately, the tears burst forth and I scooted closer to him so I could be in his warm, strong embrace.

He wrapped his arms around me, letting me cry against his bare chest as he stroked my hair. He didn't offer any words of comfort, letting me know right away he felt the same way I did. My tears fell freely for several minutes before I finally sighed heavily and tried to rein my emotions back in.

"I love you, Goody." That was the best thing

he could say to me right now. I needed all the love he had to give me.

"I love you, too. Sorry for getting you all wet."

"I'm sorry you have a reason to cry," he replied.

"It's not your fault." We lay together in silence for a few more moments before he spoke again. "After we get up and get you something to eat, I want to pack up some our things. We're going to stay at my parents' house for a while. I don't want you here by yourself and I feel safer about going to work knowing you have people around you there. Chris said he and Sheridan would even come stay with you. I'd like knowing that you have a cop in the house to protect you while I'm gone, especially since my parents will still be gone on their Mediterranean cruise."

I nodded, already prepared for him to tell me all this. I knew he wouldn't let me stay here.

"Is Oreo . . . I mean, did they . . . ." I couldn't put what I wanted to say into words.

Dylan sighed heavily. "Chris took the dog when he left, but they've taped off the family room and the patio, just in case they need to come check anything else again, today, before it gets cleaned up."

"I can't bear to look at all that, again," I said honestly. "It makes me feel queasy just thinking about it."

He continued his soothing strokes. "You won't have to. We'll get you out of here and you'll hopefully be able to relax better at my folks' place. Why don't you go take a nice hot shower and I'll make you some food? Do you want breakfast or lunch? It's almost noon."

"Breakfast, please. I don't feel much like eating, but that'll settle better I think."

"Okay, breakfast it is." He threw the covers back and climbed out of bed. I noticed he was still wearing the sweats he'd thrown on last night. I watched him as he went into the bathroom and I heard him turn on the shower. He reappeared in the doorway. "Water's hot for you. I'll have something ready for you when you get out."

I got up and gave him a big hug. "Thanks for taking such good care of me."

"It's one of my favorite things to do," he replied, hugging me back as he kissed the top of my head. "Go get in the shower." He released me, spanking my bottom as I passed and it made me laugh slightly.

"There's the sound I love to hear." I turned to look at him and he winked at me. I couldn't help smiling back. He made me feel so loved and appreciated.

Quickly undressing, I glanced up just in time to see him walk out of the bedroom, gun in hand. The weight settled on me, once again, as I climbed into the shower. Even he didn't feel safe in the house, if he was resorting to carrying his gun from room to room.

Though I was upset, the shower did wonders to help my tight muscles relax. I hadn't realized how much tension I'd been holding in. After I finished washing, I stood under the spray for several extra minutes, letting myself enjoy the luxury.

Remembering that Dylan was waiting for me to come eat breakfast, I sighed, turning the water off, and toweling dry before wrapping my hair up in it and slipping into a fresh robe and my slippers. I made my way down the hall, but stopped abruptly when I heard voices. Dylan was talking with someone.

"You're not going to like what I have to say." It was Chris's voice.

"Tell me," Dylan demanded.

"Has Cami been feeling okay lately?"

"She's been a little on the tired side with her pregnancy. Why?"

Chris sighed heavily. "All the evidence the department has points to her as the most likely suspect. They think she might be under stress and doing this herself."

"Like hell," Dylan growled.

I felt a pain stab through my stomach. *They think I am doing this? What? How?* I was trembling.

"The first incident was your pillow. It was shredded with a knife from your kitchen. Only Cami's fingerprints were on the knife. Your power was turned off and the utility company says Cami was the one who did it. When you sent her away for the week, nothing happened. But the day she came home, your dog was killed and only her footprints and fingerprints are at the scene."

"This is bullshit," Dylan said angrily. "I can't believe the department is trying to pin this on her. There's no way in hell she's responsible for this, Chris, and you know it. Cami wouldn't hurt a fly, let alone kill her own dog. What kind of motive would she have?"

"They wondered if she might be lonely and wanting your attention. Pregnancy can really mess with a woman's hormones and make them do strange things. That's why they want to know if you've noticed anything different about her."

"She didn't do it, damn it!" Dylan shouted. "What about when the alarm went off? She was with me at the Fireman's Barbecue. She has dozens of witnesses that can attest to that fact. How'd she manage that?"

Another pain stabbed me in the gut.

"I'm not saying I believe it, Dylan. You know I love Cami. But when the evidence points to a certain direction, I've got to follow up on those leads. I agree about the alarm going off. That doesn't fit, but what about everything else?"

"The police need to do their fucking job and protect my family, not try to pin the blame on my wife!" Dylan was irate.

The pain gripped me harder and I groaned loudly as I fell to the floor, clenching my stomach.

"Cami?" Dylan's concerned voice called to me.

"Help," I said breathlessly, the pain devouring me.

Both he and Chris appeared at my side. "Honey what is it?" He grabbed my shoulders.

"I think I'm having contractions." Another pain stabbed me, again.

"Call an ambulance," Dylan ordered Chris.

***

The rapid sound of my baby's heartbeat on the monitor soothed my soul. I closed my eyes, just enjoying the sound of my little Peanut living inside me.

"Drink some more water, honey," Dylan said as I opened my eyes to look at him.

"I'm hooked up to an I.V., Dylan. I think I'm getting plenty of fluids, now."

"I just don't want you to get dehydrated, again. I've been so caught up in everything else going on that I wasn't paying attention to how much you were eating or drinking. The doctor says you need to have lots more fluids than you're getting."

"I know. I'm sorry. I haven't had much of an appetite for anything, lately." I sighed heavily. "And to be honest, that's not likely to improve, either, if the police think I'm the lead suspect in their case."

"Cami, I don't want you even thinking about all that bullshit. I'm pissed that you even heard it. It's ridiculous; and I promise you, I'll see that this is taken care of. They have no right to accuse you of anything." He was extremely upset, I could tell, and it worried me.

"Well, if I didn't know it wasn't me, I'd have to say things do look pretty suspicious. Tell me the truth. If this were someone else you were investigating, what would you think?"

Leaning on his elbows against bed, he scrubbed his hands over his face. "Honestly? Yes, I'd see a connection; but the fact also remains that you had a strong alibi while you were at the barbecue. The patio doors had scratches on it. How were you supposed to be here scratching up the door and setting off alarms while you were with me at the station the entire time? It's a flaw in their deductions, one that should prove it wasn't you."

"True, but who knows if the scratches weren't there from the time before, when the intruder was in the house. He could've scratched it up then. Could Oreo have set the alarm off somehow?"

"He was penned up. I'm sorry, it still doesn't make sense; and as soon as I know you're taken care of, I'm going straight to talk with Chief Robson, because this is ludicrous. They need to be looking for who is really doing this."

"Well, we both know it's not me, so take some comfort in that. And, as you pointed out, their theory has flaws. Hopefully they'll figure it out."

"Don't worry. I'll take care of it, somehow." He slipped his hand into mine, toying with my wedding ring. "As soon as they release you from here, I'm taking you straight to my parents' house. I'll come back and pack up our things, myself. I don't want you back in that house until we figure out what's going on and catch who's behind this. Okay?"

I nodded, understanding that he was simply trying to keep me safe. "At this point, I don't want to be there. I don't like the idea of you being there alone either, though."

"I'll take Chris with me. That way no one can accuse me of tampering with the crime scene."

"I can't believe this is happening. I feel like I'm stuck in a bad nightmare that I can't wake up from."

He squeezed my hand. "Leave the nightmare to me. You just worry about keeping yourself and our baby healthy. That's all you should be concentrating on right now."

Lifting his hand, I kissed it. "I'll do my best." I promised.

DYLAN LOVE

CHAPTER TEN
Dylan-

Sitting in the recliner with my feet and arms crossed, I stared aimlessly at the television, attempting to appear normal to the rest of the crew in the station. Cami was safely stowed away in my old bedroom, texting me every hour, on the hour, to let me know she was okay. Chris was there with her, as well, which relieved a lot of my worry regarding her immediate safety. He was a crack shot and had proven, on several occasions, that he could be relied on to help take care of both Cami and me.

My mind drifted back to my earlier conversation at the police station with Chief Robson. It was probably a good thing I wasn't on the force anymore because I probably would've been fired for the way I spoke to him. My hands tightened into fists at the memory of his words.

"*Dylan, calm down. If we have leads we have to follow them, even if they implicate someone you love. Hell, we all love Cami, but you need to step aside and let us do our investigation."*

"I'm trying to," I replied hotly. "But it's a little difficult when all I see is a bunch of incompetent assholes pointing fingers at my wife!"

"That's enough, son. You need to leave before I'm forced to put you in the holding tank to give you some time to chill out."

I wanted to punch something. I felt desperate, not knowing how to make him understand. "Just try to find out who's doing this. It's not Cami. And you need to stop whoever it is before someone gets hurt or killed."

"Dylan, you okay, man?" Russ spoke up from a chair across the room, calling me back to the present. "You look a little pissed, right now."

I took in a deep breath, trying to relax. "Just have something bugging me, tonight. Trying to figure it out in my head."

The rest of the guys on the crew exchanged furtive glances. "We heard about your dog from Chief Daniels," Wilson spoke up. "That's rough."

"Anything we can do to help you out?" Charlie asked.

I shook my head and gave them a wry smile. "Not that I can think of. I guess I'm just going to have to sit back and let the police try to figure it out."

"Any leads yet?" Ron asked.

"None," I replied abruptly. There was no way I would ever tell anyone about their suspicions of Cami. "How's your new girlfriend, Russ?" I asked, deliberately knowing it would switch attention from me to him.

"Yeah, Weston. How'd your date with Daphne go?" Charlie asked. "Did you get lucky?"

"He better not have," Wilson piped up. "That girl's young enough to land him in jail if he did."

"That's not fair," Russ said, shaking his head. "She's not that young."

"Are you going to Prom with her?" Wilson asked, and everyone burst out laughing, even me.

"You guys are douches," Russ replied, picking up his soda and taking a swig.

"Ah, come on," Charlie piped up. "We're just messing with ya. All of us would love to the chance to go back and have high school sex, again."

Everyone laughed again, and then grew quiet. I watched them for a moment before I chuckled. "Every single one of you just went back to your first time, didn't you?"

"Her name was Sarah," Ron said with a nostalgic look. "I was seventeen and she was at my house for a slumber party my sister was having. She snuck into my room in the middle of the night. I woke up to her kissing me." He sighed and then laughed. "It was over quick, but it was awesome."

"My first was Candy," Charlie spoke. "I was sixteen and so was she. We were out at a bonfire party; but after making out for a while, we moved our party to the back of my pick up."

"I was sixteen," Wilson said. "Her name was

Lori and we were also at a party, but it was at her house while her parents were gone."

"Wait. Your first time was with a girl?" Russ asked incredulously.

Wilson nodded. "Yep. That's when I officially knew I was gay. I kept staring at the picture she had of her and her brother on a nightstand and I wasn't looking at her. How about you, Dylan? Who was your first?"

I sighed, giving a half chuckle at the turn of the topic. "I was fourteen—,"

"Woe ho!" Charlie called out. "Lucky bastard."

"I was playing Varsity football and all the senior guys dared me to go kiss one of the senior cheerleaders at a party. I did. She liked it and dragged me off into one of the bedrooms. She was a little loud, so yeah, everyone knew what was going on."

"And I bet you had all the girls lining up for their turn after that, didn't you?" Charlie asked.

I shook my head, laughing. "Well, let's just say I never lacked company and leave it at that."

"I knew it. You're that guy—the one we all wished we were."

"Hey now," I said. "We haven't heard Russ's story, yet. He may have us all beat." The attention shifted back to Russ once again. "Come on, Russ. Spill it."

"I pass," Russ replied, drinking another swallow of his drink.

"He's still a virgin," Wilson said and we laughed, again. "I knew it."

"Whatever," Russ said rolling his eyes.

"Then tell us about your first time," Ron said.

He sighed heavily. "You guys don't know what you're asking." He glanced up, locking eyes with me and looking worried, causing me to wonder what was going on.

"Come on, we all told," Wilson said. "How bad can it be?"

"It wasn't bad. Not at all," Russ replied, suddenly fidgeting restlessly.

"And . . . ." Charlie prompted.

"I was seventeen, almost eighteen, and it was at a party I went to, as well." He sighed again, and I couldn't for the life of me figure out was wrong. He continued, never taking his eyes off me. "The girl was hitting on my new best friend, but he left the party; so she came looking for me."

Realization hit me. I was going to be sick. "You're not telling me your first time was with Gabrielle Martinez, are you?" I asked, but I already knew the answer. "That girl was a friggin' slut."

"I tried to tell you—in my own way."

"When?" I asked, not caring that the rest of the crews' heads were bobbing back and forth between us like they were watching a volleyball game.

"I told you the reason she wanted you so badly was because no guy had ever turned her down before—I meant, including me."

Shaking my head, I stood and walked into the kitchen and opened the fridge, suddenly wishing I could have a beer. Russ appeared at my side.

"Don't be pissed, bro. You said you didn't want anything to do with her; and that was well before we knew she was involved with everything surrounding Cami."

"I'm not mad," I replied, shutting the fridge and sitting down at the table. He pulled out a chair across from me and sat, as well. "I'm just trying to get over the fact that my best friend slept with a girl I absolutely despise."

He didn't say anything, instead just stared down at his fingers.

"Please tell me it was only once," I added and he slowly shook his head, again.

"We hooked up a lot for a couple weeks after that. She kept asking me about you though; and I got tired of it, so I told her to take a hike."

I snorted. "You know she was banging Clay that whole time, don't you?"

"I do now."

"I hope you got tested for disease. If you were going to catch something from anybody, it'd be her."

"I was careful—always used protection."

Giving another grunt, I stared at him, crossing my arms across my chest. "If it were me, I'd still get tested. That girl got passed around more than a joint at a party." I sighed, again. "Why her?"

He laughed. "Dude, she was a horny girl and I was a guy wanting to experience it. How many girls have you hooked up with?"

He had me there. "Point taken. Seriously though, Russ, get tested. I'm not joking. Gabby was bad news. Who knows what else she could've been involved in?"

"I will," he replied. I hoped he was serious. "Now, tell me, what's going on with you and Cami?"

Leaning forward I rested my arms on the table, so we were closer together. I didn't want anyone hearing what I had to say. "Someone is stalking us. I have no idea who, or why."

"What do you mean, stalking you? Like are they following you around or something?"

"No. Maybe terrorizing is a better term. I came home one day and I found my pillow shredded in the hallway and all the French doors to the patio were open. At first I thought the dog had done it, but when I examined it closer, I realized someone had sliced it up with a knife. I found the knife in our kitchen."

"Wow. That's insane. Where was Cami?"

"That's what scares me. She was asleep in our bed with the dog. She claims she'd put the dog in his kennel and laid down for a nap."

"So, someone was in the house with her?" I loved Russ a little more in that moment, just because he didn't think Cami was involved.

I nodded. "When we left the barbecue early, it was because the police had called and said the alarms were going off at our house. They found signs of attempted entry at the back door—there were some scratches. Once we got inside, we noticed the power was off to the house. I called the service provider and they said someone claiming to be Cami had cancelled our service."

"Seriously? That's insane."

"Yeah, then there was this whole thing with the dog. Whoever killed him made a bloody mess out of it. They wrote the words 'Still Here' in blood on the patio."

"What the hell?" Russ exclaimed looking horrified. "Do the police have any suspects?"

Gritting my teeth, I had to pause to get my anger under control. "Chris called for a crime scene investigation. He came over this morning to tell me the findings."

"Which were?"

"They think Cami is doing it." I watched him carefully. He snorted. "Come on, man. Quit messing with me. What'd they say, really?" I stayed silent, simply staring at him, waiting for him to figure it out. His eyes widened astronomically. "You're not joking, are you? They really think it's her."

"That's the direction they're leaning."

"I'm sorry, but that's bullshit. Cami would never do anything like this. Why would she?"

"They asked me if her pregnancy was making her seem weird at all."

"You need to go talk to your old chief and tell him what's what. There's absolutely no way she's responsible."

"Already done. I even punched a hole in their theory, but they won't let it go."

"And how's Cami taking all this? Is that what started her contractions this morning?"

"Yeah, plus a combination of stress and dehydration. She's barely been eating and drinking through all of this. I've been worried about her."

"I'm assuming she's at your parents' house?"

I nodded. "Yep. Chris is there with her."

"Well, that makes me feel better, at least. I know he'll keep a good eye on her while you're not around."

A loud series of tones came through the speakers and our radios, simultaneously. "General page, general page. Engine nine dash three. We have reports of a large structure fire at 8725 W. Goldenrod Avenue."

I felt the color drain from my face and Russ snatched his radio off his belt. I watched as the rest of the guys ran for their turnouts, almost as if everything were happening in slow motion.

"Engine nine dash three copies the structure fire," Russ responded. "Can you please repeat that address?"

"8725 W. Goldenrod Avenue. We have calls reported both from people on the scene and a security company."

Russ looked at me, his eyes wide and he swallowed hard. "Dylan, your house is on fire."

***

I stared at the smoldering remains of what had once been my home. Everything was a complete loss, the baby's room, wedding pictures, clothing, and furnishings. It was all gone, everything from the first two years of Cami's and my life together. Unable to move, I stood rooted to the spot as crews rushed around me, gathering hoses and equipment.

A hand rested gently on my shoulder, and I glanced to the side, finding Chris standing beside me.

"Where's Cami?" I asked flatly.

"She's with Sheridan at the house. I told them I needed to run to the station for something. I didn't have the heart to tell either of them."

Turning back to look at my destroyed home, my vision blurred slightly, a tear escaping over the rim to fall down my cheek, before I blinked the rest away. "Do you think the police will believe me now?"

"I do," he replied softly.

CHAPTER ELEVEN
Cami-

The smile slid instantly from my face as Dylan and Chris entered the room where Sheridan and I were watching television and Chrissy played on the floor with her toys. Dylan was supposed to be at work; yet here he was, blackened and covered in soot, still in his dirty turnout pants and boots. Both of their expressions were grim and I could read sympathy in Chris' eyes as he stared at me.

"What's happened?" I asked, suddenly feeling paralyzed. My hand drifted protectively toward my stomach.

Dylan kept walking, grabbing me up in his arms and hugging me tightly to him, burying his face in my hair. "I love you so much," he whispered.

Gripping the back of his shirt in both my fists, I hung onto him, knowing he was going to tell me something bad. "What is it?" I whispered, again.

He moved his head so he could look in my eyes and I saw his mouth quiver. "Cami, our house burned down tonight."

"What!" Sheridan shouted, grabbing Chris by the arm.

Shocked, my knees started shaking and I reached for the chair behind me. Dylan held onto me, lowering me so I could sit. He crouched in front of me, holding my hands as I tried to process the news. "How?" was all I managed to say.

Shaking his head, he frowned. "The investigation stage of it is just beginning. Witnesses claim seeing smoke and then hearing some type of explosion shortly afterward. Early signs are pointing to arson with possibly some sort of explosive device."

"If you'd been home tonight, you'd have been killed," Chris said. "You were with me the whole time this evening, so no one can question your innocence. The police agree that someone is targeting one or both of you."

I couldn't even begin to wrap my mind around all this and I started shaking uncontrollably.

Dylan rubbed his hands over mine. "Goody, they're sending a squad car for us right now."

"Why?" I asked, and he sighed heavily.

"They're going to put us in witness protection while they try to figure out who's behind this."

"Witness protection?" The words seemed so foreign to me. "So, I need to go pack?"

"No," Dylan replied. "We are leaving

everything behind. Everything. Clothes, cars, personal belongings."

The reality of what he was saying began to sink in. "What about our families? Russ? What do we tell them?"

"Russ already knows. Chris will tell our parents we are safe; but as of this moment, we aren't to have any contact with them."

"But the baby? My mom will want to be there when I deliver." I glanced frantically between Dylan and Chris.

"Hopefully we'll be home long before then, honey. But for now, it's just going to be the two of us in a new place, okay? This is the best way they can protect us, for now."

"If the person terrorizing you was trying to kill someone, they'll realize soon enough that they failed," Chris said. "They could've even been watching the fire to see what would happen. We need to get you both to someplace safe before another attempt is made on your lives."

I nodded, still feeling numb and confused. "Okay. I trust you, both."

The Wilcock's house manager, José, entered the room followed by a uniformed police officer. "Mr. Wilcock, the squad car is here," he said.

"Thanks, José," Dylan replied, glancing over at the officer. "We'll be right out, Nicklaus," he added, acknowledging his old friend.. "Give us a minute to say goodbye."

Officer Nicklaus nodded. "Sure thing. I'll be waiting by the front door." He left the room with José escorting him.

"Come on, Goody. We need to go." Dylan stood, pulling me after him.

Sheridan hurried over, her face still looking as stricken as mine probably did. "I love you, Cami. I'm so sorry this has happened. Please be careful and hurry home to us."

"Thanks. Love you, too," I replied, hugging her back before turning to Chris.

"I'm coming with you to the station," he said. "So you can wait to tell me goodbye."

Nodding, I moved to where Chrissy was playing. "Come give Auntie Cami hugs, bye, bye, pretty girl." She ran over and threw her arms around my legs, squeezing me tight. Dylan came over and picked her up so we could both hug her properly.

"Be good for Mommy and Daddy, okay, kiddo?" he said. "Hopefully, we'll see you again, soon." He kissed her cheek and put her back down.

I watched as he hugged Sheridan tightly, tears filling my eyes. "Be careful, and try to keep Mom from having a heart attack when she hears about all this."

She gave a choked laugh. "I'll try." She was crying when he pulled away.

"Let's go," he said, brusquely, his voice deep with unshed emotion. Taking my hand, he led me out the door and down the hall. Pausing briefly, we both hugged José and then hurried to the waiting police car under the watchful eye of Officer Nicklaus.

I stared at the house for as long as I could, before turning to Dylan and leaning against him as my silent tears fell. He wrapped his arm around my shoulders, pulling me tighter against him. "Was it really bad?" I asked, needing to know.

He kissed the top of my head and I knew the answer before he spoke it. "Really bad," he confirmed. "We lost everything." I could hear the sorrow in his voice.

"Not everything," I whispered. "We still have the most important things." Lifting my head to look at him, I stared in his eyes and he gave me a small smile.

"You're right. That is the most important." Lowering his mouth, he pressed his lips to mine.

***

The police station was abuzz with activity when we arrived. Dylan and I were immediately shuttled into the building through an entrance hidden from public view. I quickly realized this was where they brought people who'd been arrested. We passed several rooms with big metal doors that had small windows in them. I didn't want to see who might be in there; my nerves were frazzled enough.

We waited in some very uncomfortable plastic chairs for close to an hour before we were taken to the fingerprinting room for a copy of our prints, making me feel almost like a criminal, myself. I knew they were using them to help build our new identities, but it didn't help me feel any better. It seemed as if my very life was being ripped away right before my eyes.

"You doing okay?" Dylan asked, looking at me, concerned, when we were finished. He took my arm and guided me down the hall toward another closed door.

"I guess. This all is strange."

"I understand; but it will get better, I promise. Think of it being like when we went undercover and cased out Ripper's car theft ring. This is just another undercover gig for us."

"I was still me, though. When we were dealing with Ripper, just my family was fabricated. I don't know how well I'll adjust to a completely new identity. Do you know where we are going?"

"No." He paused outside the door, resting his hand on the handle. "There will most likely only be two people here who will know where we are—Chief Robson and the detective handling our case."

"Who's that?" I asked.

"Me," Chris said, coming up behind us. "Let's go in and get things started, shall we?"

Dylan opened the door, ushering me into what appeared to be an interrogation room with three chairs at a table. He pulled one out for me before sitting in the chair next to me. Chris sat across the table from us.

"First, I want to apologize on behalf of the department for our earlier . . . accusations for lack of a better word . . . toward you, Cami. We were obviously completely in error. I hope you can trust us to keep you safe, now."

"I've always trusted you, Chris. That's never changed."

"Well, we're going to do our best. As of right now, we are making new identification for both of you. Dylan, to save time and process things a little faster, we are putting you back under your Hunter Wilder alias."

I sighed and Chris paused to look at me. "Sorry, I was just relieved. Calling him Hunter is easy for me. I was worried I'd have to get used to something completely new—another new name."

"What's Cami's name?" Dylan asked.

"Keeping in what Cami just said, we are trying to keep things as easy as possible to help avoid slip ups. Her new alias will be Camri Weathers. Do you think that will work okay for both of you?"

"Maybe I'll just start calling you Cam," Dylan said, glancing at me.

"I think that'll be okay. And I agree; it's an easy fix if I say the wrong name."

"Wait a second," Dylan said, his eyes narrowing at Chris. "You said Camri Weathers. Shouldn't be Wilder?"

Chris pursed his lips together for a moment, his gaze dropping down to the file in front of him. "The two of you won't be married during this, I'm afraid."

"Excuse me?" Dylan seemed completely frustrated.

"The Chief feels like it would be better for the two of you to not be a couple, in case anyone is searching for you, together. We're placing you in the same house, but as brother and sister."

"What?" Dylan argued. I cringed, seeing how frazzled he was becoming. "Look at her Chris.

She's six months pregnant with my baby. How are we going to explain that away? Not to mention that we look nothing alike."

"Cami's going to be recently widowed, pregnant with her late husband's child."

"You've got to be kidding me," Dylan grumbled. "This is so ridiculous."

Chris continued on as if he heard nothing. "We'll be altering Cami's appearance before your leave here, as well. The changes will hopefully help the relation thing look possible. We'll provide you with enough clothes to get you by for a few days, but you'll need to go shopping when you arrive at your new location."

"With what money? I won't have any access to my bank accounts."

"The department has funds set aside for you; but remember, I am your brother-in-law. If you need extra money, I'll see that you get it through an untraceable source."

"Where are we going?" I asked.

"Well, we're still waiting for those plans to be confirmed. Since all this has happened just tonight, we'll need to take care of some of the details in the morning; but we are looking at sending you to a very small area in the high mountains of Arizona, called Nutrioso. It's about five hours away from here, which we feel is sufficient for the time being. We can always relocate you again, if we feel it's needed. You'll probably enjoy it, Cami, because it'll be much cooler for you."

"How big is this place?" Dylan asked.

"It's extremely small. I think they had like

twenty-six people in the census I looked at. It's only twelve miles outside of the townships of Springerville and Eagar, however, so you'll still have access to anything you need."

"So, what do we do when we get there?" I asked. "Just sit around all day?"

Chris smiled. "No, we'll be hooking you up with some possible job opportunities, once we speak to our contact in the area, there. Unless you don't think you'd feel good enough to work, Cami."

"I think it would be okay, as long as it wasn't too strenuous."

"It's really up to both of you to decide. All right?" He gathered up the papers in front of him and neatly placed them in the file. "I'm sorry, but this is going to take a while to get organized. It would probably be best for you to go to bed now, and we can tackle things that'll still need to be done in the morning."

I glanced around. "Um, so where are we supposed to sleep?"

"Unfortunately, I'll have to put the two of you in one of the holding cells with bunk beds in them."

My nose turned up in distaste, thinking of all the dirty people who might have lain on the bed. Chris read my mind instantly.

"Don't worry. Our mattresses are plastic covered and sterilized between each use. There will be fresh linens for you, as well."

"Oh, okay." I still wasn't very thrilled with the idea. "Will we be able to get in and out?"

"Yes, I'll make sure it stays unlocked so

you'll have access to the bathroom down the hall."

"Unless you want to use the toilet provided in the corner of the cell," Dylan said and I jerked my head to stare at him open mouthed. He laughed. "I'm kidding, Cami."

"Is there really a toilet in there?" I asked, getting more creeped out by the moment.

"I'm afraid so, Goody."

"Come on," Chris said, standing. "I'll show you were it is. Dylan you can use the shower. There should be some clean clothes in there already for you."

"What? An orange jumpsuit?" he said sarcastically.

"Actually, yes," Chris replied, at least having the decency to look apologetic.

Dylan sighed heavily as we followed Chris out of the room. "We haven't even started this whole thing and already I want it to be over."

"Hang in there, bro," Chris said. "We'll do our best to get you back here as quickly as possible." He stopped. "Oh, I forgot one thing."

"Now what?"

We both watched as Chris went to one of the desks and picked up a box. He brought it over to Dylan. "Chief said to give you these."

Dylan opened the box and I leaned over, seeing a gun and a badge inside. He looked up, staring at Chris.

"Congratulations," Chris said. "You've just been reinstated."

CHAPTER TWELVE
Dylan-

Arms aching from holding Cami on the small bunk all night, I refused to move and wake her. She'd tossed and turned fitfully for several hours, trying to get comfortable; and I was worried she wasn't getting enough rest. After the previous scare with the baby, I felt hypersensitive to make sure she was properly taken care of. I knew she'd been under extreme amounts of stress, and that wasn't likely to improve any time soon.

Despite everything that'd happened to us, I was feeling quite blessed as I stared at my beautiful wife this morning. Images of our home going up in flames kept replaying in my mind and I knew if I hadn't sent her to my parents' house, I'd have lost her. Just the thought of something like that made goose bumps flare across my skin and my heart race. I couldn't fathom living without her. Having her in my life was like having air to breathe, essential.

A few short years ago, if someone had told me it was possible to feel this way about another person, I would've scoffed. I hadn't believed in things like love at first sight or soul mates, but I'd been proven wrong. Cami fit me perfectly, sliding into my life and becoming the piece I never knew I'd been missing.

I often pondered the fate that brought us together, leading me away from the days of my wild youth and into her arms. What if Chris had never married Sheridan? What if I'd never joined the Police Academy? Would we have still have found our way to each other, somehow?

I hated the danger my job had placed her in, but I couldn't curse it either because it had brought me to her. I didn't know who was after us right now, but I was beginning to wonder if the two of us would ever be able to have a normal life together. Was I destined to constantly be looking over my shoulder for the rest of my life, waiting for the next threat to come along?

Moving slowly, I grasped a small strand of her hair, rubbing it between my fingers, enjoying its silky texture. I simply wanted us to be happy. I wanted to be able to come home to my wife and hug and kiss her before turning to hug and kiss my kids. That was it. I could live without money, fancy cars, and big houses. Hell, I'd be thrilled to live in a tent in the middle of nowhere, as long as I had my family with me. My family was everything.

My gaze drifted to Cami's rounded belly and I thought of the child growing there, our baby, our son, made out of the love between us. I'd never realized how easy it would be to love someone I'd never even met; and I loved this little boy, plain and simple. Life truly was a miracle and something I'd never take for granted.

"Dylan?" Chris's soft voice interrupted my personal musings, and I glanced to the doorway. "Sorry to bother you, but we need to get rolling on some things. Can you both come meet me in interrogation?"

"Yeah, give us a few minutes," I replied.

"No problem."

Staring for a few more moments at her, I wished I didn't have to wake her. I kissed the top of her forehead. "Cami, honey?" She didn't move, so I squeezed her gently. "Cami. It's time to wake up."

She stirred slightly, and cuddled in closer to me. "I don't want to," she mumbled, her warm breath filtering through the orange jumpsuit I'd been forced to wear.

"I know, Goody. I don't either; but we have people waiting on us. We need to get going. I want to get out of this jail and get you somewhere we can both rest properly."

One of her hands ran up my arm, stopping at my bicep and squeezing lightly. "I love your arms," she said, still mumbling.

I chuckled. "And I love having you in them. I guess all my hours in the gym are still paying off."

"They are," she replied. "I think you get hotter every single day."

This time I laughed outright. "I'm trying to keep up with you."

"Whatever," she replied, but she laughed too.

"Come on, honey. We need to get up."

"I don't want to. As long as I keep my eyes closed, I can pretend we are still at home, cuddled up safely in our bed, together." Feeling her pain, I hugged her tighter. "Tell me it was all a nightmare, Dylan. Tell me everything is okay."

"I wish I could."

The dam finally broke and she began shedding all the tears she'd been trying so strongly to hold back, her body wracked with sobs as I held her, helpless, unable to make her pain go away. Anger and sorrow flooded through me. I hated not being able to change things for her. I hated to see her suffering. My heart ached . . . for both of us.

Chris briefly reappeared in the doorway, but I shook my head at him and he disappeared, allowing Cami the time she needed to grieve over our loss.

Remaining quiet, I simply held her as she purged herself. There was nothing I could say, and I refused to give her false hope. The fact of the matter was that our life together was about to change drastically, and it would stay that way until the danger passed. All I could do was hope time would move quickly. I couldn't handle seeing her this way. It didn't sit well, and while I had my own disappointments and grief to deal with, she was my first priority.

"Sorry," she said when her crying finally slowed. "I didn't mean to completely lose it like that."

"Don't apologize. If you feel like crying, then do it. Don't keep things bottled up inside. It's not healthy."

Glancing at me with her warm, honey colored eyes, she gave me a sad smile. "And when will you cry, Dylan?" she asked.

I held her gaze for several long seconds, before pulling her against my chest and resting my chin on her head. "Later," I replied. "When this is all over and I know you're safe."

***

Had I not know her figure so intimately, I would've scanned right over Cami as I stared down the hall at the two women standing and talking to Chris. Her back was turned to me, so I couldn't see her baby bump, but I watched in fascination as she turned to look at me.

Gone was her gorgeous curly red hair. While it was the same length, it had been straightened and dyed to a hue that was nearly as dark as my own. Her skin looked a little darker as well, and her makeup was heavier around the eyes then she normally wore it. Truthfully, I wasn't sure if I was turned on or angry. She'd always been perfect in my eyes and I hated seeing some of the characteristics I loved so much about her changed so drastically. But that being said, she still looked smoking hot.

She was wearing a short, mid-thigh, cream colored floral dress with a scooped neckline. The dress cinched just under her breasts, accentuating them perfectly, before falling loosely over her stomach. A pair of brown cowgirl boots accentuated her shapely legs, giving her a total country girl appearance. I couldn't take my eyes off her as she approached, paused, and extended her hand, smiling.

"Hi, I'm Camri Weathers. Nice to meet you."

Absently, I took her hand and shook it. "Hunter Wilder," I replied, playing along. "Wow. You look so different."

"So do you. I'm digging the ball cap, faded jeans, and button up shirt. I don't think I've ever seen you in cowboy boots."

"That's because I've never owned any. I feel like a hillbilly."

"Country boy," she corrected. "To go with your country girl." She giggled, but there was a hint of concern in her eyes. "Do you like it?"

"Yes, and no," I replied honestly. "I loved everything about you to begin with, so it's difficult to see you this way. But you're still as beautiful as ever."

Reaching up, she ran her fingers through the end of her hair. "I knew the change in hair color would be hardest for you. You're always saying how much you like it. I've never dyed my hair in my life, so it feels weird for me, too."

"I'm not going to lie; it will take some getting used to, but you wear it well."

"They chemically straightened it; so I won't have such a hard time with the upkeep for a little while, at least. Does my skin look darker to you?" she asked, holding her arms out for inspection.

"It does."

"They had me get a spray on tan. I've been to three salons today, while under police protection. Of course the salon owners didn't know that."

"Three?" I questioned.

"One to straighten my hair, one to color my hair, and one to tan. They didn't want anyone to be able to attest to my complete transformation if someone came looking."

"Well, at least they're being thorough. Are you sure you weren't followed?"

"An officer picked me up in an unmarked car and drove to a parking garage. I had to change vehicles to another unmarked car."

"Do you doubt me, brother?" Chris said as he approached. "I told you I'd make sure the two of you were taken care of."

"I don't doubt you, I'm just worried," I replied, stepping to Cami's side and draping my arm around her.

"Remember," Chris warned. "You're supposed to be brother and sister, now. Be careful of any public displays of affection."

Sighing, I hugged her tighter to me. "This big bro likes to hug his little sis," I replied, refusing to let her go as Chris eyed me. "Relax and trust me. I'm not going to do anything that will put her in jeopardy. You know that."

"Just be careful," he warned, again. "Are you two ready to go? I have suitcases loaded into the car with clothes and a few personal items for you both." He handed me a large manila envelope and I opened it to find cell phones, driver's licenses, credit cards, and resumes—all under our aliases.

"Resumes?" I asked, confused.

"We provided them in case you were there for a long time and things were going well. We thought you might want to look for jobs to break up the monotony. Hunter is now a paramedic only, and has several references that will all direct back to me, if used. Camri's resume states she has experience as a medical assistant."

"Um, I don't have any training for anything like that," Cami piped up, looking worried.

"Don't worry. Depending on where you work, it can be as simple as taking blood pressures and taking notes in charts, filing etc. Hunter can fill you in on some of the medical things. I thought with your pregnancy, it would be good to try and get a job at the hospital. Then you'd have medical care close by."

"I like that," I added. "I won't worry about you as much if you're in a hospital."

"And if you were a paramedic, you'll have reason and opportunity to visit her at work and check on her without raising any suspicions," Chris added.

I was mildly impressed. It appeared he really had thought of everything.

"Of course, all this will depend on if anyone is hiring and if you decide you want to do it. It's okay for you to stay close to your new residence, if that's what you'd rather do. As far as housing goes, we've leased a fully furnished vacation rental on a month-to-month basis. So you won't have to worry about furniture, appliances, or utensils. Everything will be provided for you except for personal items—you can purchase those yourself."

"That sounds good. How much do we have to work with in our bank account?"

He glanced around before stepping a little closer, lowering his voice. "I actually pulled a few strings and was able to get a message to your parents. They contacted me this morning from New York. They've transferred one hundred thousand dollars to the police department and that money was withdrawn and placed in a new account for you at a different bank, so it shouldn't be traceable. They said if you need anything else, they'd happily provide it."

"And my parents?" Cami asked, regret in her voice.

"They've been contacted, as well. They said to tell you they love you. They're praying for you both and want me to let them know if there is anything they can do to help."

Tears welled in her eyes immediately and I hugged her to me again, kissing the top of her head. "Don't worry, Goody. We'll get it taken care of."

"Camri," Chris corrected me. "You need to start calling her by her alias, *Hunter*."

"Fine," I replied. "As of this moment, Camri and Hunter are alive and going strong."

"Perfect. Let's go. We have a long trip ahead of us. I'll be driving you as far as Show Low, where we'll stop and pick up a rental car for you to use. After that, you're on your own. I'll give you the rest of the directions you need to get to your final destination. Make sure you keep that gun and badge of yours somewhere safe and where no one will find it. It could blow your cover." Chris stepped past us and began walking toward the exit.

"Got it. Let's get out of here. I'm looking forward to sleeping in a real bed and it's going to be very late before we get there." I gestured for Cami to go first. "After you, Camri." She sighed and followed him. Neither of us was looking forward to this.

CAMI LOVE

CHAPTER THIRTEEN
Cami-

"Oh, it's a log cabin," I exclaimed as the headlights hit the house when we pulled in the driveway.

"A nice one, too, from the looks of it. Check out those big windows. I bet it has incredible views. Chris has good taste."

"It is a bit on the remote side, though." I hadn't seen any other houses for at least a mile or two.

"I think he did that on purpose. This way when we're home we can be us—together without prying eyes to watch us. I like it."

"Well, when you put it that way, I do, too."

"Do you have the code for the lockbox on the door so we can get the keys out?"

"Yeah. I put it in my new phone so I wouldn't forget it."

"Awesome." Dylan parked our black, extended cab Chevy in the driveway. He totally looked like he belonged out here in the wilderness. "Let's get you inside and check this place out," he continued. "Then I'll come get our things."

Before long, we had the front door open and Dylan fumbled for the light switch. Flipping it, two lamps illuminated the space with soft light.

"Oh my gosh! Look at this place! I love it!" I said.

"It looks pretty nice." Dylan agreed.

Vaulted ceilings with polished wood and beams gave the room and open, spacious feel. Two large leather sofas were angled facing the giant floor to ceiling windows that flanked either side of a great rock fireplace. A distressed wood coffee table with matching end tables, each holding lamps with shades in a material made to resemble cowhide, completed the living area. A very plush white rug covered the polished wooden floors.

The kitchen, with custom cabinets and granite counter tops, along with a stone-topped table and wrought iron chairs also opened into this space. On the far wall, a beautiful staircase, made of the same polished wood, ascended into what appeared to be a loft area.

"Come on. Let's look," Dylan said, offering me his hand. We went up the stairs found a king size bed, along with nightstand and a dresser, there. "I bet the view in the morning is great from up here," Dylan said as he looked over the railing down to the living area below. Upon further inspection we found another bedroom with a king size bed and furniture, as well as a bathroom, located next to the laundry room.

"Small, but sweet," I said, feeling very comfortable and cozy. "I love the way they've decorated everything. It has a very chic country feel."

"So, you think you can handle being stuck with me here every day with nothing to do?" Dylan pulled me toward him and I wrapped my arms around his neck.

"Oh, I can think of plenty we could do."

He laughed, looking more relaxed than I'd seen him in days. Even I felt the same, like we'd stepped out of one world and into another. "Well, if that's the case, then I'm proud to be a country boy. We might have to be careful in front of these big windows. If the blinds are open, anybody who happens by would be able to see straight in here."

"So, we'll close them if we need some privacy. We'll make it work."

He gave me a quick kiss before releasing me and heading toward the door. "I'll let you take the downstairs bedroom so you don't have to climb up and down the stairs and it gives you more privacy."

"We're seriously sleeping in separate bedrooms?" I asked, disappointed.

"Hell no," he responded with a laugh. "I meant just for the keeping up of appearances. I'll keep my things upstairs and you can have the downstairs. I plan on using both beds, though." He winked at me before disappearing outside and I relaxed. That was the husband I knew and loved.

***

"Check out this view," Dylan whispered in my ear; and I blinked rapidly trying to wake up.

"Do I have to?" I mumbled into my pillow. "I think this bed is made of clouds from heaven. I swear I heard angels singing as I slept."

He laughed and leaned over, kissing me on the cheek. "I'm glad you got some rest. But I promise it'll be worth it."

Groaning, I stretched my limbs out while yawning widely. I sat up on the loft bed so I could see what he was talking about. "Oh wow!" I exclaimed as I took it all in. The triangular windows, directly across the great room from the loft, revealed a lush green valley surrounded by tall pines with mountains behind them.

"See that herd of animals moving out in the field?" he asked, pointing.

"Yeah."

"Those are elk."

"Really?" I said excitedly, throwing back the covers. "Let's go outside and look closer." I grabbed my robe, tying it as I descended the staircase, not even waiting to see if he was behind me. Flinging the front door open, I made my way out onto the wrap-around deck, going to where the view was the best. Dylan came through the door wearing only a pair of shorts, his hair tousled, but he still looked as sexy as ever.

Moving behind me, he wrapped his arms around me. "Man, I wish I had some binoculars right now. I'd love to see the herd up close."

"Well, you know they're here now, why don't we go into town and get you some? There has to be some place that carries them."

"Good idea."

I shivered a bit in my silky robe. "Can you believe how cool it is here? It's downright chilly this morning."

"I'm sure it will warm up more as the sun gets higher, but Chris was right. It's much nicer than Tucson."

"What happens if we fall in love with this place and want to live here forever?" I asked, looking at him and he shrugged, chuckling a bit.

"I don't know. I guess we'll cross that bridge when, and if, we come to it."

Leaning my head against him, I sighed. "I love how peaceful it is here, already. I could sit out here all day reading books and listen to the birds and the breeze blowing through the pines."

"Well, judging from the nice swing hanging on the end of the porch, it looks like you aren't the only one who thinks so." Letting go of me, he walked around the corner, disappearing. "There's a built in barbecue and fire pit over on this side of the property," he called to me and I went to join him.

"Oh, I can tell already you're going to love this, aren't you?" A nice circular area, built out of what appeared to be sandstone, made up the patio, fire pit, and built in barbecue. In addition, a short wall of same material ringed the outer edge, providing plenty of seating. "Too bad we don't know anyone. We could have quite the dinner party here."

"Yeah," he replied. "Russ would love this place."

Russ. Just hearing his name made me instantly homesick and brought the reality of our situation crashing back down upon me.

"Maybe we should've brought him with us," I said, trying to lighten the mood.

Dylan gave a small laugh. "I was hard pressed to leave him behind as it was. Russ was with me when Chris said he was going to put us in a protection program and I thought he was going to pitch a fit about not being able to come. He wasn't very happy about it; but with the danger surrounding us, he knew there was no way we could remain in contact with him."

Hearing the regret in his voice, I moved to his side, wrapping my arms around him. "I'm so sorry for everything that's happened, Dyl . . . Hunter." He chuckled after I stumbled over his name in the reverse, and I couldn't help laughing with him. "Would you please stick to one name so I know what to call you?"

"I told you to keep calling me Hunter if that was the name most comfortable to you," he reminded.

"I know, but I thought it would be weird around your family. I was so nervous to meet them."

Sliding his hands behind me, he stared at me solemnly. "And now you know all that worry was for nothing. Just like I told you it would be. My family loves you a much as I do."

"I love them, too."

"Do you ever regret it, Cami?"

"Camri," I reminded him and he sighed.

"How about Cam? That might be a little

easier for me."

"I'm good with whatever. Now what did you mean, do I ever regret it?"

"I mean do you regret staying with me through everything? I know you love me, but knowing me has brought so much heartache and danger into your life. I hate that."

A small pain stabbed through my heart at his words. "There are no regrets at all for me. I'd follow you through anything and everything. Don't you know that?"

Frustration appeared in his eyes. "I know you love me, but I keep wondering if your life would've been better off without me."

"Hunter, what would've happened if you hadn't been around to stop Clay?" I asked. "He was sick, we know that now, but there's no guarantee that things wouldn't have happened just like they did, even without your involvement. I could've dated anyone and it would've produced the same results in his behavior. He could've raped me with no one to stop him. Then what?"

"True. But then I pulled you into the whole thing with Ripper, and then Roberta went after you—now this. It's seems like, despite my feelings for you, all I've done is put you in harm's way."

"We don't know who, or why, this is happening; so you can't take the blame. It could be some random crazy person that targeted us because one of us is the first person they saw. You know, like a gang initiation or something. As far as the whole Ripper thing, I could've chosen not to come meet you when you contacted me. I put you in just as much danger, of blowing your cover, by showing up. We are equally responsible for that mess."

He shook his head. "Simply put, I wonder if it will ever stop? I left the force so we could live a safer life and now look at us—I'm suddenly a cop again and we are hiding out in the middle of nowhere. What kind of life is that?"

"Look at this view," I said, sweeping my hand across the scene in front of us. "I really wouldn't call what we're doing a hardship at the moment. Would you?"

"Yes, because we had to leave everything else we love behind."

"Would you rather go back?" I asked.

"No. Not until I know you're safe."

I snorted. "You keep talking about keeping me safe. What about you, Hunter? You deserve to be safe, as well. This move is for both of our protection, not just mine. Quit singling me out."

"The reason I'm singling you out is because my life is nothing without you in it. Do you hear me? If something happened to you and our baby, I'd die a thousand deaths, everyday. I wouldn't want to live without you. So yeah, I'm gonna put you first."

"Oh, so it's okay for you to be killed or injured as long as I'm fine? That makes a whole lot of sense. I feel the same way about you that you feel about me. So, we are either in this together or not at all, got it? I'm tired of running and being scared. From now on you and I are on the offensive. We're taking our lives back and we are going to enjoy living here for as long as we need to be here."

Dylan burst out laughing and he stroked a hand over my hair. "I love it when you're feisty like this. It turns me on."

I shook my head. "You're such a . . . man!" I spewed, walking past him toward the front of the house.

"What's that supposed to mean?" he called after me and I turned to face him, again.

"It means you can take any conversation and turn it into something about sex! I want you to take me seriously, dang it!" I folded my arms, shooting daggers at him as he approached.

"I get everything you're saying, Goody, trust me, I do. And I don't want you to ever feel like your opinion doesn't matter. It does; and I hear you, loud and strong. Be happy, live our lives, don't fear. Got it." He stroked the side of my face, gently running his thumb over my cheek. "Sometimes I just feel like I've done you a horrible injustice by claiming you for myself."

My irritation with him melted away the moment he touched me. "Well, get over it, because you didn't and it's my opinion that matters. I love you and I want to be with you. When you talk like that, it makes me feel afraid—like you want to leave me or something."

He stepped closer, pulling me against him and enveloping me in his arms. "I'd sooner cut my own heart out than purposely leave you. You have my word on that. And, as far as my earlier comment, you're just going to have to get used to the fact that there are certain things you do that turn me on. I can't help it. If that makes me some insufferable man, then so be it; because I like it."

I sighed in defeat, shaking my head. "And we're back to the sex."

"Yes we are." He laughed. "What're we going to do about that?"

"What do you want to do?" I asked, refusing to give in so easily.

"Well, I've never had a brunette wife before." Grinning mischievously, he stared down at me with a wicked gleam in his eyes. "I'd kind of like to sweep her off her feet and take her for a ride."

"Ugh." I rolled my eyes. "A ride? That is so not romantic, Hunter." It surprised me how easily I was reverting back to the name I originally knew him by. If he noticed at all, he didn't comment on it.

"What's romantic then? How would you seduce me?"

"Pfft. That is the easiest thing to do on the planet. It's not even a challenge."

"Really? Then tell me. What would you do?"

"Mmm . . . let's see. I could brush my teeth, or my hair for that matter. Both of those have turned you on before. Washing dishes always seems to do it for you, too. Oh, and of course there's sweeping, vacuuming, and any time that I need to change my clothes. And—,"

"Okay, okay. I get it. I'm a horny bastard." He was grinning from ear to ear.

"I wouldn't exactly use the term bastard. Maybe a sexual zealot?"

Laughter burst from him and he scooped me up in his arms and headed for the front door, continuing to chuckle the entire way.

"What are you doing?" I asked, unable to keep the smile off my face.

"Carrying you off to bed with sexual zeal," he replied. "Is that okay with you?"

"I see I can add talking to the list of things that turn you on."

He laughed again, kicking the door shut behind us as we entered the house. "Yes, you can. Face it, Goody. Everything about you turns me on. You're just gonna have to learn to live with it."

"I thought I already had been. Hello? Got pregnant on birth control, here, unless you've forgotten?"

Hurrying up the stairs as if I weighed no more than a feather, he lowered me to my feet when we reached the top and grabbed for the tie on my robe. "I haven't forgotten." As soon as the knot was loose, he moved his hands inside and slid the robe off my shoulders. It fell in a pile on the floor.

"Then what are we going to do for birth control in the future?" I asked as he bent to kiss the side of my neck.

"Don't know," he said against my skin, as his hands ran over my arms before dragging me flush against him. "Just have lots of kids, I guess, because I'm not stopping this."

My breath hitched as he tugged at my earlobe with his teeth. "Well, then. With the loss of our house, I'm predicting you will need to build a much bigger one after all," I teased.

His hands slid to the sides of my face and he stared at me seriously. "I'll build you a castle to fill up with our children if that's what it takes." Pressing his lips to mine, he walked me backwards until the back of my knees hit the bed. Laying me carefully on the mattress, I released a moan as he continued kissing his way down my body.

Tangling my hands in his hair, I gave into the sensations that followed. "I love you, Dylan," I said, not caring that I wasn't supposed to use that name.

Apparently, he didn't care either. "I love you too, Cami. More than you'll ever know."

DYLAN LOVE

CHAPTER FOURTEEN
Dylan-

"Well, at least now we'll be able to see the town a little better than we could last night," Cami said. "Hopefully, there's more in the other direction from the stoplight than what we saw going this way."

"I wouldn't get your hopes up." I laughed. "But it looks like a nice mom and pop mountain town." Glancing to the right, I saw the building I'd been looking for with a sign that read 'Red's Cafe' painted across the top of the adobe style building. "How about this restaurant? I saw it when we passed through here last night. There are lots of cars. That usually means the food is good."

"Sounds good to me. I'm starving." As if to confirm her words, her stomach growled and I chuckled.

Parking, we went inside, finding a very country western atmosphere, complete with old artifacts hanging on the walls and the floors and booths made of wood. We were quickly seated by a friendly waitress and given our menus. "What do you recommend?" I asked, wanting to know what the favorites were.

"Are you looking for breakfast or lunch?" she asked cheerily.

"Breakfast," Cami piped up and I nodded.

"Well, if you want a lot to eat, then I recommend the Early Cowboy Platter. It has biscuits and gravy with sides of eggs, bacon, sausage, and Texas toast. Our Rodeo Pancake stack is also a big favorite, as well as our Buckin' French Toast Breakfast."

I snickered when Cami moaned. "That all sounds so good. How will I decide?"

"Let me go get your drinks first, and that'll give you a few more moments. What would you like? Water, juice, coffee?"

"I'll have an orange juice," Cami said happily.

"And I'll take a coffee."

"Perfect, one orange juice and coffee coming right up. I'll go get those."

"Have you decided what you want yet?" I asked Cami. "Or shall I just order one of everything on the menu?"

She rolled her eyes at me. "Ha, ha, ha. You're so funny. I'm not that bad."

"Your growling stomach says otherwise," I disagreed.

"I haven't eaten since we left Tucson yesterday, and you kept me busy for the better part of the morning. Can you blame me?"

I shook my head. "No, but I have been right

there with you. How about you narrow it down to your two favorites and I'll order whichever one you don't. That way you can have some of both. How's that?"

She sighed. "Have I told you how much I love you?"

I winced as the waitress approached our table, clearly in earshot of her words. "What are big brothers for?" I asked lightly, hoping it would cover up her blunder.

"Here you go," the waitress said, placing our drinks in front of us. "There's free refills on the coffee too, so just wave at me if you want some more. I'll try to keep it coming, but we're a little busy this morning, as you can see."

"Busier than usual?" I asked. "My sister and I are new to the area so we don't really know much about the community."

"Welcome to Springerville," she said brightly. "We're always pretty busy, but this weekend is our Old West Days celebration, so there's lots of people from out of town."

"Old West Days? Sounds interesting. What's that all about?"

"It's to celebrate our pioneer heritage and the ranching that goes on in the area. There's rodeos, ice cream socials, tours of historical homes, softball tournaments, dancing, barbecue, all kinds of stuff. We have some flyers here about it. Would you like one?"

"Sure, that would be great." She hurried over near the register counter and picked up a folded pamphlet.

"Did you narrow your choices, yet?" I asked

Cami.

"If you'll get the Early Cowboy Platter, I'll get the Buckin' French Toast Breakfast."

"Deal," I replied as our waitress returned.

"Here you go, sir." She handed me the flyer.

"Thanks. Sorry to keep asking you questions, but could you happen to tell us where we can find a grocery store, too?"

"Of course. Just keep driving down to the stoplight and take a left. There is a couple of big grocery stores on that road. One is pretty close and the other is a little farther down the way in Eagar. If you aren't familiar with the area, the towns of Springerville and Eagar run together. It's not a very big place, but everything can be found in just a few short miles. If you want any of the bigger chain department stores though, you'll need to go to Show Low."

"Thanks. I appreciate the information."

"Anytime. I'm happy to help. Are you ready to order?"

"We are." I gestured for Cami to order her food and then I ordered mine. The waitress took our menus and disappeared.

"Well, what you think so far?" I asked as I glanced down at the flyer.

"It sounds like a far cry from Tucson, but kind of quaint, too. Can I see the flyer?"

I passed it to her. "Would you like to attend some of the celebrations?"

"I think it sounds fun. Do you want to?"

"I'm game if you are."

"What's logging events?" She crinkled her nose, perplexed, as she read over the brochure.

"I think it's where they toss big logs, log rolling, saw pulls, chopping, and climbing. Basically anything you can do with wood, logs, or trees."

She stared at me. "And how do you know all this?"

I chuckled. "I saw some lumberjack world championship thing on television once."

"They have world championships?" she asked incredulously.

"Apparently."

"Hmmm. You learn something new every day." She glanced back at the flyer. "The ice cream social sounds fun. And I love history. I wouldn't mind touring some of the historic homes."

"I thought the rodeo sounded fun too, but it's up to you. I don't want to wear you out."

"I'll let you know if I get too tired, but I'm excited to see what there is to do here. As long as we get groceries and gas at some point today, then I'm good."

"All right. We'll go check things out." Starting to reach across the table to squeeze her hand, I suddenly remembered that I couldn't. I pulled back and she stared at me, noticing what I'd done.

"It's harder than I thought it would be," she said, her voice low. "I didn't realize how many times a day we touch each other. It's not natural for me to suddenly stop."

"I know. Hopefully it won't be this way for long. And if we keep to our property . . . ." I let my voice trail off knowing she would get my meaning without me having to voice it.

"I miss our old life." Her face was sorrowful.

"You'll have it again. I promise."

"I know. I trust you. It'll all work out, somehow."

The waitress reappeared with our food and the light reappeared on Cami's face as she picked up her fork to dig in. Her eyes rolled back and a moan escaped her as she chewed.

I chuckled. "Anything in particular you'd like off my plate? I don't want you to starve or anything."

She shook her head. "I changed my mind. This is fabulous and it's a huge plate. I'll be lucky if I can even finish it."

"Okay." I continued to watch her, feeling amused at her antics. "Let me know if you decide otherwise."

***

We chose to drive around town to see where things were located and what kinds of activities were going on.

"Some of these restaurants look like they might be fun to try. And check out that big dome." Cami pointed to the left. "I wonder what it is?"

"That must be the high school football field. It's my understanding that several teams come up here for summer training."

"Wow. It seems so huge for a town of this size. Oh, but look! There's the city park and it looks like a lot of stuff is going on there."

"Shall we stop and check things out?"

"Yes, please. Look at all the vendors out

there. I want to go see what they have."

"Great. Shopping."

She laughed as I drove to an open parking spot. "Don't you even start with me. You shop as much as I do."

"When?" I asked in astonishment.

"Seriously, have you seen your closet? You hardly have anything in there that isn't from some designer label."

"That's not shopping," I argued. "That's just having good taste in nice clothing."

"Yeah, well, you could probably feed a small country on the stuff you have."

"Not anymore."

She sighed and looked out the window. "Sorry. I didn't mean to bring it up, again."

"We can't avoid reality, Cami." Glancing at me, she narrowed her eyes.

"What's my name?"

"Fine. Camri. Is that better?"

She smiled. "Yes. Now let's forget about all the bad stuff for a while and go have some fun."

"Sounds good." I loved her upbeat attitude. "Try to leave some money in my wallet, okay."

"Okay." She giggled.

"I'll come get your door."

"Would a brother do that?" she asked.

"He would if he had a very pregnant sister."

She considered this for a second before she nodded. I hopped out of the truck and went around to help her. It was odd to walk together, side by side, and not hold her hand or put my arm around her. It actually made me pretty uncomfortable. I couldn't count the times we naturally reached for each other only to yank our hands back as we slowly walked along, looking at the booths.

"Oh, look at this necklace, D—." Cami immediately launched into a fake coughing fit to try and cover her blunder.

Unfortunately, she caught the attention of a man standing outside a first aide tent. "Are you okay, ma'am?" he asked, stepping toward us.

She waved her hand. "Yes, thank you. My brother is a paramedic," she said smoothly as she gestured toward me. "He's taking good care of me."

"Really? You're a paramedic?" the man asked, holding his hand out. "My name is Mark Young. I'm a paramedic. Are you from around here?"

"Actually, we just moved near here, out in Nutrioso."

"Really? My grandpa has some land out that way. Where you from?"

"The hot desert of the valley," I replied, reluctant to give out too much information. "My sister hated the heat down there, so we thought we'd try out the mountains for a change and get away."

"I'm Mark," he said, turning to shake Cami's hand.

"Camri Weathers. And my brother's name is Hunter Wilder."

"Nice to meet you, both. So do you have other family here with you?"

"Nah," I replied. "It's just the two of us."

His eyes drifted to Cami's protruding

stomach. She shifted uncomfortably and cast her gaze downward. "My husband was killed in a car accident a few months ago." She recited the story line that had been drilled into us. "Hunter has been trying to help me out with things." She glanced up adoringly at me. "I couldn't have asked for a better brother." Patting me lightly on the arm, she smiled.

"You're my baby sister. Of course I'm going to be there." I smiled back at her.

"I'm sorry to hear about your husband," Mark apologized, running a hand over his short buzzed blond hair. "That's rough. I actually lost my wife to cancer last year. It's not a fun thing to experience. My sympathies."

"Thank you. I appreciate that. I'm sorry about your wife, too."

"Well, life goes on. Sometimes even when we don't want it to." Mark glanced from Cami to me. "Listen, I didn't mean to interrupt you for so long, but when I heard you were a paramedic, it caught my attention. We have a spot on our department we've been trying to fill recently after one of our medics moved away. We've all been working extra hours to try and keep things covered. I don't know if you're looking for work, but if you might be interested then feel free to fax me your resume." Reaching into his back pocket, he retrieved his wallet and pulled out a card, handing it to me.

"Thank you." I took it from him and removed my wallet to store it. "I'll talk it over with Camri and see if it might be something I'm interested in. She's my first priority at the moment. Do you have any recommendations for an OB doctor?"

"Hmmm." He stroked his chin. "Doc Wilson has been around for a while. I think he's delivered half the babies in this area. Thomas Wilson. We all just call him Doc. His clinic is over by the hospital. Do you know where that is?"

"Yes, I noticed it when we were driving around earlier today," I replied.

"Yeah, he's located right behind the hospital."

"Mark," a woman in uniform motioned for him. "Someone fell a couple of tents over. They're calling for our help."

"Got to run," he said, waving at us. "It was nice meeting you. Enjoy the festival."

"Thanks! You, too!" Cami called after him before turning to me. "He was nice. What do you think about that job?"

I shrugged. "I'm not sure. I know Chris set things up for us, in case we wanted to work, but I don't know if I'm willing to do that, yet." We continued walking, casually passing each tent and browsing through the items for sale. "You're my first priority. Besides, I'm not sure I want to give that guy any other opportunity to be around you."

"Why? What do you mean?" She seemed thoroughly confused and I laughed.

"I think he liked you. You both have that whole "dead spouse" connection. It's given you common ground with him."

Shaking her head, she rolled her eyes at me. "I think you're seeing threats where there are none. I didn't get anything like that from him."

I lowered my voice, leaning in closer to her. "Yeah, and you didn't know I was into you either, in the beginning. Or Clay. Or Ripper."

"All right, fine. You don't need to rub it in. Still, I think you're imagining things."

"I hope we won't have to find out." The guy was nice enough, but I'd seen the look in his eyes when Cami had mentioned the death of her fictional husband. It had sparked emotion in him. Not that I would blame him. He must be lonely without his wife, but that didn't mean he could have mine.

"This is a really nice event," Cami said, obviously not concerned in the least about Mark. "I love that this community likes to pay homage to their heritage. It looks like it draws a pretty good crowd, too. There is even a news crew from the valley walking through here getting footage."

"Where?" I asked, the blood suddenly draining from my face.

"They were filming around those tents behind us while we were talking to Mark. Why?"

"We need to go right now." Taking her by the elbow, I steered her back toward where we'd parked the pickup, my gaze darting about looking for the news crew.

"Is everything okay?" Cami asked, sensing my urgency.

"We can't risk ending up on film somewhere."

"They weren't looking at us, though. They were filming some of the booths."

"Better to not take any chances. Let's go do

the grocery shopping we needed to do and head home before we run into anymore trouble."

"Sorry. I didn't even consider the cameras."

"I'm sorry to be so picky about it. It makes me uncomfortable, though. Better safe than sorry, in my opinion."

"I agree," she replied as I opened the door to the truck and helped her inside. Glancing covertly around the lot, I checked to see if there was anything else I needed to be concerned with. Cami was right. Living this way was irritating.

CAMI LOVE

CHAPTER FIFTEEN
Cami-

Stretching, I sat up in bed and immediately noticed the delicious smells coming from the kitchen. Getting up, I shrugged into my robe and went downstairs to find Dylan cooking eggs, bacon, and toast.

"Good morning, sleepyhead," he teased.

"You have to be the best husband ever!" I said, hugging him from behind. "That smells heavenly. I'm so glad I don't get queasy in the mornings anymore. What time is it?"

"Ten."

"Ten! Why did you let me sleep so late?"

"I figured you needed it. And it's not like we really have that much to do around here."

"Well, I want to do something with you," I said rubbing my hands lightly over his pecs and abs as I continued to embraced him from behind.

Raising an eyebrow, he glanced over his shoulder at me. "Right now? Or can I finish cooking first?"

I stepped away and smacked him on the shoulder. "I didn't mean *that*."

"Oh," he said with a chuckle, continuing to scramble the eggs. "I almost got excited there for a second. Guess I should've known better than to think you'd choose me over food."

I shrugged, going to the cupboards and looking for plates. "It's the baby's fault."

"Next cupboard." He shook his head. "Poor baby isn't even born yet and already he's getting blamed for stuff."

"Well, you sure don't seem to mind when my pregnancy libido kicks in. I blame that on him, as well."

"Now see, that's where you and I differ. I prefer to think that my charisma is simply too much for you to handle. Which, by the way, is totally okay with me. I have no problem with you using me to take care of your physical needs."

"Ha! Ha! Ha! If that isn't the pot calling the kettle black, then I don't know what is." I set the plates on the counter and went looking for silverware.

"Second drawer on the right," he said, anticipating my moves. "And I have to say, I don't hear you complaining much. If you need a reminder, I can give you a repeat performance of last night. Maybe I can record you on my phone so I can play it back to you later for proof."

Pursing my lips, I shook my head, feeling the heated blush flood my face. "That's okay. Really.

I'll take your word for it."

He chuckled, removing the last couple pieces of bacon from the pan before sliding the eggs to the back burner and turning off the stove. Quick as lightning, his arm snaked out, grabbing me around the waist and pulling me to him until my stomach collided into his. Glancing down, he shook his head before returning his gaze to mine. "This baby is really starting to come between us."

I couldn't help but laugh. "That was really lame. Now who's blaming the baby? Besides, it's all your fault that he's here to begin with."

Smiling, his features softened as he placed his hands on each side of my face. "You're the most gorgeous pregnant woman I've ever seen. Thank you for deciding to stay with me after our crazy wedding."

"There was no choice." I couldn't look at him without loving him more. "You were always the one for me. Ever since that day in class when you labeled me Little-Miss-Goody-Two-Shoes."

Leaning forward, he kissed me gently on the lips. "And you were so incredibly offended." His eyes twinkled with humor.

"I thought you were making fun of me."

"How could I possibly make fun of perfection, Goody?" he asked, kissing me lightly, again.

"I'm far from perfect."

"You're perfect for me, and that's all that matters. I wanted you for myself, even before then. It killed me to think I'd never have you."

"Well, I think you've conquered that fear. I

can't count how many times you've had me."

He kissed me, laughter rumbling through him. "Now who's turning the conversation back to sex?" he asked, his lips brushing mine as he spoke.

"I know what you're trying to do," I said grinning.

"What's that?"

"You're trying to distract me into forgetting about breakfast so you can have your way with me." I rubbed my hands over the sides of his shirtless waist.

"Is it working?"

"Not even a little. I'm starving and that food smells really good."

Sighing, he released me. "Can't blame a guy for trying."

I laughed and moved toward the stove to dish up our food, but he grabbed my shoulders and turned me toward the table.

"Sit. I'm taking care of you this morning." Walking me over, he pulled out a chair for me.

"Wow. I'm liking the service at this place."

"I bet you are," he replied as I rolled my eyes, even though he wasn't looking. "You just rolled your eyes at me, didn't you?" he added.

I merely laughed instead of answering him. He carried our plates to the table and placed one in front of me.

Smiling, he handed me a fork. "Dig in, honey. I don't want you to starve to death."

"Have you seen me lately? I'm as huge as a barn. I hardly think there's any danger of starving to death."

"You look amazing. Now eat."

"Thank you for making this."

"You're welcome." He took a bite of his eggs, staring at me the whole time. "How are you feeling today?" he asked when he was finished.

"I'm okay, why?" I nibbled on a piece of bacon, eyeing him suspiciously.

"I was thinking we could go for a walk. Maybe hike around a bit and explore the property. I'd like to get a little better lay of the land. See if there are any close neighbors we don't know about, things like that. Plus, it's just a nice day. I thought you might enjoy getting out and into nature. I have that backpack I bought yesterday when I got the binoculars. We could fill it with a few picnic items. What do you think? I don't want to wear you out."

"Honestly, I think that sounds fabulous. Maybe we'll see some elk." I paused for a moment. "Do you think there are bears?" That idea didn't thrill me at all.

"I have no idea if this is bear country. I'd imagine it's always a possibility, though. And maybe even some mountain lions or bobcats."

"You're not making me feel any better. That kind of makes me want to stay put right here."

He laughed. "Tell you what. I'll bring my gun and an extra clip. Will that make you feel safer?"

"Much," I replied.

"So you'll do it?"

"Yes, but you have to let me get showered, first. I won't take long."

"I still need to shower, too. We can do it together to conserve water."

Shaking my head, I stared at him. "For someone who is so hell bent on conserving water all the time, why is it that every shower I take with you lasts ten times longer than normal?"

Chuckling, he stabbed at his eggs. "Come on, Goody. It's not that bad."

Quirking an eyebrow at him, I took another bite of bacon. "I'm just thinking you may not make it out on your hike if you shower with me."

Reaching across the table he grabbed my hand and squeezed it. "I'll be a good boy. I promise."

"Mmhmm. I'll believe it when I see it." A ringing phone broke the silence, making me jump. "I wonder who that is?"

"There's only one person it could be," Dylan said. "Chris is the only one with this number." Quickly rising, he ran up the stairs to retrieve his cell phone. "Hey, Chris," he answered. "What's up?"

I held my breath, trying to listen to the conversation, hoping desperately that everything was all right. A million different scenarios were running through my mind.

"Okay. I figured as much." He finally spoke up. "Yeah. Sounds good," Dylan said, and I relaxed a little. He didn't seem concerned. "Everything is great so far. The place you got us is really nice. Gorgeous views, too. Cami's been freaking out over all the elk that come into the field near here every morning." He laughed loudly. "No, I haven't been shooting them, but I did buy a pair of binoculars. We plan on hiking around today and seeing the area." Another pause. "Yeah, it's beautiful here. You and Sheridan should come check it out someday. How's the family, by the way?"

I continued eating while I waited for him to finish the call, listening as they spoke about his parents and how badly his mom was concerned for him. Truthfully, I could imagine her tearing the police department apart trying to find her son. She was probably pretty hard on Chris, trying to get information from him.

I was finished by the time Dylan made it back to the table. "Is everything okay?" I asked as I rinsed my dish and loaded it into the dishwasher.

"Yeah. He was calling to tell me they had finally received the files of all the arrests I made or assisted in, and cases I testified on. The department is going through them one by one to see if they can find any leads that way. So far, everyone they've looked into has checked out, but they're still working their way through."

"Is that really going to help?" I asked, still worried. "I mean, really, if you were stalking someone or harassing somebody else, would you be doing stuff out in the open where others could tell?"

"No, but they can cultivate a list of people who were living in our area during the attacks. They can also check and see if anyone has recently violated their parole, too. If they get a hit on someone, they can get a court order to delve deeper into things, like checking credit card usage, and track people that way. You'd be surprised how many people aren't where they're supposed to be. They've also pulled all my EMS and Fire Department files. I've testified on a few cases there, too."

"That will take forever!" I exclaimed. "You've been on lots of calls since you started working for the fire department."

He shrugged. "They're doing the best they can with what they have to go on." He sighed. "The fire investigation on the house came back as arson, as well. Gasoline was used an accelerant and they believe the explosion people heard was actually containers of gas that were ignited."

"How does no one notice someone carrying around a bunch of gas cans?"

"I don't know, but it was later in the evening. How often do we pay attention to what's going on at the neighbor's?

"That's true." Giving a dejected sigh, I sat back down at the table. "We're going to be here a while, aren't we?"

"It's looking that way. But don't let it get you down. We'll make the best of it."

"I just want to be married and not have to hide it. I hate pretending you're my brother."

"So do I, but we don't have to mix in with society that often. We can stick together out here and be ourselves, if that's what you'd like."

"We need some books and movies or something, or we're going to go crazy."

"Well, maybe we can go look for a library, or better yet, we can order you an eReader and you can load it up with books. There's a wireless keyboard and a modem under the television, there." He gestured toward the entertainment center. "I'm assuming that means there's Internet access here, as well. If it's not on, I'm sure we can get it turned on. Then you can watch movies or read to your heart's content."

"Okay," I said. "We can check it out after our hike. At the rate we're moving this morning, our picnic is going to be more of a late lunch or early dinner."

"I'll hurry," he said, digging back into his cold food.

"Do you want me to heat that up for you real quick?"

"Nah, it's fine," he replied.

"All right. I'm going to get in the shower, then."

"I'll join you shortly."

Standing, I slowly made my way toward the bedroom that held my things.

"Cami?" he called after me, and I sighed, knowing it was useless for us to try and keep up our aliases when we were alone.

"Yes?"

"Are you sure you're okay? You seem upset."

Going back over to him, I bent to kiss his head. "I'm fine. I just hoped we'd be able to go home sooner is all." I laughed wryly. "I don't know why. It's not like we have a home to go home to."

"You will, honey. I promise," he replied. "I give you my word, I'll make things right again, somehow."

DYLAN LOVE

CHAPTER SIXTEEN
Dylan-

"I'm glad we did this," Cami said as she stood on the rock beside me, staring out at the view.

"Here. Look through the binoculars." I handed them to her, but my eyes didn't leave her, watching as the breeze ruffled her hair, causing a few strands to blow around her face. The sun hitting it made the red tones underneath the dye job come out, allowing me a glimpse of the color I loved so well. She looked strong and beautiful. I knew she was missing home, but I could totally get used to living with her in an environment like this. I enjoyed hearing her "ooh" and "ah" over different discoveries we'd made. "If you check down the hill there, it looks like there's a pretty nice stream. Would you like to go sit there for a while and eat?"

Lowering the glasses, she followed to where I was pointing. "Yes! That looks amazing!"

Offering my hand, I helped her off the rocks and we carefully made our way down the hillside. I'd taken things extra slow today because I was worried about her getting tired and falling, but so far she'd done pretty well, going almost full circle around the property. We now knew we didn't have any neighbors who were close enough to see us on the property, though we could easily see a couple houses in each direction across the meadows. However, they were probably still a mile and a half away from our cabin. We'd also seen some fenced fields in the distance that looked to have horses and cattle. Apparently ranching was still going strong out here.

While portraying this outing as something to do for fun, I'd mainly wanted to know what was going on for security reasons. As near as I could tell, the house was on the ridge of a hill covered in pine trees that sloped down into vast meadow valleys. There were other rises, like ours, around us, and I was pretty sure there were houses I couldn't see hidden within the trees. This could be both a good and bad thing. Good because we were remote enough to be able to retain our privacy, but bad because if we needed help of any kind, it would take a significant amount of time for anyone to arrive. To that extent, I was happy about being reinstated and knowing I had some legal recourse to fall back on if needed, even if I wasn't in my jurisdiction.

"That place looks good over there," Cami said, pulling me out of my musings. "It's grassy and shady under those trees, but still close by the water."

"I agree," I replied, following her. Shrugging off my backpack, I unzipped it, removing a couple bottles of water and handed one to her. I sat in front of a big pine tree and she sat between my legs, leaning back against my chest.

She started laughing and picked up my hand, placing it on her stomach. "The baby is moving."

A hard knot formed beneath my hand. "What do you think that is? A foot? An arm?"

"I don't know. Maybe it's his baby bottom."

I patted her there. "Does that mean I'm spanking the baby?" I laughed. "That's such an incredible thing. Sometimes I roll over in the night and you cuddle against my back and I can feel the baby kick."

"Really?" she asked, seeming surprised. "I had no idea. I guess I sleep through it."

"Yeah, it caught me by surprise the first couple of times it happened, but I enjoy it. I like having you both close to me like that."

She ran her hand over mine, linking our fingers. "I think you'll be an amazing dad."

I chuckled. "I hope so. My dad was always good to me. I know I definitely have big shoes to fill."

"You'll be a natural. You're already so caring and aware of other people and their needs. I love how compassionate you are."

I laughed. "You make me sound like I'm a saint or something."

"To me, you are." Letting go of my hand, she

reached up to pat the side of my face. "You're amazing and I love you."

I set my water bottle down and wrapped my arms around her. "I love you, too." I kissed the top of her head. "So, have we decided what we're naming this kid of ours for sure, yet? What if you have him while we're still here? Is Hunter going to be a confusing name?"

"I don't think so. I'll call you Dylan when we are alone."

"I know; but if we are in public, it might be a little weird to say you named your baby after your brother."

"Hmmm. I didn't think about that. What if we use Hunter for his middle name then, like yours? We can pick a different one for his first name."

"That's fine with me. What names do you like?"

"What if we did "D" names so he can have the same initials as his daddy?"

"Okay. Give me some."

"Well, there's Darren, Daniel, or Drew."

"Hmm. I don't know if I like any of those with Hunter. But I do like the names with more than one syllable."

"There's Dalton, or Denver. How about Dennis?"

"If I had to pick one of those it would be Dalton, but it's not my favorite, either."

"How do you like Devon?"

"Not sure." I was thoroughly enjoying myself as she spouted off different names. It was very relaxing and peaceful sitting here and talking about our future and the baby, as I held her in my arms. "Not to be difficult, but I have to say I'm not really digging any of the "D" names. How about "C" names instead, like his pretty mom? That way he can be named after you and me. Something like Cameron?"

"Cameron Hunter Wilcock," she said, testing it all out. "I love that, Dylan! I really do!" Turning in my arms so she could face me and kneeling, she stared at me, joy radiating from her face. "Do you like that?"

"I think it sounds nice. Is that it then?" I stroked my hand over her back.

"That's it! I love it!" She grasped my face, planting a kiss firmly on my lips. "We just named our baby." She kissed me, again, and I pulled her closer, deepening it. Knowing she was so excited made me excited, too. I loved her so much.

"Here," I said, shifting my legs so she could straddle me, making her more comfortable.

"Did you bring me into the woods to seduce me?" she asked with a giggle.

"Is it working?"

"Yes. This is all very romantic."

"Well, I'm glad you're enjoying it. Now kiss me, again." Doing as I asked, she wrapped her arms around my neck and pressed her mouth to mine. Her lips parted and I dipped my tongue inside, tasting the sweetness that was uniquely her. Pulling away, she tipped her head back and I trailed my mouth is a series of sucks and kisses down her neck.

"No hickies," she whispered. "I'm a single

woman, remember."

I chuckled and commenced with lightly sucking on her neck anyway, before drifting down to her collarbone. "What if I put it where no one can see it?" I teased.

"Oh, well that's different, then." She laughed again, as I opened the first couple buttons of her shirt, kissing closer to her cleavage. Her soft moan signaled that she was enjoying it.

A distant sound caught my attention and immediately I stiffened—all my senses on high alert. "Cami, get off me." To her credit, she moved without asking why, quickly redoing the buttons on her shirt as I reached for the backpack that held my gun.

A cow came tromping through the trees, followed immediately by someone on a horse cursing at the animal. Cami scrambled behind the tree and the rider drew his horse up when he saw us.

"Sorry! I didn't know anyone was out here." I recognized him instantly and had to fight not to groan. "Hey, Camri; and Hunter, right?"

"Yeah," I replied. "Nice to see you again, Mark," I lied. "What are you doing way out here?"

"My grandpa owns a cattle ranch down towards the end of the meadow. I come here on my days off to help him out. This cow got out of a broken part in the fence and I've been chasing her for about an hour now. Damn cow. Grandpa said he'd heard someone had rented the Miller's vacation place. I'm assuming that's you two?"

"Yes," Cami said. "We're just out hiking

around today and enjoying the scenery. Hunter has been seeing lots of elk in the field in the morning, and sometimes in the evenings. He went and bought some binoculars so we could try and see some of the wildlife."

"Any luck?" Mark asked with a grin.

I shook my head. "A bald eagle. And now a cow."

Mark laughed heartily. "Yeah, I better get along and go catch her. Keep your eyes open, though. You never know when you might run into something else."

"Are there bears here?" Cami asked, suddenly.

He leaned forward, resting on the horn of his saddle. He sure didn't look like he was in a hurry to go catch that cow. "Sometimes." He nodded. "But you don't see them too often. Sometimes we run into wolves, though."

"Wolves?" Cami's eyes grew wider.

"Yeah. There has been a project going on for a few years. They released Mexican wolves into the Blue region hoping to rebuild the packs there. They're an endangered species, so they don't want people shooting them. And I've seen a couple mountain lions; but they tend to keep to themselves. It's pretty rare to see one." His eyes never left my wife and suddenly I felt invisible.

"Well, thanks for the info." I broke in, more than ready to send him on his way. "We'll let you get back to catching that cow before she's too far gone. Camri and I need to get headed back to the house, anyway. I think I've had her out hiking enough, today. Our mom will kill me if I don't take care of her."

"It was nice running into the two of you. Hopefully I'll see you again, soon."

"Thanks. Have a nice day," Cami said cheerily with a little wave of her fingers.

"You, too," he replied, giving her a wink before spurring his horse into action and riding off.

"Now do you believe me?"

She laughed. "I do believe you're jealous."

"You bet I am. That guy likes you and he's not afraid to show it."

"Well, why should he be? He doesn't know I belong to you."

"Then he should have some respect for the dead, at least. You're supposed to be grieving. I mean, obviously your husband didn't die that long ago for you to be as pregnant as you are."

She giggled, bending to pick up her water bottle. "I like seeing this side of you. It's fun."

"I don't see anything fun about it at all," I grumbled, grabbing the backpack.

"It makes me feel special." She smiled.

"What? Because it drives me crazy every time another guy looks at you?"

"Yeah. It's sweet. It proves you still love me."

"Have you looked at yourself lately? I think there's plenty of proof about how much I love you." I gestured to her belly.

"All this proves is that you loved me six months ago."

I snorted. "Whatever." I held my hand out so

I could help her climb back up the hill. "You know I love you."

"Yes, I do. But it's fun to see you get possessive. It makes me feel cherished."

"I'll always cherish you, Goody. You don't need the appearance of a strange guy to prove that."

"Oh, so now he's strange?" She laughed.

"In my book, yes."

"Well, you and I don't have the same book. I think he was just being neighborly."

"Of course, as he scares you with tales of wild beasts roaming the forest. He was probably hoping you'd jump on his horse and ride home in his lap."

"Hey, now. There's only one cowboy I ride in these here parts," she said with a country drawl and I couldn't help laughing.

"Well, keep riding him. He likes it."

CAMI LOVE

CHAPTER SEVENTEEN
Cami-

"Let's do something fun tonight. I'm feeling a little stir crazy. We need to get out of the house for a while." Clicking off my new iPad, I tossed it onto the couch beside me.

"I thought you were enjoying your reading time," Dylan said, glancing up from the game he was playing. "That *Loving* whatever book you told me about."

Sighing, I curled up on the couch. "*Loving Liberty*, by Belinda Boring, and it was really good. I finished it already. The story made me think about the way we define other people and what our expectations of them are. But it also made me feel like I'm being held captive here. I don't want to just sit around, anymore. I want to take our lives back. I want to go out and do something different. We've been cooped up in here for days."

Turning his game off, he placed his iPad on the end table. "Your wish is my command. What would you like to do?"

"Go home." I didn't even hesitate.

"Okay, your wish—within reason—is my command How's that?" he replied, scooting closer to me and rubbing his hand over my knee. "Any other ideas?"

"Can we go into town? Maybe do dinner and a movie?"

"That I can do. What're you hungry for?"

"Pizza, I think. It's been a while since we've had that." I rubbed my stomach as I considered. "Of course, some pasta might be good, too."

Dylan laughed and picked up his iPad again. "Let me see what I can find around here, close. How about you look up the movies and see what's playing?"

Thirty minutes later, the two of us were in the truck, headed down the road toward town.

"What did you decide on?" Dylan asked.

"I have no idea what's playing. I couldn't find it. All I found was a thing that said they're only open on the weekends after six thirty p.m."

"Guess we'll have to see when we get there. If it's something you don't want to see we'll go for a drive or something."

"That's fine with me. I just needed to get out." I glanced at him. "I've even considered using the resume to get a job like Chris suggested, but I'm afraid there will be days I don't feel good and I won't be reliable. Plus, if we are still here when I have the baby, I'd want to take maternity leave. Who's going to want to hire someone just in time for them to leave?"

"I understand." Reaching across the seat, he

squeezed my hand, flashing me a sympathetic look. "Is there something else you'd like to do? What about volunteering someplace? Or maybe you could knit a blanket for the baby."

I stared at him pointedly before I burst out laughing.

"What?" he asked, a confused smiled on his face as he glanced between the road and me. "When have you ever seen me knit anything? I'll tell you when. Never. I wouldn't even know how to hold the needles, or hooks, or whatever they are."

"Just trying to help. What are some other things you'd like to do?"

"Honestly? I miss singing."

"Do you want me to buy you a piano?"

I laughed, again. "Quit being a smart mouth. Where in the heck would we put a piano? Not to mention that they're kind of difficult to move around."

Grinning at me, he shook his head. "Okay, so a piano is out; but I bet we could get a nice keyboard for you to play on. Then you could write some music, sing, make your own karaoke, or anything you want."

"I'm only singing karaoke if you do it with me."

He shook his head. "That's where I draw the line. No one wants to hear me sing. It's like cats...screeching."

I giggled. "We've been married all this time, and I've never heard you sing."

"I know; and there's a reason for that. I refuse to mar your opinion of me." He chuckled.

Flipping on the radio, I found a rock music station playing a popular song. "Come on," I encouraged him. "Sing with me. I'll even turn it up loud."

"No," he replied, shaking his head as he grinned. "But I'd love listening to you sing it."

"Just a little bit, please?" I begged. "A few bars. You can do it."

"Not a chance."

"Maybe that's what I could do! I could teach you to sing." I sat up excitedly.

"Goody, I'd rather pull my own teeth out."

Slumping back against my seat, I sighed. "How'd the two of us ever get together?"

Glancing over at me, he smiled. "Starting to regret it? I was wondering when you'd figure things out."

"What's that supposed to mean?" I asked.

"It means I got the best deal in this relationship." He squeezed my hand again.

"Don't lie to me, Dylan. There's no one else like you. You're an amazing husband and I love you."

"Even if I don't sing?" he asked and I nodded, smiling back at him.

"Even if you don't sing."

***

Biting into my pizza, I heard Dylan groan and I glanced at him before following his gaze to the door where Mark Young stood in his paramedic uniform, with a radio on his hip. Another man was with him, obviously his partner.

"That guy is seriously everywhere," Dylan

grumbled. "I swear he's following us."

That actually made me feel a bit nervous, due to the fact we did know someone was trying to find us, but I quickly brushed it aside. "Paramedics need to eat too, as you well know."

"Yeah, but what are the odds of him choosing this restaurant?"

"Really? This town only has like twelve restaurants and only two of them are pizza places. So, if he wanted pizza, the odds are fifty/fifty."

"I still don't like it."

"Be nice," I whispered, seeing that Mark had noticed us at our table in the corner. He waved. Tapping his partner on the shoulder, he pointed at us, and his partner nodded. They made their way toward us.

"Great," Dylan muttered, trying to compose what I assumed was supposed to be an affable expression, but it didn't reach his eyes.

"Hey, you two," Mark said in a friendly tone. "We meet again."

"Crazy, isn't is?" Dylan replied. I kicked him under the table.

"How are you, Mark?" I asked, hoping he wouldn't notice Dylan's iciness.

"Doing good. Just grabbing some dinner. This is Jake Ronald. Jake, this is that paramedic I've been telling you about, Hunter, and his sister, Camri."

"Nice to meet you both," he said, extending his hand to shake each of ours. "Mark says he's been hounding you to come work with us."

"He's been trying to," Dylan replied, still

smiling like someone had painted it on him.

"We definitely need someone else," Jake said.

"I keep telling him that, but he doesn't seem interested." Mark glanced at me. "But he's here taking care of his sister, so I can understand that, too."

There was an awkward pause as they stood there for a moment. "Would you like to join us?" I asked. "We just started eating and we have plenty of room."

"That would be great. Thanks." Mark pulled out the chair next to me and sat down. Immediately, I glanced across to Dylan, noticing the ticking in his jaw. He was not happy. Jake sat beside him and a waitress came to take their order.

"So, how long have you both been paramedics?" I asked, trying to keep the conversation going. I was desperate for some socializing.

"I've only been doing it for two years," Jake said.

"And I've been doing it around five," Mark spoke up. "My dad used to run the department before he retired and turned the reigns over to me. There are a few full-time positions, but we also rely heavily on volunteers. We have a few of those, but most of them are basic EMT's. We're needing another paramedic in a full time spot." He glanced at Dylan. "Too bad you don't live closer to town. We could've had you respond to calls from home on a volunteer basis if you didn't want to work full time."

"I'm sorry you're having a hard time filling it. I love the work, but I've promised my time to Camri right now. She's been through hell lately."

I knew he was being serious with that comment. "You're doing a great job," I replied. "I appreciate it."

"Mark mentioned your husband," Jake said. "Sorry for your loss."

"Thank you." I felt horrible about playing on the sympathy of others with a lie. Even if it was for our protection, I didn't like it. "Tell us more about the area. Is there anything we should go see or do?" I asked, eager to move on to a safer subject.

"I, personally, like nature things," Mark replied. "I go fishing a lot at Big Lake, which isn't too far from here. It's a beautiful area still, even after the fire we had."

"I remember watching that on the news," Dylan said. "This place was almost wiped out. I noticed how close the burn line came to the edge of town. It's a miracle they were able to get it put out before it came through."

"It really was. There were a lot of scared people around here. They evacuated the whole place."

"That must've been terrifying."

"Well, I can safely say I don't ever want to go through anything like that, again."

"That isn't the only fire you've had up here either, is it? There was another big one over in the Show Low area, if I remember correctly."

The hard edge to Dylan's voice had disappeared and I knew he was completely immersed in the conversation. If there was one thing Dylan knew, it was fire. Some of his buddies on the department also worked for hotshot crews and they were routinely sent to wildfires all over the country. They'd shared horror stories of the battles they'd fought. After hearing about the group of Arizona firefighters who'd died battling a wildfire, I'd been afraid for Dylan to even go to work. It scared me. Large fires could get out of control so quickly.

I continued eating quietly; listening to the conversation as they swapped stories of the things they'd seen on the job. Dylan actually seemed be enjoying everything the longer they spoke, and I was happy to see him relaxing. Tonight had been a good outing for him, too.

Loud tones burst into the air from both their radios, followed by the voice of a dispatcher. "An ambulance is need for a child who's been bitten by a dog . . . ."

Mark and Jake both stood, throwing some cash down on the table. "Sorry to cut things short, but we've got to go. It was nice visiting with you."

"Have a good night," I said.

"Hopefully we can get together again, soon." He winked at me before turning to hurry out the door.

Dylan was shaking his head as he stared at me. "And I'd almost convinced myself to like him."

I laughed. "At least you got to have some fun. I could tell you were having a good time. You miss work, don't you?"

"I enjoy the job, but I enjoy being with you more."

"It's completely okay with me if you want to take the job. I think you'd like it."

"I won't leave you home, alone, and I can't very well bring you to work with me. It's okay. You don't need to worry about me. I'm happy where I am." He smiled. "Did you decide if you wanted to go to that Disney movie we saw playing at the theater?"

I laughed. "The more accurate question is can you handle a Disney movie? It's a cartoon and a musical—and you know how much I love musicals."

He grinned. "As long as you don't make me sing. Besides, if there's going to be a little tike running around, I may need to get used to those kinds of movies."

"That's true," I agreed. He paid for dinner and we left, walking out to the truck, together.

"Mmmm. Smell the air," I said, relishing in the differences being in the country brought.

Dylan glanced up and the darkening sky. "Let's hurry and get to the theater. It looks like it's going to rain."

DYLAN LOVE

CHAPTER EIGHTEEN
Dylan-

"We are drenched!" Cami laughed brushing her sopping hair back from her face, and I smiled as I grabbed a dishtowel to wipe my gun and cell phone. They'd both gotten a bit wet in the run from the truck to the house.

"It's really coming down out there, isn't it?" I asked my clothes dripping.

She stood at the window staring out at the dark night, brief streaks of lightning illuminating her face. "That lightning and thunder is scary. I'm glad we're inside."

"Me, too. We're lucky we made it up the driveway. It's going to be a muddy mess out there, tomorrow." Placing my gun on the table next to my keys, I dropped the towel to the floor to soak up the puddle of water I'd made. "Let's go take a warm shower and get cleaned up," I suggested. "We need to get you out of those wet things."

Suddenly the giant window shattered,

sending shards of glass into the room. "Cami!" I shouted as she fell to the floor. She didn't move. "Cami!" Running toward her I was brought up short by a popping sound and stabbing pain in my arm. Glancing down, I saw where the outer edge of my skin had been torn.

"Shit!" I dove to the floor, realizing I'd been shot. Scrambling behind the furniture, I rushed to the table, grabbing my gun and training it on the open window. Cami lay unmoving in the spot she'd fallen, but I could see some cuts she'd sustained on her arms from my position. We were sitting ducks in here. I couldn't see who was out there, but they could see in. Turning my gun toward the lamp, I fired, shattering the bulb before turning and knocking out the second one. Two bullets down and my extra clip was upstairs. There was no time to get it. I had to get Cami someplace safe before whoever was out there came looking in here.

Crawling military style, I moved to her side, not caring that the glass was cutting into my elbows and chest.

"Cami, honey!" I shook her as I whispered sharply. "Goody, can you hear me?" There was no point in keeping up pretenses. Whoever was after us had found us.

She uttered a small moan and relief raced through me. "The baby," she said softly. Running my hand across her soaked body, I felt her stomach, terror coming over me when I felt the warm, sticky liquid there.

"Hang in there, Goody. I'm going to get you out of here, but it might hurt. I'm sorry."

Reaching for the back of her shirt, I grabbed the collar and fisted as much fabric as I could. Taking advantage of the dark, I quickly stood, dragging her behind me and out of the way of the window. Pieces of glass crunched around us as we moved and she moaned in pain.

Pop. Another shot whizzed past my head. Pulling her around the corner into the hallway, I knew we were out of the line of fire, but I still had no idea who was out there. The only thing I could think to do was go out the back, but who knew if anyone was waiting in that direction for us, too.

Cursing, I realized I'd left my phone on the kitchen table. Cami's should still be in her pocket, but first I had to get her to safety. Hopefully, whoever was shooting couldn't see us anymore, either.

I slid the gun into my pants and bent to gather Cami in my arms, she was a dead weight, her head rolling back and her arms flopping out to the sides. Carrying her to the back door, I scrambled to turn the knob with my wet hands, finally swinging it open. I waited for a second to see if anyone would fire at us before dashing out into the pelting rain. Across the backyard, past the patio, I ran straight into the woods for cover. The truck was parked out front where the shots had been fired. There was no way I would risk going to it. There was only one other alternative I could think of, and that was to try and call for help, then see if I could make it the distance to Mark's grandfather's land.

Slipping and sliding, I scurried my way down

the hill, trying my best to stay upright. Reaching an outcropping of rocks, I sat down and scooted against them, holding Cami in my lap. Digging in her pocket I found her cell phone. Trying to shield it from the water, I hit the speed dial that would go to Chris. He answered on the second ring.

"Cami?" he asked, sounding concerned.

"It's Dylan," I huffed out, my voice shaking. "They shot her Chris! They shot her! I need help! Get an ambulance and the police here, now!"

"Where are you?" he asked. I could hear him talking to someone else.

"In the woods behind the house," I panted. "It's raining really bad, but it was the only direction I could go. The keys are in the house still. I'm on foot carrying her. I'm afraid they'll try to follow us."

"Is there anywhere you can go?" he asked.

"There's another farm about a mile and a half from here. I'm heading in that direction. I need to go, Chris. She can't wait. She's unconscious and I'm afraid she's losing too much blood."

"There's tracking on your phone. I made sure of it. Check and make sure your location app is on." My hands shook as I did what he asked, fearing that the phone was going to get damaged and die on us.

"It is." A burst of lightning made me jump, illuminating the dark stain spreading across Cami's white shirt.

"Keep moving. The police are on their way

and they're dispatching an ambulance and a helicopter to your location, but the helicopter is coming from Show Low, so it's going to take a bit for it to get to you. You need to get as far away as possible from the house. The medical teams won't be able to come in until the scene is cleared for them to arrive."

"She doesn't have that much time, Chris." A sob escaped me and I could feel my tears mixing in with the rivulets of water running down my face.

"Get going. I'll get help to you, I promise. Be careful."

I slipped the phone into my front pocket, before pulling my shirt off and tearing it into strips. Tying them together, I wrapped them around Cami's stomach, hoping I was doing something to help staunch the blood flow. Crawling to my knees, I picked her up again, wishing I could toss her over my shoulder in a fireman's carry, but her pregnant belly wouldn't allow for that. I continued on, in what I hoped was the right direction, working my way down the hill toward the stream and the meadow.

Falling in the mud, my knee slammed into a rock and I winced, sliding about some more before slipping on my butt a good part of the way down the hill. It wasn't a comfortable ride, but I managed to hang on to Cami. I didn't think I was too far away from the stream now. Lifting her again, I stood and hurried forward. Another flash of light revealed the water rushing by. The storm had obviously raised the water level and what used to be a smooth babbling brook suddenly appeared much more treacherous.

"Damn it!" I cursed, panting as I tried to figured out what to do. Gently, I laid Cami on the ground, digging the phone out of my front pocket again, relieved to find it still working." Chris answered immediately.

"I'm at the base of the hill by the stream," I gasped out. "It's risen significantly though, and it's moving pretty fast. I don't know if I can cross it and hold on to her, too."

"We've got you up on the maps. According to this, if you keep to your left and follow the stream, it will take you back toward the highway.

"There's a slope from the house to the meadow in that direction," I replied. "If anyone was out looking for us they'd be in that direction."

"The sheriff's department is near your location, now, if we can get you to a road to meet them. Ambulance is coming fast behind them. You've got to try to get to the road. Do you have your gun?"

"I do. Leaving now." I put the phone back into my pocket and leaned over Cami.

"Cami!" I shouted, shaking her. "Wake up, honey! I need you to wake up!" Nothing. Reaching to her neck, I felt her pulse beating, but it was faint. The clock was clicking down rapidly. Not wanting to waste anymore time, I gathered her in my arms again, moving as fast as I could along the edge of the stream. Thankfully the sounds of the water and the storm would be enough to muffle any sound I was making. I couldn't see a thing, except for when the lightning flashed briefly. Stumbling through brush and thick stands of trees, I could feel my skin ripping as branches tore at me. Fatigue was quickly spreading though me and I could feel my arms and legs trembling as I struggled to remain upright. Fire seemed to spread through my lungs with each breath I took. I felt like I'd swallowed a gallon of water and my eyes were stinging from trying to see through the rain.

None of that mattered. I had to get Cami to safety. She'd been unconscious the entire time and I was praying for Divine intervention with every step.

Wanting to weep with delight when I saw the several pairs of code lights flashing in the distance, I noticed the bobbing of flashlights as people ran in my direction. I heard the low flying chopper the moment before the searchlight illuminated me in its brilliant glow. It seemed like hours had passed, but suddenly there were officers everywhere. Two men quickly took Cami from me, carrying her off. I fell to my knees in exhaustion, gasping for breath, as I watched them moving with her toward the waiting vehicles. Strong arms grasped me on each side, lifting me back to my feet and two officers slid under my arms, attempting to help me along. I did my best to run and keep up with them, my eyes never leaving the men that carried Cami.

"He's injured, too," I heard the officer at my left side call out to the ambulance crew. A medic turned and I saw it was Mark, his eyes wide in horror.

"Don't worry about me. Take care of Cami," I gasped out. "She's my wife."

"The helicopter is going to land in the staging area just down the road," another officer barked out. "They want to know if this is going to be a hot load?"

"Yes, it's a hot load. She's in bad shape. Tell them to get ready for two patients. One on a backboard and one in the jump seat."

I couldn't stop the sobs that wracked my body as I watched them put her on a gurney and put her into the back of the ambulance to get her out of the rain.

"Start up two large bore IV's with blood tubing," Mark shouted to Jake as he started hooking her up to the heart monitor. "We need to get some fluid in her and get her pressure up. How far along is she?" he called to me.

"Six and a half months," I managed to choke out. "She's twenty years old."

I started shivering hardcore, recognizing the signs of what was happening to me. "I think I'm going into shock," I mumbled, feeling my vision sway before me.

"Take him to the front seat," one of the officers shouted. "And get this rig turned around and head for the chopper. We don't have time to waste!" I was shuttled to the front of the ambulance and helped inside. Slumping against the seat, I heard all the doors start slamming as another officer climbed into the driver's seat. Making a U-turn we headed down the road to the waiting chopper, it's blades whirling in the air.

Another Sheriff signaled for us to stop and the flight crew jumped out and ducked, running toward us. I could hear Mark shouting out vitals and information to two crewmembers, as the sheriff and another medic helped me out and began shuttling me toward it. The heavy sound of the blades whipped loudly through the air as we approached. The medic jumped on-board and pulled me inside, helping to seat and buckle me into the harness. "Are you hurt anywhere else besides your arm?" he asked loudly. I shook my head, glancing down and seeing that the wound was deeper than I'd originally thought. He started wrapping some gauze around it, but I didn't care; my gaze drifting, instead, to the gurney that was being rolled toward me. Cami had been intubated and was being bagged. I couldn't stop the gurgle that rippled through my throat, and I felt like I was going to strangle on the spot. She was slid on a backboard into the gurney spot and locked into place. The other two medics hopped in after her and the doors were closed.

"Where we headed?" the pilot called over his shoulder. "Are we bypassing Show Low to go to Flagstaff?"

"She won't make it to Flagstaff," the medic replied, and my I felt my body convulse in a shiver. "We need to go to Show Low and get her stabilized."

"Roger," the pilot responded, picking up his radio. "Dispatch, Eagle One headed to Summit Regional with level one trauma and second patient on board."

"Copy Eagle One, en route to Summit Regional with level one trauma. Twenty-one thirty-two," the dispatcher's voice came back using the military time.

The medic leaning over Cami slipped his headset on. Another headset was gently placed on me. I heard a voice crackle through the radio as the chopper powered up, lifting off the ground into the air, leaving the mass of swirling code lights behind. "Eagle One, requesting patch through to Summit Regional," he said.

"Copy Eagle One, patching through to Summit Regional." A few seconds passed and then the radio crackled, again.

"This is Summit Regional. Dr. Gunter speaking."

"Summit Regional, this is Eagle One. We're flying into your facility with two gunshot wounds. Patient one is a level one trauma, gunshot wound to the abdomen on a twenty-year-old female approximately twenty-seven weeks pregnant. Patient is intubated with large bore IVs times two with blood tubing. Acquiring vitals at this time. Patient two is a," he paused, glancing at me.

"Twenty-four," I said, my teeth chattering. I couldn't control myself.

"Twenty-four year old male," he continued, "with a gunshot wound to the left lateral arm. We have an estimate time of arrival of twenty-five minutes."

My heart stopped and I could barely breathe. Twenty-five minutes. I didn't think Cami had that long.

DYLAN LOVE

CHAPTER NINETEEN
Dylan-

X-rays of my knee hadn't shown anything and the wound to my arm had been cleaned and stitched. I'd been given an IV, but refused any pain meds. I didn't want to be sedated while Cami was in surgery.

After being treated and released, I sat in the surgery waiting room, waiting for news. Now, dressed in the pair of scrubs I'd been given, I stared at the bruises and scratches on my arms as I leaned against my knees. Every few minutes, I glanced up at the clock, sure that another hour had passed. Time seemed to be moving at a snail's pace, each second slipping slowly by. She'd been in there forever.

A door opened and I was surprised to see Chris enter. I stood to greet him. Wrapping his arms around me, he hugged me tightly. "I'm so sorry, Dylan."

"Don't be. If it wasn't for you . . . ." Letting the sentence trail off, I couldn't say anymore, fearing the news that was still to come. He released me and we both sat down. "How'd you get here so fast?"

"I managed to snag a helicopter of my own. Your parents and Sheridan are catching a fixed wing flight, probably as we speak, and Cami's are trying to get here, as well. I didn't want you here alone, since we still don't know who's behind this. Did the police come to get a statement?"

"Yeah, while I was in the ER." I glanced at the clock, again. Every minute that ticked away seemed to take a piece of my soul with it. I knew the longer she was in there, the worse things were. "What's taking so long?" I asked in frustration.

"Take it as an encouraging sign. It means they're still working on her, right?"

At that exact moment, the door opened and a doctor in surgical gear stepped through. "Mr. Wilcock?" he asked, looking straight at me.

I stood. "Yes?" My heart was beating a million miles a minute and I briefly wondered if this was what it was like to wait for execution.

"I'm Doctor Talley. I performed the surgery on your wife. She's in recovery, now." I felt faint, relief seeping through my limbs. She was still alive. "I'm not going to mince things," he continued. "She's not doing well." My relief was short lived. "She coded once on the table and we had to revive her. She was right on the brink, due to the significant amount of blood she lost into her abdomen. We've had to give her quite a large transfusion to replace it, but the bullet has been retrieved and the area repaired."

"And the baby?" I asked, still reeling from the fact Cami had coded.

The surgeon shook his head. "I'm really sorry, but the baby's umbilical cord and placenta suffered trauma from the bullet. We weren't able to save him. He died in the womb and we had to perform a C-section on your wife."

Raising my hand to my mouth, I attempted to calm the overwhelming grief, but I was unable to stop the choked cry that escaped. My body shuddered as tears ran down my face. Chris put his arms around my shoulders, squeezing me tightly for support.

"Does Cami know?" I managed to ask.

He shook his head. "She's not awake, yet. We're keeping her sedated to try and let her body recover a little from the shock it's been through. I'll send someone out to get you in a few minutes, after they get her situated." He paused, staring at me sympathetically. "I feel the need to warn you. She's not out of the woods, yet. I'll be having her admitted to the surgical intensive care unit after recovery. We'll see how things go in the next day or so and reevaluate, as needed, from there."

I nodded. "Okay. Thank you for your help."

He shook my hand. "Sorry we had to meet under these circumstances."

"Me, too," I replied. I stood there numbly, staring at the door as he disappeared through it, trying to process everything I'd been told. "If she makes it through this, Chris, losing that baby is going to kill her. I don't know how she'll overcome it. Hell, I don't know how I'm going to overcome it."

"We'll just take things one day at a time, okay? Small steps until we can work our way back up the ladder."

Anger suddenly coursed through me. "I can't lose her. I want you to find the bastard that did this to her and string him up by his balls. Do you hear me? I mean it. I want whoever's responsible for this to pay, just like she's having to pay."

"Hey. Hey, Dylan." He grabbed me by both shoulders, staring me straight in the eyes. "I don't want you worrying about any of this. I promise you, I'll see that it gets taken care of. And as far as Cami, we'll get an officer stationed outside her door and anyone who doesn't have clearance won't be given access to her, okay? We're gonna get to the bottom of this. I swear it."

"You won't need an officer," I growled. "I'm not leaving her side for a minute until the perpetrator is caught."

"You're too close to the situation. Come on, man. Take a deep breath. Let the police do their job."

"Because that's worked so well for us?" I saw the hurt in his eyes and felt bad; knowing he'd take the blame, personally, for what happened. But I couldn't deal with that right now.

A nurse appeared in the doorway and my attention snapped in her direction. "Mr. Wilcock? If you'd like to follow me, I'll take you to see your wife, now." She glanced at Chris. "I'm sorry, but we only allow once person back at a time."

"No worries." He patted me on the shoulder. "Go see Cami. I'll take care of everything on my end."

I nodded, leaving him to follow the nurse down the sterile looking hallway. She led me through a swinging door into an area that had a bed sectioned off with a curtain. Stepping behind the curtain, I froze, hardly recognizing Cami. Her hair was tucked up in a surgical cap and her face looked gaunt, and sallow. Several bandages were on her arms, covering cuts from the window glass. She was still hooked up to a ventilator, and listening to the sound of it breathing for her made ice creep into my veins. Wires and tubing were running all over her. I didn't even know where I could touch her without disturbing something. Glancing to her stomach area, I could tell it was obviously flatter, and intense pain stabbed me in the heart, making it all real.

Moving to the bed, I leaned down next to her ear. Placing my hand on her covered head, my thumb drifted to lightly stroke her forehead. "Cami," I whispered hoarsely. "Cami, honey. I'm so sorry I didn't protect you well enough. Please, I beg you, don't leave me. Give me another chance." The knot was back in my throat and my tears fell onto the bed. "I can't live without you."

The only reply was the beep and sound of the machines she was attached to, but I didn't care. Standing beside her, I continued to stroke her forehead, occasionally bending to kiss her there, as well. I didn't want to ever leave her side. I didn't even want to sleep, because it meant I wouldn't be able to look at her.

"Mr. Wilcock?" I turned to find the nurse standing beside the curtain. "Can I speak with you over here for a moment? I need to ask you a few questions."

Reluctantly, I moved away from Cami, following after the nurse as she led me toward the big desk in the middle of the room. "I'm sorry to pull you away from your wife, I know you want to be with her right now. I'm just always reluctant to speak about certain things in front of the patient. You never know what they might hear."

"Okay." I had to admit, she had me a little on the nervous side. I didn't know if I could take any more bad news tonight.

"We need to know what you'd like to do with your baby's remains." Her words struck me hard, leaving me feeling like I'd been stabbed in the chest. "This situation varies from couple to couple," she went on. "Some choose to have the remains disposed of by cremation. Others ask for a chance to see the infant first, and some have even buried them and held small graveside service for them. I just need to know how you'd like to proceed with this."

Staring at her, I couldn't even manage to form words. How was I supposed to make a decision like this without Cami? I scrubbed both hands over my face, as if the action would somehow clear my mind.

"I know this is a difficult situation," she added. "Would you like a few minutes to consider things?"

Glancing toward the curtain that hid Cami from me, I tried to place myself inside her and what she would do.

"Is it okay . . . I mean, can I see him?" My heart was pounding so loudly my ears were throbbing.

She nodded. "If that's what you'd like."

I'd imagined the moment of meeting my son so much differently. Never in million years would I have come up with this. I swallowed hard as I weighed my feelings. "That's what I'd like." Glancing over to where Cami lay, I continued. "I don't know when she'll wake up, but I know she will want to see him too, if possible."

"We can keep the body, if needed, until you better know your situation."

"Okay, but can I see him now?"

"Certainly. I can take you to a private room, or you can choose to see him here with your wife."

"With my wife, please. I always imagined we'd be together when we met him for the first time. I'd like to have that, at least." Never had I known my emotions could rip me up so badly from the inside out.

"All right. Did you have a name for your son?" she asked, and immediately the knot was back in my throat.

"Cameron Hunter Wilcock," I responded.

She smiled softly. "That's a beautiful name." She pointed to a rolling chair at the desk. "Why don't you grab that and go sit in with your wife. I'll bring Cameron out to you in a few minutes."

Nodding numbly, I did as she asked, sitting rigidly beside Cami as I tried to prepare my mind and heart for what was about to happen. I'd seen plenty of dead bodies before in my line of work, but none of them had ever been my son.

The curtain fluttered and I glanced up to see the nurse enter, carrying a very small, blanketed bundle in her arms. "He's really tiny," she said. "So don't be alarmed. He only weighs a couple of pounds."

I nodded, unable to speak as she held her arms out. Carefully, I took him from her. "Here's a paper with his name and little footprints on it for you to keep." She placed the paper on Cami's bed. "I'll give you some time alone."

Staring at the blanket it my arms, I lifted a trembling hand to open it. I had to blink several times before I could see his tiny face through my tears, so sweet and innocent. Opening up the blanket the rest of the way, my fingers traced over his tiny fingers and toes, all so perfectly formed. A bracelet circled one of his legs and I saw the nurse had written his name on it. Gently brushing my fingers over the dark peach fuzz on his head, I thought he was beautiful, perfect in every way. Turning toward the bed, I carefully lifted him, placing him in the crook of Cami's arm, where he belonged.

"Here's our baby, Goody," I said. Unable to hold back my emotions any longer I slipped my hand into hers, laying my head against her arm as uncontrollable grief threatened to consume me. "I'm so sorry." My face was wet with the steady stream of tears. "Please forgive me for failing you both. I'm sorry. I'm so sorry. I tried so hard to get you both to safety. I'm so sorry."

I knew begging her to forgive me was asking for the impossible. How could she forgive me, if I couldn't even forgive myself? And I would never forgive myself for this.

DYLAN LOVE

CHAPTER TWENTY
Dylan-

Stretched out on a slim, not-so-comfortable recliner in the ICU, I continued to stare at Cami, watching for any voluntary signs of life. The respirator continued its rhythmic breathing for her, the noise somewhat comforting. I was at least guaranteed she was still breathing. Several nurses were repeatedly in and out of the room to check on her, even though the wall was made entirely of glass and they could watch her from the desk. Thankfully, they seemed to recognize my need to sulk in the corner, choosing to disturb me as little as possible.

My gun had been returned to me in my bag of belongings from the ER and it lay on the table beside me, easily within my reach if the need arose. Apparently everyone had been made aware of what was going on, because no one questioned me carrying it.

A police officer had been stationed outside the door to the ICU and no one was allowed in without being cleared for entry, first. Chris was also seated outside the glass doors to the room, which gave me a lot of relief; however, my mood seemed to darken with each passing moment.

I was exhausted, but I couldn't sleep. Every time I closed my eyes. I saw Cami being shot over and over again. Repeatedly playing events over and over in my mind, I pondered every different scenario imaginable—looking for some way I could've changed the outcome. Mentally, I knew this was wasted effort on my part, but my heart refused to accept the reality of the situation.

Another nurse came into the room, standing by the machines as she waited to get another set of vitals. I'd been watching the monitor, making sure her blood pressure stayed within the proper parameters, along with her pulse and oxygen levels. Picking up the chart, the nurse quickly jotted things down, before glancing at me.

"Can I get you a blanket, water, or anything?"

"No thank you. I'm okay for now."

"How's your arm doing? Do you need anything for pain like some Tylenol?"

Even though my arm was throbbing a bit, I shook my head. "I'm good. Thanks for asking."

"Let me know if you change your mind. We want you to be comfortable, too."

"I appreciate it; but right now my biggest concern is her." I nodded toward Cami. "Just keep taking care of her like you are, and I'll be great."

The staff here had been very caring and accommodating. I appreciated their compassion for us both.

Chris got up from his chair and stepped into the doorway. "The guard outside just called. Your parents are here. They're coming in."

Closing the chair, I stood, spotting them coming around the corner. My mom whispered something in Spanish before making the sign of the cross and casting a glance toward Heaven. I didn't have to ask about her prayer, I knew it was a prayer of thanks knowing how concerned she always was for my safety.

"Dylan," she whispered coming to me, her arms outstretched. I enveloped her in mine, resting my chin on the top of her head, as I closed my eyes. "I'm so sorry for everything, *niño*." My emotions were too close to the surface for me to respond, though.

"Son, we sure are sad to hear about all you've been through," my dad said, and my mom stepped aside so he could hug me, as well. "I know how important family is to you."

A knot was back in my throat and I nodded, my lips pursed as the damn tears resurfaced once more. "Come in," I managed to spit out, gesturing for them to go see Cami.

They moved to the side of her bed. "Oh, my pretty girl," Mom said, grasping one of her limp hands. "Honey, you've got to come back to us, okay? We love you and all of us are waiting to help you through this. Our family needs you. Dylan needs you."

Good hell, there was no way I could stop the stuttering in my chest, listening to my mom talk to her like this. I'd never allowed my emotions to rule me, until now. This was a whole new level of hurt and heartache. I couldn't bear it, or control it, it seemed. It bubbled out of me at will, almost as if it represented the bleeding of my heart.

Wiping at my eyes with the back of my hand, I stepped closer. "They're keeping her sedated for tonight. The doctor said they'd try to pull her off the ventilator tomorrow and see how she handles it. She needs her rest right now, though."

They both nodded. "What happened with the baby?" Dad asked softly.

"We, I, got to sit with him for a while, today. I let Cami hold him even though she won't remember it. One of the mortuaries came and picked up the body since the hospital doesn't have a morgue."

"Will you have services then?" Mom asked and I nodded.

"I think Cami will need it for closure. Probably just a graveside service of some sort." I sighed heavily. "She doesn't know yet, so I'm waiting to discuss things with her when she wakes up." I knew that the doctor had warned me that she wasn't out of the woods yet, but I refused to believe I could lose her, too. As long as there was breath in my body, I'd do whatever was needed to secure her fate—one that belonged with me.

"Well, we're here to help with anything you

need—whether it is funeral arrangements or someone to sit with Cami so you can get some rest. Just tell us what you need us to do."

"Thanks, but I won't leave her. I need to be here when she wakes up." My tone brokered no argument and both she and my dad nodded.

"That's wise, I think," Dad said. "She's going to need you when that happens."

"Maybe one of us can sit here with you while you sleep, then. If she wakes up, we can tell you. I worry about your health too, Dylan. No offense, but you look almost as bad as she does."

"I'll be okay. Just some emotional stress catching up with me." I attempted a half smile, trying to lighten my words. "Do you have a place to stay?"

"Yes, there's a nice hotel just down the road from here. We booked a room there so we can come back and forth, if needed. I also brought some of your clothes from our house, in case you wanted to get showered and cleaned up. I brought some of Cami's, too."

"They let me use a shower here after I was released from the ER and gave me these scrubs to wear. I'd torn my shirt into bandages in an effort to stop the . . . ." Cami's limp body spread out before me in the pouring rain flashed through my mind. I flinched.

"Son. Don't worry about the details," Dad said. "Take the time you need. When you're ready, we'll be here. We also heard that Cami's parents are driving in from Copper City. Is that true?"

"Yeah." I glanced at the clock. "I don't expect them to arrive for a couple more hours."

"They're going to be tired after driving all night. Your dad and I would like to book a room at the hotel for them, too. Do you think they'd mind?"

I shook my head. "I don't think they'll mind at all. That's very considerate of you. Thank you for thinking of them." My mind had been complete mush for the last few hours. I could hardly form a coherent thought.

"I'm going to go back out," Dad said, coming to hug me, again. "Your sister is waiting to come in. They'll only let a couple of us in at a time. I love you, son."

"Love you too, Dad. Oh, and Chris went to get our rental. So he has the keys. You might need a vehicle while you are here and you might as well drive it."

"All right. I'll ask him about it."

Sheridan appeared a few moments later, throwing her arms around me, weeping openly, and not even trying to hide her emotions. She didn't speak a word; she couldn't because she was crying too hard, but I understood everything she wanted to say.

"I love you. Thanks for coming," I choked out, allowing my tears to fall, again.

***

It was after noon before the doctor came in with nurses and someone from Respiratory to take Cami off the vent. I stood to the side, watching tensely as they prepared to remove it. I understood why they were doing it while she was still out, so she wouldn't fight it; but they'd also decreased her sedation levels, which meant she could wake up during the process. I was aware that if she didn't show the ability to sustain breath on her own, they'd put her back on. Cami's mom and dad stood beside me in the corner, trying to stay out of the way. They'd arrived in the early hours of the morning just before dawn and they both looked as tired as I felt.

We watched as they prepared her, raising the level of her head so she was sitting up more in bed. "Okay, let's test her," the doctor finally said, and we all waited.

My heart rate increased as each second ticked away. It felt like an hour. Sucking in a breath of my own, I hadn't realized I'd been holding it. My eyes didn't leave her, watching for any sign. Nothing happened. The doctor shook his head in defeat.

I couldn't take it anymore. "Come on, Goody! Breathe!" I yelled at her, making everyone jump, but I didn't care.

All of a sudden her chest expanded as she took a breath. My heart soared. That breath was followed by another, and then another. Glancing up at the monitor, I watched the numbers as, they continued to climb to the proper levels and Cami's mom wrapped her arms around me, all of us with tears in our eyes.

"Looks good," the doctor said, smiling. "I guess she listens to you." He glanced over at me. "We'll remove the tube from her throat and keep monitoring her progress. I'm going to order sedation to stop, as well, but I'm going to take it slow and reduce it over the next several hours. I want to ease her back into things. She had a rough night and day, so I want it to be as gentle of a transition as possible. We'll see if we can get her to wake up and then we'll reevaluate cognitive skills and things like that."

"Will she be comfortable?" I asked, concerned she'd be in pain now.

"We'll make sure she's resting easy. I've ordered regular doses of pain meds. Once she wakes up, if she does okay for a couple hours, we'll probably move her out of ICU to the regular Med/Surg floor."

I was elated with this news, knowing it meant he was hopeful of her to making a full recovery. The vise that'd been gripping my heart so tightly loosened a little and suddenly it felt easier to breathe, as if I'd just been relieved of a gigantic weight that had been sitting on me.

"Thank you for all your help. You have no idea how much it means to us," Cecily, spoke.

"Yes, thank you," I echoed.

"Happy to help," he replied. "I'll be in and out to check her progress." He shook hands with each of us before leaving the room. There were still people sitting by the bed, working on removing the tube from her throat and charting her progress.

"Since it's going to be a while, why don't the two of you go catch some sleep at the hotel," I suggested, addressing my in-laws. "I promise to call as soon as anything happens. That way you can feel refreshed when she sees you. She's going to need her parents in a bad way."

"I hate leaving her," Cecily replied. "But I think you may be right. We'd help her better if we were properly rested."

"It's definitely been a draining experience," Brandt said, turning his gaze from his daughter to me. "However, I think you should take some of your own advice and get some rest, too. She's going to want you more than anybody."

"I'll try," I replied, knowing I'd do no such thing. I intended to be awake when she woke up. And after she realized the truth, I could only hope her dad was right—that she'd still want me once she realized how badly I'd failed her.

CHAPTER TWENTY-ONE
Cami-

Blinking slowly, I tried to shake the fuzziness from my mind.

"Cami?" Dylan's voice broke through the haze and I felt his hand slip into mine, comforting me immediately. "Cami? Can you hear me?"

"Dylan . . . ." I attempted to smile, but suddenly the sensations inside my body grabbed me—I was in pain . . . bad pain. "Dylan, I hurt," I whispered, feeling confused. My throat was very dry and sore. I tried to swallow as I looked up at him.

"It's okay. You're going to hurt for a while. You've been through a lot." I could clearly see both pain and worry etched in his eyes. "What happened?" Searching my mind, I kept trying to remember, but the last thing I could retrieve was standing in front of the window, watching the rain.

"You don't remember?" his voice was tight. I

watched him swallow hard, his Adam's apple bobbing with the action.

"I remember it was raining." It was then I noticed the beeping of the machines around me and I glanced up, seeing IV poles hanging at the head of my bed and a monitor. Suddenly, I was scared. "Dylan, what happened?"

"Shhh," he coaxed, reaching to lovingly stroke his hand over my head. "Everything is going to work out." He sighed, and I felt my panic levels rising. "We had a little . . . altercation."

"Tell me what happened," I demanded, too tired to try to decipher his vague comments.

"You were standing at the window and someone shot you."

"They found us?" My mind was reeling.

"Yes, but that's not all," he continued, gripping my hand tighter. "The bullet," he paused staring at me sympathetically as he stroked my head. "Honey, the bullet hit you in the stomach."

Unable to take my eyes off him, I tried to absorb the meaning behind his words. Shakily, I lifted my hand, drifting across the blanket to the pain in my stomach, only to discover my rounded belly was missing, replaced with soft squishy flesh. I started shaking, fear gripping me in it's clutches as tears sprang into my eyes. "The baby," I whispered. "Where's my baby?" My hoarse voice grew louder as I frantically clutched at the covers.

Tears rapidly fell from Dylan's eyes. "Oh Cami, honey. I'm so sorry. They couldn't save him."

A loud groan of terror escaped me and I grabbed his shirt, weeping as the pain in my stomach grew even stronger. "Tell me you're lying," I shouted at him and he clenched his mouth so tight his jaw ticked, but he didn't take the words back. "Dylan! Ahhhh! No! Tell me you're lying!" Giant sobs enveloped me, wracking my body, as my wails filled the air bringing a flurry of people rushing to my bedside. I clutched at my chest, feeling like my heart was being ripped out of my body and I gasped for air. "You're lying! You're lying!" I shouted again, slamming my fists into his chest as he tried to hold onto me. "No! No! This is just a bad dream. I need to wake up. Help me wake up!"

"Goody." Dylan grabbed me holding me against him tightly, and I could feel his body shaking violently. Suddenly, I felt relaxed and the room tipped in front of me, causing my vision to swirl dizzily.

"Cami, we've given you a sedative," another voice, one I didn't recognize, slurred. My head lolled to the side and I saw a nurse holding my IV tube.

Dylan didn't release me, his face buried in my hair. "Cami, I'm so sorry," he said, his voice thick with emotion. "Please. I love you so much. Please don't hate me. I'm so sorry."

I opened my mouth to ask him what he meant, but I couldn't get the words out before the darkness consumed me.

DYLAN LOVE

Chapter Twenty-Two
Dylan-

Rushing into the bathroom, I closed and locked the door behind me before hurrying to the sink. I turned on the faucet and bent over, splashing the cold water vigorously against my skin.

There was a knock on the door. "Dylan? Are you all right?" Chris's muffled voice came through.

"I'm going to need a minute, please," I replied, my voice strained under the pressure I was feeling.

"Okay. I'm here if you need me."

Leaning on my arms against the sink, I stared at the mirror, barely recognizing the stranger staring back at me, the sunken eyes with dark circles, in bad need of a shave. But none of that mattered. Cami had taken the news much worse than I thought she would. Her terrified screams were still echoing loudly in my ears, where they would continue to haunt me for the rest of my life.

Rage boiled through me and I slammed my fist against the sink. I couldn't take this anymore. I couldn't stand the suffering and the ache in my rib cage that wouldn't cease. Desperately, I wished for normal—wished we were safely in our house in Tucson, planning for the arrival of our infant son. When had things gone so horribly off track?

Determined, I stormed to the bathroom door, throwing it open and finding Chris waiting there. "Give me the list," I demanded and his eyes widened.

"Dylan," he said his gaze flicking around the hallway in concern.

"Don't Dylan me. Give me the damn list!"

He shook his head. "I can't do that. You're too close to the situation."

"I don't give a shit!" I yelled drawing the attention of some nurses. "Give me the fucking list!"

Raising his hands in submission, he backed away. "Let's go outside and talk about this. This isn't place."

"So help me, Chris, if you don't give me that damn list you're gonna live to regret it." I stepped closer, threatening.

"I'm afraid of what will happen if I do give it to you." At least he was honest.

"I'll tell you what will happen. I'm going to go down that list and find out who the asshole is that did this to my wife and baby. And then I'm going to make him pay! I'm tired of waiting around for the department to just drag their feet on this. Whoever this is—they've gone too far. They might've started it, but I'm going to finish it!" I snarled, poking him in the chest.

"We have no proof that this is someone from your past," Chris argued. "The list could be a dead lead for all we know."

I snorted shaking my head. "You look me in the face and tell me you don't think this is revenge, pure and simple. They are targeting *my wife* to get to me!"

"You're right. They are targeting your wife. But how do you know it's not someone from Cami's past? What if she is the target? How would that relate to any of your past cases? You'd be going off and after the wrong people."

His words hit me hard and I stepped backward, staring at him as my mind raced a million miles a minute. "You're right, Chris," I agreed, my whole tone changing. "Quick! Let me see the list." He stared at me as if I'd lost my marbles with the abrupt shift in attitude, but I didn't have time for any of that. Something he'd said had triggered a hunch I couldn't let go of. "Chris," I pleaded, gesturing for him to hurry along as I strode toward Cami's room. Pausing, I turned to find he wasn't following me. "I need to see the list." I tried to say it as calmly as possible, hoping he'd trust me.

Hanging his head dejectedly, he stared at the floor for a second and I knew I'd won. Walking past me, he went to the briefcase on the floor beside his chair. Picking it up, he handed it to me, but he didn't release it. "This is everything. Every stitch of evidence we've gathered during all of this, including the list. See if you can see anything we can't."

Taking the briefcase, I moved to the chair in Cami's room and sat, opening it on my lap. Hurrying through the files, I found one marked "possible suspects." Reaching inside, I yanked the list of names out of the folder as Chris watched me from the door. Quickly flipping the pages to get to the letter I wanted, I scanned my finger down the page, pausing when the name I'd been looking for jumped out at me. Closing the briefcase, I carried it over and handed it back to Chris, who held it flat in his arms. I slapped the paper down in front of him and pointed.

"There's your shooter," I growled, never feeling more certain about anything—my gut confirming my feelings. I never ignored my gut.

He stared at the name before glancing at me. "I hate to admit it, but you might be onto something. This could really make sense."

I chuckled wryly. "Don't play it down, Chris. I can see the puzzle pieces falling into place in your head, just like it is in mine."

Sighing, Chris pulled out his phone and hit a number on speed dial. "Give me the Chief," he said to whoever answered.

"Hello?" I heard Chief Robson's voice come loudly through the speaker.

"Hey, Chief. It's Chris."

"Napier! Anymore news on Cami?" he asked, sounding concerned.

"She still having a rough time," he replied, and I felt like that was the understatement of the year. "Listen, I think I've got a possible suspect on this case. I need you to put out an APB on a Gabrielle Martinez. You'll need to send it to the police in Copper City and see if they can find anything on her, too."

"Gabrielle Martinez. Isn't that the girl who was messed up in Dylan's drug case?"

"One and the same," Chris replied, his eyes drifting to mine. "You might want to put approach with caution on there, too. If it is her, she's definitely armed and dangerous."

"I'm on it. I'll let you know if I turn up anything. Tell Dylan and Cami we are all praying for them."

"Thanks. I'll let him know." Chris hung up. "Happy now?" he asked.

"No. Not until Gabby's caught and dealt with."

"Let the police deal with it," he warned, his expression stern.

"The only reason I'm still here is because she needs me." I pointed at Cami. "And I promise you, if the department can't do the job right, then I'll be doing it for them. I have to know Cami's going to be safe, and I'm certainly not going to let some little spoiled bitch with an axe to grind come after her. That girl was messed up, Chris. Probably just as bad as Clay was. Who else would sit on a murder and an attempt on someone else's life like that? And she was jealous of Cami, too."

"She was jealous because Cami had you."

"Cami still does. And what does Gabby have after all this?" I stared at him. "Nothing but prison time. I'm telling you, I wouldn't put any of this past her. She was just as sadistic as Clay. Even when I'd try and talk to her and tell her to back off, she just continued on like she hadn't even heard me. I tell you, it was bizarre. Ask Russ if he thinks she could do it. He'll back me up on this, I promise you. He knows her. As in knows her, knows her. Ask him."

"You don't have to convince me. I think you may have something, but we also need some hard evidence to back this up. We can't just arrest her because of her past. She's served her jail time for that already."

Sighing, I walked back toward the chair, suddenly feeling so tired. I slumped into the recliner. "I'd start by finding out if she's been spending any time in Tucson lately. That would be something—if you could tie her to that location at the same time all of this was happening. If you can get that, ask a judge if you can subpoena her financial records. It would be easy to trace purchases off of that, say things like fire accelerants."

Chris nodded. "You stay here and take care of your wife. I'm on this." I watched as he walked through the door before turning around again and staring at me. "We miss having you on the force, Dylan."

I gave him a sad half smile. "I miss it, too; but I left it precisely to avoid this kind of thing." I gestured to Cami. "I won't risk her, Chris. She's lost too much now, as it is."

"I get it," he replied. "I'm going to make some phone calls and see what kind of things turn up. The other officer is still at the entrance. Are you okay here?"

Reaching for my gun on the table, I rested my hand on it. "I've got it covered."

***

My guard went up instantly when I noticed Cami starting to stir. Panic rose inside me and I attempted to stamp it down. She needed me to be strong for her right now. I needed do what I could and accept any blame she placed on me. All I cared about was helping her get to a place of peace where she could deal with this as rationally as possible. I wasn't deluding myself, though. We both had a long road of recovery ahead of us.

Scooting my chair next to the bed, I grasped her hand in mine, rubbing it softly, hoping it would soothe her. Her head turned toward me, but she didn't open her eyes, though her fingers tightened around mine. I didn't rush her, wanting to let her take her time. After a few moments, her other hand moved, coming to rest against her stomach. Tears began leaking from her closed eyes. Her chest caught and heaved as a sob escaped.

"Dylan." It was the only word she said, and it was all that was needed. Moving from my chair, I sat on the edge of her bed and carefully gathered her in my arms. She leaned against my chest and wept freely, tearing my heart out more each second.

A nurse came and nodded at me before closing the curtain in front of the glass wall, giving us some privacy. Continuing to hold Cami to me, I kissed the top of her head, as I mourned with her for our child.

When her tears finally subsided, she didn't try to move away from me. We stayed that way for a long time, just clinging to each other.

She sighed heavily. "I'm sorry," she said and her words struck me like stones.

"What in the world do you have to be sorry about?" I asked incredulously.

"For flipping out earlier. I just can't . . . I don't know how . . . ."

"Goody, rest. That's what is important now."

"I can't rest. I need to know what happened."

I swallowed hard; knowing the next few minutes might make or break her feelings toward me. "After you were shot, I had to get you out of the house. I shot out the lights so whoever was out there," I omitted Gabby's name for the time being, "couldn't see us moving around. I couldn't get you to wake up so I carried you out into the rain. I tried stopping the blood by tearing my shirt in bandages, but I knew I had to get you to safety. Thankfully, you still had your phone in your pocket and I was able to get in touch with Chris. He dispatched police and medical teams, as well as a helicopter, to our location; but it just took too much time. I moved as quickly as could, but too much time had passed." A tremble passed through me and I took a deep breath before I continued. "The surgeon told me they had to revive you in the operating room. He also said the bullet had torn through the placenta and severed part of the baby's cord. He was already gone." She shuddered in my arms, fresh tears falling. "I'm so sorry, Cami. I understand if you're mad at me. I'm mad at me, too. But I want you to know I love you."

Raising her head, she stared at me with swollen eyes. "Why would I be mad at you?"

Stroking the side of her face, I sighed heavily. "I promised I would protect you both and I failed miserably."

"Dylan," she replied reaching up and touching my face. "I wouldn't be here if it weren't for you. You did the best you could under the circumstances." She dropped her hand weakly, but didn't break eye contact with me. "This has all been too horrible for words, but you need know . . . I don't want to be anywhere that you aren't. I love you." She moaned, her hand going back to her stomach. "Can I have something for pain?"

As gently as I could, I removed myself from her and laid her gently back against her pillow. Bending, I kissed her forehead. "I'll go get the nurse."

CAMI LOVE

CHAPTER TWENTY-THREE
Cami-

If I were being truthful, I was feeling more than a little overwhelmed. I simply wanted to sleep, but I couldn't bear to tell my family to leave, knowing how worried they'd been about me. Dylan hadn't taken his eyes off me since I'd been moved from the ICU to the regular Med/Surg floor, after my status was upgraded, except for briefly going into the bathroom to change out of the scrubs he'd been wearing and into a pair of jeans and a t-shirt his mom brought for him. It was as if he were afraid to blink because I might disappear. He looked exhausted, unshaved, messy haired, and refused to rest. I could tell he had some deep aching going on inside and I wished we had some time to just be alone, together.

Shifting uncomfortably in the bed, I tried to find a place that didn't hurt. I was covered in cuts and bruises from the window shattering, apparently. But none of those hurt as badly as my stomach area, which was definitely the worst.

"Is it time for more pain meds?" Dylan asked, not missing my discomfort. I nodded. I saw him give a subtle nod to Sheridan and she stood suddenly.

"Why don't we all go get some dinner and let Cami get some rest?" she asked. "She looks so worn out."

"Thank you," I said, not denying it. "It's definitely been a rough time. I could use some sleep." One by one, they came and gave me a hug and kiss.

"Sweetheart, you call me if you need anything. I don't care what time it is, okay?" my mom said, concern evident in her eyes.

"I will, Mom. Thanks." I sighed when the last of them were out the door, feeling relieved.

"I'll call the nurse and have her bring you some pain meds," Dylan said, reaching for the call button.

"No!" I said a little harshly, stalling him.

"What's wrong?" he asked, instantly on edge.

"You are."

"What do you mean?"

"No offense, Dylan, but you look like death. I have no idea how you've stayed up so long."

He sighed. "I needed to make sure you were all right. You were my first priority."

"Look at me," I said. "I'm fine. Maybe a bit emotionally worse for wear, but I'm not going to die if you close your eyes to go to sleep. You're driving yourself into the ground worrying about me. I don't like it." I shifted again, the pain irritating me.

"I'm calling for your medication," he said, reaching for the button again and I placed my hand over it, preventing him.

"I'm not going to take any more pain meds unless you agree to go to sleep. They make me sleepy, so you aren't going to miss anything. You got shot, too. You need some rest so you can recover."

He snorted. "This is nothing. A graze. I'll be fine."

"I mean it." I wasn't going to take no for an answer. "The nurse brought you some bedding and that couch turns into a bed. I want to see you make your bed before I'll take anything. And you need to hurry because it hurts."

He sighed heavily, but I knew he wouldn't refuse me. I could be just as stubborn as he was. Dutifully removing the bedding from the small closet, he began making his bed.

I watched him move, thinking how grateful I was to have him in my life. We'd been through so much together—some of those experiences being really bad. But the good times far outweighed the bad. I had confidence that someday, after our hearts had a chance to heal, we'd find our way back to a good place.

Earlier, we'd briefly discussed funeral arrangements for the baby. I was glad he'd chosen that option. I needed my own closure, still. He told me he let me hold the baby, even though I was unconscious, and I cried a whole bunch more. Truthfully, I was scrubbed raw on the inside. I felt like I was barely holding it together.

"There. Is that good enough to satisfy you or do want me be able to bounce a quarter off it like they do in the military?" A smile quirked at the edge of his lips and that did more to warm my heart than anything. I loved his smile and I'd missed seeing it. He'd been agitated and restless, sorrow heavy on his features.

"Do it again," I said.

"Seriously?" He looked completely perplexed as he glanced between the bed and me.

"Not the bed, silly." I laughed and immediately groaned, placing my hands on my abdomen.

Instantly, he was at my side, carefully touching me. "What is it? What can I do?"

Placing one of my hands over his, I stared at him. "You can stop being so worried," I replied. "I just wanted you to smile, again. You've looked so sad; it was nice to see a bit of humor back on your face."

"I shouldn't be making jokes around you at a time like this."

"Yes! You should! There's a reason they say laughter is the best medicine. It might hurt a little right now, but I need some cheerful things, too. I can't stand seeing you so . . . broken." I winced as a sharp pain stabbed through my stomach.

Reaching across me, he pushed the call button for the nurse. "Can I help you?" a voice came over the speaker.

"Can my wife get some more pain meds,

please?" he asked.

"Certainly. I'll send your nurse right in."

He stared at me, resting his hand on the rail of my hospital bed. "I thought I'd lost everything, Cami. I still worry that the more you recover and the clearer your mind becomes, that'll you'll blame me . . . like I blame myself. I should've kept this from happening."

The nurse entered the room, carrying a syringe and we stopped talking as she administered the medication in my IV. We waited for her to check a few other things and chart it, before she left. I felt myself growing drowsier.

"Dylan." I needed to get this out before I drifted off again. "Would you blame me if the situation were reversed? What if I was supposed to be protecting you and I failed? Would you hate me?" I blinked several times trying to stay focused.

"Never," he whispered; his voice so low I could hardly hear him.

"Exactly. So quit expecting me to do it to you." I continued before he could say anything. "Now I'm sleepy, so go get in your bed. I can't close my eyes until I know you're in bed."

My eyes were heavy as he kissed me on the forehead. "I love you, Goody. Thank you."

I watched as he climbed into bed. "Close your eyes," I ordered and he did. Then I closed mine.

***

Dylan's exhaustion was pretty evident to anyone who came into the room. He slept like the dead. I kept looking at his neck to see if I could see a pulse there, he'd been asleep for so long. I wasn't even sure if he'd moved since I'd awakened. Nurses, techs, and lab people tiptoed in out of the room, getting vitals and taking blood. I appreciated everyone trying not to disturb him. When breakfast came, they brought a tray for him, too. I had them place it on a small table stand while I tried to decide what to do. My breakfast contained mostly liquid items, since my diet was still restricted after surgery, but his smelled wonderful. I briefly wondered if he'd even had anything to eat since this whole fiasco had taken place.

"Dylan," I called to him. He didn't move. "Dylan, can you hear me?" Still nothing. Now I really was getting worried. This was the guy who could jump out of bed in two seconds to run to an emergency call. "Dylan," I said even louder as I picked up my spoon and banged it loudly against the tray.

He jumped, sitting up almost instantly and reaching for his gun in the windowsill behind him.

Smiling, I raised my hands in the air. "Don't shoot! I'm just trying to feed you."

Groggily, he dropped his hand and shook his head, as if he were trying to clear the fatigue.

"You've been really out of it," I said with a slight chuckle, clutching my belly. It was incredible how many muscles the human body used, ones I'd never noticed until they were suddenly sore.

Dylan slumped back against his pillow.

"Sorry. I didn't mean to sleep so long."

"Don't be sorry. You needed it. Here, come get your food. It smells wonderful. I think they brought you French toast."

"You look better this morning," he said, staring at me for a few moments. "Your color is better than it was yesterday."

"Yours, too. It's amazing what a little rest can do, isn't it?"

"Are you trying to trap me into telling you how right you are? Because I'm way too tired to figure out anything like that, right now." He smiled. That's what I'd been waiting for. I smiled back, even though my heart and body felt like they'd both been run over by a bulldozer. I knew there was a lot of grieving and healing ahead of us, but as long as I could see him smile once in a while, it made everything better.

Of course, maybe I was just being a little sappy over the whole smiling thing. People did that kind of stuff after a near death experience, or so I'd heard. After this, I would be inclined to agree. It made you realize what the most important things your life really are. And I knew Dylan was on the top of my "Most Important List." He was my love, my anchor, and my hope.

"You okay?" he asked, continuing to stare at me.

I nodded. "Just thinking about how lucky I am to have you in my life. I don't know if I'd be able to get through all this without you." I teared up. Yep, my emotions were all over the place, running out of control.

"Aw, don't cry, honey. It hurts my heart." He got up and dropped the side rail to the bed and sat down next to me, wrapping his arms around me.

"I'm sorry. I'm happy, but I'm so sad at the same time. I don't know how to handle it. One second I'm in the depths of despair and the next I feel so grateful for everything. How is that okay? I can't feel grateful after I just lost my baby. That would make me a bad mom."

"No, it doesn't. It means your human and you've been through a terrifying ordeal. It's going to take time to process everything, Goody. And you can take as much time as you need. We both can."

"I just feel stupid, or confused, or something."

"That's okay." He kissed my head. "The hospital has grief counseling services. I met one of the counselors when you were brought into the ICU. His name was Kevin and he was really nice. I think maybe we would benefit from talking to him or someone from that department. Would you be okay with that? I don't want either of us ending up with post traumatic stress disorder. We need to be smart about this."

I nodded. "If you think it will help, I'm good with that. I mean, I'm not like going crazy or anything, I don't think; but I just feel like it's all stuff I can't control. Know what I mean?"

He gave a small grunt. "I know exactly what you mean. I feel the same way, myself. I hate waiting and not being able to take care of things."

"Have the police found any leads?" I asked. "You haven't really talked about all that."

"That's because I don't want you worrying about any of that stuff. You have plenty of other things demanding your attention right now."

"Don't shield me, Dylan." I knew what he was doing, I'd seen it often enough. "I'm involved in this and I need to know what's happening."

"Not a whole lot. The police have someone they want to bring in for questioning, but they haven't, yet."

"They have a suspect? That's great news, isn't it? Why don't you seem happy about it?"

"Because whoever it is wanted to hurt you and that upsets me."

"Do you know who it is?"

He sighed, clearly not wanting to divulge anything.

"Dylan," I said again in frustration.

"Yes. I know who it is. I'm the one who suggested they be checked out."

"Who?" I asked nervously, feeling my insides clench painfully.

"They're trying to find Gabby Martinez."

Gabby. Feeling the color drain from my face, I instantly reverted back to the memories of Clay and the horror he'd put me through and Gabby's involvement.

"I thought she was in jail."

"She served her time and was released. Oddly enough, not too long before all this stuff started happening."

"And she definitely could be carrying a grudge against both of us." I sighed. "This isn't good, but it makes sense."

Dylan didn't reply, instead he grabbed a cup of juice from my breakfast tray, and took the lid off. "Drink your breakfast," he ordered. I took it from him and he started removing lids from some of the other containers. I knew he was trying to redirect my attention, but I didn't mind. I was sick of this whole thing. I simply wanted someone to tell me it was over. "Looks like you've got some Jell-o and broth, too."

"I don't know if I can handle all of that, but you need to eat your breakfast too, Dylan."

"Do I? Maybe I just need to pull the same stunt on you that you pulled on me. I'm not going to eat until I see you making a valiant effort to get yours down."

I was at a loss for an argument and he laughed.

"Sucks to be on the receiving end of those ultimatums, doesn't it?" he asked.

"Yeah, kinda." But I wasn't upset at all.

DYLAN LOVE

CHAPTER TWENTY-FOUR
Dylan-

"I need to talk to you," Chris said in his all business voice. He had that "look" and I knew he was onto something.

I got up from Cami's hospital bed. "Be right back," I told her.

"You could just talk in front of me, you know?" she called after me. "I'm not twelve."

I flashed a smile at her. "In a minute." Following Chris out into the hall we walked a few feet away, but still had Cami's room in plain sight. "What's going on?" I asked, folding my arms.

"We got a hit from the hospital switchboard operator. Someone has called in several times to ask about Cami. For security reasons, Cami's not officially listed as a patient here unless whoever is calling identifies themselves with a password. The person calling obviously isn't aware of this. Also, the caller was a woman. The switchboard has denied that there is a Cami

Wilcock registered here each time, but the woman keeps calling."

"Do we have a phone number?" I asked, seeing where he was going with this.

He nodded. "We do. We traced the number to a pay phone near one of the older hotels downtown. The front desk there has verified a woman matching Gabby's description was staying there, but they don't have anyone registered under that name. Show Low PD is forming a team right now to go check things out. They have her previous mug shot, so they can get verification if it's her. There's a female officer going in under the pretense of checking in, so they won't alert anyone who's watching."

"I want in," I said without hesitation.

"No. Absolutely not," he replied firmly. "Don't even argue with me about it. I'm here telling you this as a courtesy because I know you've been going crazy about everything. There's no way any cop in his right mind is going to let you on that scene."

I sighed heavily. "Are you going?"

He nodded. "I'm just waiting for them to call and tell me they're ready. Don't get your hopes up, though. It could be a false alarm."

"Pretty coincidental, if you ask me. Calls from a random phone near hotels that none of the family is staying at? Outside of the emergency services people, no one else even knows we're here. It'd have to be someone who was involved in this."

"I agree. There's definitely someone who's not with us that's doing the inquiring. I'm simply saying the girl at the hotel may not be Gabby. And if it's not her, we don't have any witnesses to who has been using the pay phone."

I ran a hand through my hair, frustrated. "The waiting is driving me crazy, Chris."

"Then I suggest you do something to keep yourself busy. Go to the store next door and buy some clothes, get a razor and get cleaned up. I'm sure that would help Cami feel better, too. She'd like to see you looking like your old self and not some homeless guy who just came in off the street."

"If you're leaving, I can't go, too."

"Seriously, Dylan. It's across the street. They aren't even letting staff into this department without a password. Plus, I'm expecting someone any minute who would be happy to come sit with her."

"Who?" I asked, wondering why he was being so secretive.

"So, are you guys like actually watching her door?" Russ's voice interrupted. "Or should I just walk in?"

I turned, unable to help the smile that crossed my face. "Russ!"

"Hey, bro!" He grabbed me in a bear hug, patting me hard on the back. "Man, Dylan. I'm so sorry to hear about all of this." I felt myself getting choked up, again. It was so good to see him. It'd been hard for both Cami and I to leave him behind. He was just as much part of our family as any of our blood relatives. My dad even claimed him like a son, mostly because Russ's last name was Weston, which, of course, was Dad's first name. Dad had said, "Never met a Weston I didn't like!" when they were introduced and they'd been fast friends ever since. I was so happy to have him here, and if anyone could cheer us up, it would be him.

Releasing him, I glanced at Chris. "Thanks for doing this. It means a lot."

He patted me on the shoulder. "Anytime, kid. I'm taking off now. I'll let you know something when I know something."

"Be careful," I said and he gave me the thumbs up sign as he walked away.

Turning back to Russ, I wrapped my arm around his shoulders. "Come on. Let's go see Cami." Leading him into the room, Cami's eyes were closed and I realized she'd fallen asleep in the middle of eating.

"Let her sleep," Russ whispered. "I'll sit here with her and you can run to the store and get whatever you needed. That way she won't miss you."

I shook my head. "I hate leaving her. I can wait until later."

"Dude, no offense, but I thought you were like one of the Duck Dynasty guys when I walked up. Do us all a favor and go get a razor. I'll stay with her. Get showered or whatever you need. She's sleeping and I want to help. That's what I came here for. You know you can trust me to protect her. Besides, you're gonna have to leave her sometime. You can't stay with her every second."

Sighing heavily, I felt my heart twist, but I nodded. "I just feel really over protective of her."

"That's understandable, and no one is telling you can't do that. All we're saying is it's okay to ask for help. You need to take care of yourself, too, or you can't take care of her. Besides, you shouldn't be scaring her like this every time she wakes up." He waved his hand gesturing to my appearance. "She'll be okay long enough for you to shower."

I knew Cami was in good hands with Russ, but I was still hesitant. "Did Chris fill you in on the case?"

"Yep, about Gabby and everything. I know who to watch out for and I've got your back."

"All right," I replied, giving in. It would feel nice to get cleaned up. Going over to the closet, I retrieved my wallet and badge Chris had given me, tucking the wallet in my pocket, and then clipping the badge to my waist.

"Don't forget your gun," Russ said, grabbing it from the window and handing it to me. I took it and tucked it into the back of my pants, pulling my shirt over to conceal both it and my badge. No need to make anyone unnecessarily nervous about my being armed.

"Okay. I won't be long," I said, glancing at Cami.

"Shoo!" Russ said in a loud whisper, flicking his hands at me as he herded me to the door. "Don't come back until you find the 'real' Dylan!" I shook my head and chuckled as I headed down the hall.

Leaving the hospital, I jogged across the small two-lane street and into the Wal-Mart store parking lot on the other side. It felt good to run after being cooped up for so long, so I continued to jog across the large parking lot, knowing the faster I was finished, the faster I'd be back with Cami. Not that I didn't trust Russ, I simply wanted to be with her. I needed to be with her.

I entered the store, grabbing a cart before glancing around at the signs for the different departments, choosing to go to the personal hygiene section first. After quickly picking out the items I needed there, I made my way to the men's clothing section to get another couple of shirts and pants to wear, since the clothes I was wearing were the only ones my parents brought. The rest of Cami's and my stuff was still part of the crime scene in Nutrioso, which was a good hour and fifteen minutes away; so there was no way for me to go get anything from there anyway, without taking an incredible amount of time.

Once I was finished, I headed toward the registers, suddenly I thought of a couple more things. I wanted to do something nice for Cami. Going to the book section, I was intent on finding a romance book she might like to read. However, once I got there, I was overwhelmed with the selection. I had no idea what she might want. One called *Big Apple Dreams*, by Kamery Solomon finally caught my eye and I picked it up, quickly reading the blurb. As soon as I saw it was about a girl whose dream was to perform on Broadway, I tossed in the cart. That was totally something Cami would like.

I continued out of the aisle, ready to head back up front where I'd seen some roses when someone caught my eye, making my hackles rise. I knew the girl at the end of the main aisle. Staring hard at her, I was sure it was Gabby. Well, almost sure of it. Her long dark hair was just like it had been in high school and she didn't look like she'd aged a day, still very pretty and put together. She was intently looking at something on the shelf and not paying any attention to the people around her, so I could only see her from the side. Turning my cart in her direction, I did my best to remain calm as I walked toward her. Absently, I felt my pocket for my phone so I could call Chris before realizing I didn't have it.

Damn.

The girl moved, turning away from me and walked into the hardware section. I needed to see her straight on to be sure. I hadn't seen her in a couple years, and I didn't want to scare some innocent bystander out of her mind, so I pushed my cart just past the aisle she went down, not wanting to draw attention to myself. I paused at the end where a bunch of red toolboxes sat, pretending to be interested in those while I watched her covertly. Lifting her head, she turned to glance at the other side of the aisle and I knew for certain. It was her. I wasn't wasting another second.

Very slowly, so I wouldn't startle her, I casually walked into the aisle. "Looking for a hammer to bludgeon someone with?" I asked casually; and she looked up, giving a startled cry. She tried to run past me and I grabbed her arm, swinging her into the rack of hammers, causing merchandise to pop off and fall everywhere. Whipping my gun out, I trained it on her in the beat of an eyelash. "I should kill you right now," I said, as she looked at me fearfully.

"You already have." She spat back, a defiant look crossing her features as she lifted her chin. "Might as well go ahead and pull the trigger and finish the rest of the job."

Yep, she was still bat shit crazy. "What the hell are you talking about, Gabby?"

"You and Cami. It was because of you two that I ended up in prison."

"You ended up in prison because you were dealing drugs and covered up a homicide. That was all you. Not me, not Cami, and definitely not our baby." Rage poured through me and my finger itched to pull the trigger. One shot, placed just right, and this would all be over. Cami could have her life back. She'd be safe, again. All I had to do was pull the trigger.

"Do you know what happened to me in prison?" she asked, her chin quivering. "Those women, they were mean. They assaulted me in terrible ways you can't even imagine. I begged them not to, but they liked the begging. Then, when they were done punishing me, the guards started coming onto me too, dragging me into empty cells so they could do vile things to me. Every time that happened, I promised myself I'd make the two of you pay for it."

"Are you sure it wasn't the other way

around?" I asked sarcastically. "Maybe you were coming onto them. If I remember correctly, there were at least a dozen times you propositioned me, not to mention every other guy in the school. I'd say prison sounds like it was right up your alley."

"You bastard!" she yelled, in a snarling scream. Ripping her hand out from behind her she threw a hammer at me, before grabbing another and launching herself at me like some possessed demonic creature.

Ducking to dodge the missile, I jerked to the side to avoid her attack, her weapon grazing my arm. I didn't stop to look, turning quickly as she jumped to attack me, again. Zeroing in on her chest, I pulled the trigger. One, two, three, four, I emptied the rest of my clip into her as she jerked backwards, slamming into the shelves, her body knocking more things down as she fell into a heap of hardware.

Screaming erupted throughout the store and I could hear people running in all directions, but I didn't move, my gun still trained on Gabby as her blood spread across the floor.

I had no idea how much time passed before I heard people closing in on my location. "Drop your weapon," a loud voice came from behind me.

"I'm a police officer," I replied calmly, bending to set my gun on the floor. Kicking it away from me, I also pulled my badge off and tossed it toward them. Immediately, I was tackled from behind and pinned to the floor by two men. I could feel the stitches in my arm ripping as it was twisted back behind me. Someone else was shouting orders for workers to get people out of the store safely, but all the sounds of chaos around me meant nothing. I stared at the widening pool of blood that was moving across the floor. Whatever happened to me now was up to fate. The only thing I cared about was taken care of. Cami was safe.

CAMI LOVE

CHAPTER TWENTY-FIVE
Cami-

The room was so quiet. I opened my eyes to see if everyone was still gone.

"Ah! There's sleeping beauty."

"Russ!" I exclaimed, forgetting my predicament for a second and leaning forward way too fast. "Ow!" I wrapped my arms around my stomach and slumped back against my pillow.

"Easy there, slugger. You're supposed to be resting." Standing, he moved across the room. "See? This is how it works." He gestured to his legs. "I come to you. You stay in the bed like a Disney Princess. But again, I won't be kissing you. That's Prince Charming's job."

I couldn't help my laughter and the simultaneous tears that leaked from my eyes. "I've missed you so much. When did you get here?"

Sitting on the edge of the bed, he leaned forward and gave me a huge hug. "Late last night. I got a room at the same place your parents are staying. I saw them this morning and they said to tell you they'll be here a little later." He paused and sighed. "Cami, I can't tell you how sorry I am." His voice was soft and he didn't release me and I relished being in the embrace of one of my very best friends.

"It's been so hard, Russ. It seems so unfair for me to be able to keep on living without my baby." Tears continued to fall, dripping onto his shoulder, but he didn't seem to mind.

"I know it's got to be hard, but you had to keep living or Dylan wouldn't have made it through. You know he'd rather be dead than live without you? I mean, I would be a pretty good substitute, but there are certain places that I draw the line."

I burst out laughing again, followed by a painful moan. "This is what I love about you, Russ. You can always make me laugh, even through the most dire of situations." He squeezed me tighter before letting go and settling in the chair beside me.

"I'm just glad Chris called to let me know what was going on. Of course, that might have been because I've been hounding him day and night for information on the two of you. Which, I might add, he refused to tell me. Life has been terribly boring without you guys. Turns out, watching you and Dylan make out is one of my favorite pastimes after all. You don't know what you've got until it's gone."

I giggled again, this time holding the extra pillow they'd given me to my stomach. "I'm sure it hasn't been that bad. Not with your new girlfriend hanging around. I'm hoping you've been getting a few make-out sessions of your own, lately."

"Yeah, about that." He shook his head. "She's not around anymore."

"What?" I exclaimed. "But you two liked each other so much, what happened?"

He shrugged. "Sometimes it's just hard for girls to handle all of this." He waved his hand over himself. "I think my super awesomeness scares them off."

"That must be it." I smiled at his joking around, but I felt sad for him. "What really happened?"

"Our mothers. They wouldn't leave us alone. It got to be a little too exuberant for Daphne and me. I guess it proved we didn't like each other enough to keep putting up with it."

"Well, I'm sorry." I really was. Russ was such a great guy—wonderful personality, good looking. He'd be a catch for any girl.

"Don't be. I'm still looking for my "Cami"." He made quotation signs in the air. "I just haven't found her, yet. I'm starting to think Dylan walked away with the prize in that department."

My emotional state was getting to be too much. Eyes watering again, I felt completely touched by his words. "Thank you, Russ. But I hope you find someone better than me. I'm far from perfect."

He snorted. "You need to get a better mirror then—one that reflects what the rest of us see.

I've watched Dylan for the last two and a half years. There's something inside him that lights up every time he looks at you. I want that, too."

I sighed. "I'm afraid he doesn't light up anymore. All I see there now is worry and concern. He blames himself for everything. I don't know why, either. He did everything humanly possible to save me and the baby." I glanced down at my hands, realizing I'd been subconsciously rubbing my hand over the pillow where my belly used to protrude. "I've never seen him like this, Russ. I'm worried this has broken him. He barely smiles. I see him struggling with his emotions when he thinks I'm not awake or paying attention. He's hurting badly and I don't know what I can do to fix it."

Russ leaned forward, laying one of his hands on the bed offering it to me and I slipped mine inside. He gripped it, rubbing his other hand across the top of mine. "You can't fix it, Cami. He needs to work through his grief and he's the only one that can do it for himself. The same goes for you. You need to grieve in your way and not worry about whether or not it's hurting him. I know how you both are. Each of you will mask your pain in order to make things better for the other. That's not going to work this time. You need to talk things out and be truthful with each other about what's going on inside." I nodded, agreeing with everything he was saying. "And as much as I hate saying this, neither of you are ever going to get over this. It'll become easier to deal with in time, and maybe not consume your every thought, but you're still going to cry every time you think about it. It's just the way it is. You've both been through hell and this experience has changed you."

Sniffing, I reached for a tissue. "I hate change, Russ."

"Nah, that's not true. You just hate bad changes. Everyone does. You have a lot of good changes to love in your life still, and the important thing is you and Dylan have each other. In the end, isn't that what matters most?"

"Yeah, but I'd be okay with the sunny rainbows and fluffy bunnies version of life."

He chuckled. "I'm with you on that. I think everyone in the world feels the same." He released my hand and sat back in his chair. "I don't know why bad things have to happen to people, but I can say this—it certainly makes us learn to appreciate the good days."

"That's true." Russ might be a jokester, but his heart was always in the right place. I knew Dylan trusted him more than anyone, with the exception of Chris, perhaps. He loved Russ.

The sound of wailing sirens filled the air and Russ shook his head. "I swear, no matter where I go I can't seem to escape those things. Dang hospitals and emergencies."

I gave a short laugh. "Yeah, you and Dylan are always out in the thick of things. But you've both done so much service for others. That has to feel good."

He nodded. "It does. As far as jobs go, this has been a rewarding one."

"I'm glad you and Dylan get to work

together, now. It makes me feel better knowing you're out there with him." More sirens filled the air, catching my attention again. Staring Russ in the eyes, fear suddenly surging through me. "Where *is* Dylan, Russ? He's not usually gone this long."

"He ran to the store across the street to get a razor and some other things so he could get cleaned up."

As even more sirens joined the others, I began to panic. "Those sirens aren't coming to the hospital. They're going past us. Go find him, Russ, now!"

Russ shook his head. "I can't. I promised Dylan I wouldn't leave you for any reason. I won't go back on my word."

Still, I could see the worry evident in his eyes. Standing, he paced toward the window before giving a disgusted sigh. "I can't see anything from here."

"Please, go find him!" I begged, hoping I was working myself into hysterics over nothing.

"I can't. But we can call Chris and see if he knows what's happening." Digging his phone out, Russ quickly dialed a number.

"Put it on speaker please." I wanted to know exactly what was going on. No more sugarcoating things.

"Hello?" Chris answered and the wail of a siren could be heard in the background.

"Chris, do you know what's going on around the hospital? We're hearing a bunch of sirens and it's upsetting Cami. Dylan went to the store a little bit ago and he hasn't come back."

"Damn. We have reports of a shooting there. I'm on my way over with another officer now. They're evacuating the building. I was concerned because the location was so close to the hospital."

Russ glanced at me and my chest constricted so hard, it felt like it was going to cave in on me. My knuckles turned white as I clenched my pillow. "Can you please let us know if he's okay as soon as possible? Cami's on the verge of hysterics. I don't know how much more she can take."

"I'll call as soon as I know what happened. Tell her not to worry. They're most likely asking people to stick around so they can interview them and see what they can find out. I'm sure he's fine. You know Dylan—ever the cop. Those instincts die hard."

I knew he was trying to appease me, but I wasn't going to believe it unless Dylan came walking through the door. Hoping for exactly that, I glanced in that direction, willing him to appear.

"Will do," Russ answered. "Talk to you in a few minutes. Be careful." The call ended and he came to sit beside me on the bed, wrapping his arm around my shoulders. "Don't worry, Cami. I'm sure he's okay. Try to breathe. Come on, in and out, in and out, nice and slow."

His coaching suddenly reminded me of Dylan at my Lamaze class. I'd give anything to be back at that day right now. Leaning my head against Russ, I let him attempt to comfort me while I watched every second ticking by on the clock.

Soon we heard the wail of another siren.

"That's probably Chris. Hang in there. We should hear something soon."

"I hope so. I mean, I'm sure Chris is right and I'm just overreacting. It makes sense. If something happened, Dylan would want to make sure everyone is okay. He is a paramedic after all. He wouldn't pass by someone needing attention. I'm just feeling over stimulated with everything else that's happened." I wasn't sure who I was trying to convince, Russ or me.

Hearing a deep voice talking outside my door, I turned, relief pouring through me, but it was my parents who entered.

"Good grief! It's a mad house out there. We were lucky to get in when we did. Apparently there was a shooting next door and the hospital is on lockdown until it's resolved. The guard had to vouch for us," Mom said.

"Hi, Russ. How are you?" My dad stepped over and shook his hand. "Good to see you, again. If anyone can cheer up Cami and Dylan, it's you." He glanced around. "Where is Dylan?"

"He's next door at the store." I stared helplessly at my parents.

"Oh, dear." My mom's grim face told me she was thinking exactly the same thing I was. "Brandt, go see if you can find anything out for us. I'll stay here with Cami and Russ."

"All right. I don't know if they'll be giving out any information over there, though."

"Tell them your son-in-law is there. That has to be good for something."

Russ's phone rang right then and he glanced

down. "It's Chris." He answered the call, putting it on speaker. "Chris? What's going on?" he asked.

Chris sighed heavily. "Try not to panic, okay? I'm trying to take care of things. Dylan's been arrested. He shot and killed Gabby Martinez."

CHAPTER TWENTY-SIX
Dylan-

The door opened and I glanced up from where I was seated in the interrogation room, waiting to be . . . well, interrogated. Chris entered, quickly closing it behind him.

"They're granting me a professional courtesy and letting me talk to you first. I also told them you needed to have a lawyer before they questioned you." He sat in the chair across from me. "No one is in the booth behind us and I'm holding the key to that room, so you can talk to me freely. This is off the record, strictly brother-to-brother."

I shook my head, glancing at him. "How's Cami?"

"Honestly? She's about to go insane. I promised her answers. So let's hear them."

"There's not much to tell. I went to grab a few things at the store. As I was leaving, I thought I saw a girl that looked like Gabby, so I followed her."

"You didn't think to call me first?" he asked incredulously.

"Of course I did, but if you'll remember, I'm currently without a phone, thanks in part to you."

Chris sighed and ran a hand through his hair. "Go on."

"As I got closer, she walked into another department. I saw her go down the aisle in the hardware department. I continued past, pretending to be studying some toolboxes at the end. I waited until she turned and I was positive it was her. She still didn't see me, so I approached her and ask her if she was picking out a hammer to bludgeon someone with."

"You didn't?" Chris said, shocked.

"On my word. That's exactly what I said. She glanced up and saw me, then tried to run, but I grabbed her arm and pushed her back. She stumbled against some of the tools and a whole bunch of things fell, but she looked like she was going to bolt again, so I pulled my weapon on her."

"And what, exactly, was your plan at that point?"

"I didn't have one. After briefly considering how easy it would be to pull the trigger and be done with it all, I figured I'd keep her talking until someone noticed me holding her at gunpoint. I'd tell whoever that was to call security and the cops."

"And did she talk?" he pressed. "Did she say if she was involved in any of this?"

"She did. She blamed Cami and me for her

arrest. Apparently the jail she was in had some extra friendly inmates and guards, if you get my meaning."

He sighed. "I do."

"You might want to run her history and see where they were keeping her. It sounds like bad things are being done to the prisoners there."

"I'll be sure to pass this information onto the state. What else did she say?"

"She said every time something happened to her, she plotted ways to get revenge on Cami and me."

"So she admitted her involvement."

"Pretty much, yeah."

"Then what happened?"

"I made some comment about how after knowing her in high school, I'd have thought she'd enjoy a place like that. She got pissed and threw a hammer at me and then came after me with another one, claw side out. She swung and grazed my arm, but I managed to dodge my way past her. " I shifted so he could see the long welted scratch going down my arm. "She turned and came at me again and I loaded her up."

"I'll say. What'd you do, empty the clip on her?"

"I did. It was self-defense; but I'm not going to lie, Chris, I wanted to make sure she was dead."

He leaned back in his chair and sighed heavily. "Well, all I can say is I'm glad Chief Robson had the foresight to reinstate you. Hopefully that'll pull some weight. As far as

Gabby, the department here had a crew at the hotel we believed she was staying at. They did find a gun, but the serial number is filed down. We'll send it to a ballistics team to see if they can retrieve it, but if we can tie it to the bullets pulled out of the wall in the cabin, that will make things a whole lot tighter."

"Get the security video from the store. They have those cameras everywhere in there. It'll confirm my story."

"Already being done. Anything else I can do for you today?" he asked a bit sarcastically.

"Yeah. Tell Cami I'm okay and I love her."

"That poor girl is about to crawl out of her own skin, Dylan. She can't take much more. I'm worried about her. She's had so much thrown at her so fast. And this didn't help any."

I nodded. "I know, but at least she's safe now."

"Yeah. That's a good thing. And now you can stop beating yourself up about all of this. I know how your mind works. None of this is your fault. You pointed us to the guilty party, and in the end, you took care of it. Call it done and move on. Your wife needs you, and you need her. And both of you need to take some time to mourn your baby properly, together." He stood and headed for the door.

"How long do you think I'll be here?" I asked, hating being away from Cami.

"As long as it takes for them to interview you and to verify everything you said. I'll do whatever I can to get you back to your wife as soon as possible; but you know how these things go. This isn't my jurisdiction, so I'm at the mercy of others. I'll get on the phone with Chief Robson and see what he can do from his end to help things along." He turned the knob. "Do you need anything to drink? Coffee, maybe? I imagine you're in for a long day."

I shook my head. "No, thanks. I'll be okay. Just make sure Cami is taken care of until I can get back."

"Russ hasn't left her side and her parents are with her. Your parents and my wife, however, are waiting in the lobby. So, while you sit all safe in here, I get to go out and face the firing squad."

I couldn't help chuckling. "Good luck."

"Thanks. I'm gonna need it.

***

As strange as it seemed, I never realized how happy I'd be to see this hospital. Getting out of the car, I turned to Chris. "Thanks again, for everything."

"No problem. Now get in there and see your girl. Oh! And just so you know, the guards are still stationed here, as a safety precaution. They didn't want to pull them prematurely until they had time to organize and go through the items found in Gabby's hotel room. They're bagging everything to send to forensics."

"Sounds good." Despite what I'd been through, I actually felt all right. After my testimony checked out and I'd filled out a mountain of paperwork, they released me. Chris was waiting with fresh clothing, razor, and other personal care products. We stopped off at the hotel on the way back so I could assure my parents and Sheridan all was well and borrow their shower before heading back to Cami.

I was anxious to see her, hoping we could start putting the whole stalker thing behind us. The guard let us in and I hurried around the corner, only to be brought up short.

Cami was walking down the hallway in the opposite direction. Russ was guiding her along. Just seeing her there, out of the bed and moving again, made me feel overwhelming gratitude. I was so happy she'd survived. From this view, though, I could still imagine her with her pregnant belly poking out in front. Sorrow flooded through me. This is what it should've been like—walking around the halls to help things progress faster while she was in labor.

"Are you okay?" Chris asked softly, placing his hand on my shoulder.

I sighed. "Just feeling equally happy and sad at the moment."

He nodded. "I can understand that."

I simply stood there, watching her move, observing her progress. They reached the end of the hall and turned around to come back. Then she saw me.

"Dylan!" she cried out, letting go of Russ. Picking up her pace, she started jogging toward me, discomfort etched on her face. Terrified she was going to fall; I rushed to meet her, catching her in my arms as she threw hers around me. It had to have hurt her.

"Goody. Take it easy, would you? You just had surgery. You shouldn't be trying to run down the hall. I swear you're going to take years off my life."

"Shut up and hold me. I've been terrified for hours, wondering what was going on with you."

I wasn't going to deny her request, embracing her close, but carefully, so I wouldn't hurt her. The two of us swayed lightly back and forth. "I missed you," I whispered.

"I missed you, too." She didn't release her hold on me—practically a death grip around my neck.

"I'm sorry for scaring you. That was never my intention," I said, attempting to ease her worries.

Lifting her head, she locked her gaze with mine. "Are *you* okay? I mean it couldn't have been easy for you to—,"

"Cami." I cut her off, not caring to re-live the experience ever again. "I'm fine, but I'd love to forget all this crap and concentrate on the two of us, now. Is that good with you?"

She sighed. "That would be wonderful. I'd like that."

"Have you seen the doctor this evening?" I asked and she nodded.

"He said if everything looks good tomorrow, he'll release me. But I had to prove I could walk to the end of the hall and back, which I've done several time with Russ' help. I was so nervous about everything, I had to get it all out. No offense to anyone here, but I'll be so happy to leave this place."

I chuckled. "I don't think anyone would blame you, honey. You've had a rough time."

She pushed away from me abruptly, staring at my arm where it was bandaged. "You're bleeding, again. What happened?"

"It's nothing. After," I paused, trying to decide how to continue, "everything. I was tackled to the ground by a couple of very exuberant security guards. They pulled my arm back and pinned it behind me and I felt some of the stitches pop out."

"Did they hurt you?" Her eyes were flaming with some of her old spirit and I thought she looked beautiful, despite everything she'd been through.

Shrugging, I smiled at her. "Well, it wasn't a day at the spa or anything, but I don't know if I'd say it hurt. Mostly just uncomfortable, like it would be for anyone who had two guys, over a couple hundred pounds, laying on them."

"Why did they do that? Didn't you show them your badge?"

"Yes, but if it were you, would you believe a badge or control first and ask questions later?"

"That's true." She sighed once more, running her fingers over my bandage. "Do we need to go get these redone?"

I shook my head. "Maybe, but not right now. Right now, I just want to be with you."

Glancing around, I saw that Russ and Chris had disappeared, leaving us alone for our private reunion. "Shall we get you back to bed? I don't want you getting too worn out."

Shaking her head she stared at me pointedly.

"What?" I asked, recognizing that look.

"Here I am, in the hospital, and you're still trying to get me into bed."

Laughter escaped, uncontrolled, and it felt good. "You're a funny little girl." Bending, I very gently scooped her off her feet and carried her back to the room. A blush spread across her face as we passed the nurse's station and they all chuckled at us, watching me carry her.

"That's so romantic," one of them said after we stepped through the door to her room and we both laughed, again.

"Still hauling her off to bed like a barbarian, are you?" Russ said as I carefully laid her on the bed.

"Always and forever," I replied.

CAMI LOVE

CHAPTER TWENTY-SEVEN
Cami-

It seemed fitting to me that the skies picked today, of all days, to start the Arizona monsoon season. Dylan held a big umbrella over both our heads, his free arm wrapped tightly around my shoulders as he clutched me. My tears fell with the rain as I stared at the very tiny casket that held the body of my precious baby. Glancing around our small group of ten, I saw many others whose eyes weren't dry either, and I was glad our family was here with us.

"It is often said, there is no loss greater than that of a child . . . ." The priest began. He stood at the head of the grave, reading his sermon, as he huddled under an umbrella that Russ was holding for him. "In this case, it is especially so, because the child wasn't lost by natural means, but by the actions of another."

Dylan squeezed me tighter and I leaned my head against his chest, thankful to have his support.

"One may think it's hard to get past carrying a burden of this magnitude, something that weighs your soul so heavily you feel as if you might perish. In Matthew, chapter eleven, the words of our Lord and Savior bring comfort to those who morn: Come unto me, all ye that labor and are heavy laden, and I will give you rest."

Unable to swallow past the knot in my throat, I wondered if I would ever feel that way about this. Would I ever find rest? Would I ever find peace in my heart?

I was angry—angry that this miracle of life had been robbed from me—angry that the proof of Dylan's and my love was going to be lowered into the ground. The elation we'd felt together at the idea of being pregnant and welcoming a little one into our home was gone, replaced with agonizing sorrow. Now that the immediate threat against our lives was over, the loss of my child ached bitterly inside me. The pain was much worse than the pain in my body, where my baby had been ripped from my womb.

No, this pain was black. It crept along in my veins like venom searing me as it poisoned me to the core. There was no relief from it, either. Gabby's death wasn't going to bring my baby back. It didn't make me feel better that justice had been served at the hands of my husband. I simply had to content myself to sit by and live with this for the rest of my life, knowing that every time I thought of this child, I would get to relive the anguish I felt right now. Memories of my baby would consist of a few short minutes in a funeral home, knowing the only time I got to spend with him was as he lay in a casket. It would haunt me for the rest of my days.

So, Gabby had won after all. Dylan told me her desire was to make us pay for what she'd suffered at the hands of others. Well, it had worked. Maybe not in the way she'd planned, but this was way worse than death. And she could rest in peace knowing she'd left Dylan and me aching and raw inside with grief.

I couldn't understand how someone reached that point in his or her mind. How did enacting a personal hatred against another right another wrong? It was an absurd way to think; yet uncountable battles had been fought for the very same reasons—people who disagreed with one another chose hate, death, and war to try and bring punishment and justice to someone else. How is that justice? What does it accomplish? If everyone on this planet set out to get revenge for every offense done against them, there would be no people in the world at all. Why can't we try to teach love and work things out? Why can't forgiveness be offered freely between people?

Well, now I was the one who had been wronged. Did this give me the right to punish someone else for my pain? Should I hunt down Gabby's parents and slaughter them for bringing my baby's killer into the world? Even the sarcastic thought made me ill. Truly, how could a human being, with any sort of feeling at all, do something like this to another human being?

"As we lay this infant, Cameron Hunter

Wilcock, to rest today," the priest's words drew my attention back, "we ask the Lord to help us find His promised peace in our hearts. Let us turn to one another for help and compassion, strengthening ourselves in the bonds of love. Let us pray."

I stared at the tiny casket and the spray of lilies on it that almost dwarfed it, as the priest recited his prayer. And then it was over, just like that.

"On behalf of Cami and Dylan, I'd like to thank you all for joining us today to express your sympathies," the priest said. "This ends our service. There will be a small luncheon provided by Weston and Connie Wilcock at their home."

I stood numbly as our loved ones filed by once more, hugging Dylan and me as they passed, making their way to the vehicles parked a short distance away. We thanked the minister and he stepped aside, allowing Dylan and me the opportunity to say our goodbyes in private.

"I didn't think it'd be this hard to walk away," I said in a choked whisper as the tears fell down my face. He didn't reply, simply continued to hold me tightly, leaning over to kiss me briefly. We stood there, in silence, for several long minutes, unable to bear leaving.

He squeezed me lovingly. "I love you, Goody." His words were soft.

"I love you, too," I replied.

"I was right, you know. You're a beautiful mother."

A choked sob escaped me and the floodgates I'd been trying so desperately to hold, broke. So many emotions where churning inside me. I felt like I was going to explode. Dylan wrapped me in his arms and I clung to him like he was my only lifeline in a tempest sea.

"We need to go, honey," he finally said. "There are people waiting to finish things up and I don't want to risk you getting sick in this rain while you're still recovering." Slowly, he released me and we both turned to look at the casket one more time.

Stepping out from under the umbrella, I placed my hand on the beautifully carved box, bending to kiss it lightly, saying my last words to my son. "Mommy loves you, Cameron. Sleep well."

***

The comfort of both our families around us had helped our hearts today, but I was ready for some alone time with my husband. I wanted to spend the rest of the evening and night wrapped in his arms in his old bedroom. We were staying with his parents for now, until we figured out what we were going to do about our living situation. I still hadn't been by to see what was left of our house. Dylan refused to take me, insisting that I keep resting. He kept saying he would take me later, when I was more recovered. I'd believe that when it happened. He'd been extremely overprotective of me, barely leaving my side; not that I could blame him after all we'd been through.

Catching his eye from where he was talking to his dad and Russ by the large granite fireplace, he excused himself and made his way back to me. "How're you holding up?" he asked, concerned.

"Would it be bad for us to leave and go up to your room?" I asked, reaching out and squeezing his hand. "I think I've had about all I can handle of this drama for the moment. I just want to go hole myself up with you somewhere."

"I think that's fine. Everyone will understand. Plus, this is the most you've been up and about since we came home." He helped me stand. "Hey everyone," he spoke louder, capturing the attention of the others. "Cami and I just want to say how much we love you all and we appreciate all the things you've done for us this past little while. Thanks for being with us, today. But my pretty girl is feeling worn out, both physically and emotionally, so I'm going to take her back to our room."

"Cami, sweetheart," my mom said, hugging me. "I guess your dad and I will head home if you're going to bed. The service was beautiful. If you need me, I'm just a phone call away."

"Thanks, Mom. I appreciate it." She kissed my cheek and moved to hug Dylan.

"Love you, Pumpkin," Dad said, giving me a giant hug. He kissed my head. "You've grown up too fast for my taste, but I'm so proud to see the woman you've become. Keep your chin up. Things will get better."

"Love you, Dad."

Waving to the others, we headed toward the doorway leading out into the soaring hallway.

"Let me know if either of you need anything," Connie called after us.

"We will," Dylan replied. "Thanks." When we reached the staircase, I paused, taking a deep breath as I gathered the energy I needed. Before I could take a step, Dylan quickly, and carefully, swept me into his arms and began climbing.

I shook my head, rolling my eyes.

"What?" he asked.

"My legs work just fine. I can walk up the stairs by myself."

"I don't want you to strain yourself. Besides, as you've so aptly pointed out before, I enjoy carrying you off to bed." He winked at me and it made my heavy heart feel a bit lighter.

Entering the bedroom, he deposited me on the bed, before going back to shut and lock the door so we wouldn't be disturbed. "Would you like one of those new pairs of pajamas my mom and Sheridan got you?" he asked, disappearing into the large walk in closet.

"Yeah, that sounds nice." I kicked off my shoes and reached for the zipper on the back of my dress, but the action pulled my stomach and I winced.

"Here, let me get that," Dylan said, reappearing, and he hurried over to unzip it for me.

"I feel like a dang invalid," I said. "It's irritating."

He kissed my neck. "Don't feel bad. I like helping you." Unsnapping my bra, he took it from me and handed me the loose pajama top, his eyes trailed over my body, pausing at the bandages on my stomach. "How's everything feeling? Why don't you lie down and let me check your dressings for you. They may need to be changed, again."

I chuckled, doing what he asked. "They're probably fine. I think the paramedic in you just likes to play with bandages, as often as you seem to want to change them."

He didn't share my humor. "I don't want to risk anything getting clogged up or infected around your incisions. Plus, I like to make sure everything still looks okay. It's important for you to stay as healthy as possible. You're body has been through a lot. That's why I keep telling you to rest and take it easy."

"I can't lie in bed all the time. Even the doctor said to get up and walk around more each day.

"Exactly—walk—not plan or attend a funeral or visit with and entertain all the guests afterward." He laid out the supplies to change my dressing, sliding his hands into a pair of latex gloves. "And between all that walking needs to be resting, and lots of it."

I was too tired to argue with him, choosing, instead, to let him inspect and bandage me up, again.

"Looks good," he finally pronounced, pulling off the gloves. "Would you like your pajama pants, or do you just want the shirt for now?"

"I'll take the pants, too." Setting them beside me, he grabbed the old dressings, disposing of them before putting the other supplies back in the basket on the shelf. Turning back the covers, he waited for me to climb in and then covered me. "Are you going to join me?" I asked as he loosened his black silk tie, pulling it free. He began unbuttoning his dark gray shirt, slowly revealing his sculpted body beneath and I couldn't take my eyes off him.

"That's my plan, if it's okay with you."

"Yes, I just want to snuggle." I wanted to wrap up in his arms and not think about anything; but I knew there was no escaping the thoughts rumbling around in my head. He shrugged out of his shirt, tossing it on the bed before unbuckling his belt and letting his suit pants hit the floor and stepping out of them. Sitting on the end of the bed, he kicked off his shoes, before going for his black socks.

Glancing at me as he removed them, he gave me a half smile. "You sure seem to be watching with avid interest. Do I still make you blush?" Smiling softly, I nodded against the pillow, drawing the blankets up closer around me.

Leaving his clothes and shoes where he'd dropped them, he came around to his side of the bed, climbed in and scooted over beside me, slipping his arm under my head. I rolled over, curling into the warm cocoon he created.

"What's worrying you, Goody?" he asked, not missing a thing. "I can practically see the gears shifting in your head. Talk to me."

Tracing my finger over one of his pecs, I sighed. "I'm just having a bit of a pity party today is all."

"You've earned a pity party. Am I invited?"

I gave a small laugh. "You always are."

"Are you thinking about what the doctor told you?" he asked, pegging my reason for worrying with ease.

Nodding, I closed the mere millimeters between us, wrapping an arm around his waist as he hugged my shoulders, rubbing my back in a soothing manner.

He sighed heavily. "I know it's not an easy thing, but I think you should concentrate on getting better and we'll deal with each step as it comes. What if all the worrying is for nothing? Then you've wasted all that time and energy on it."

"Dylan. I don't think I could ever get over not being able to have any more kids. My arms ache for my baby. To think there may never be another, it's almost more than I can bear."

"Listen. We're going to do the best we can. We'll let you heal for at least a year and then, if everything checks out, we can try again. The doctors can reevaluate the scar tissue and we'll go from there."

"And if it doesn't work?" That was my real fear.

He held me tighter. "I promise you, I'll get you a baby one way or another– even if we have to adopt."

"But I want *your* babies—you and me together."

"Then we'll hire a surrogate if needed, but I don't want you worrying about this right now. I know it's scary for you, and it's a terrible thing for me to ask, but I want you to focus on now and getting better."

"Will you be disappointed? Will you regret your choice?" I asked, my voice small, a crazy need to hear him say whatever he was feeling overcoming me.

"Cami, honey, I want you no matter what. If you had told me you couldn't have kids when we got together, I still would have chosen you. If you were maimed, blind, deaf, or dumb, I'd still want you. Just having your presence in the same room with me is enough. I love you. You're perfect for me now, right here, in this minute."

I smiled against his skin, his declaration warming me. "So, you're saying you wouldn't change anything about me?" He paused, and my breath caught, wondering why he was hedging. Lifting my head, I stared up at him. "What's wrong?"

Locking gazes with me, he smiled softly. "Nothing, but there is one thing I'd change."

My heart fell a little with his words. "What's that?"

"Can we please get your hair put back to your natural color? I miss my redhead."

I laughed and pinched him.

"Ow! What was that for?" He grinned.

"For scaring me. You," I searched for a word, ". . . big meany."

Laughter rumbled through him and I snuggled against him. "I could never be mean to you, Goody."

DYLAN LOVE

CHAPTER TWENTY-EIGHT
Dylan-

"What do you think?" I asked Cami. "I know it's only temporary, but it can be ours while we decide what we want to do, whether buy or build." Watching her as she stood on the sidewalk, her gorgeous red hair stirring in the slight breeze, I thought she looked beautiful as she stared up at the house. "I know it might be a bit more modern than our style, and it's not quite as big as our other house, but it's loaded with all the bells and whistles. And we can swim everyday—not to mention it's furnished, which is a huge plus for us right now." I waited, hoping she'd say yes.

She glanced over at me. "You aren't fooling me one bit, you know."

I smiled, knowing she was teasing me. "And what does that mean?"

"You're in love with the man cave in the basement. That theater room is calling to you like the song of a siren. Right now, you're imagining all the action flicks you and Russ could watch together, or all the video games you can play on that screen."

Laughing, I pulled her into my arms. "And you. Don't forget I can do all those things with you, too."

"Mmhmm." She narrowed her eyes at me. "Do things with me? Is that code for yelling at me to bring you more popcorn?"

I laughed harder. "You have no faith in me. Don't you remember that baby grand piano you ran your fingers across so lovingly? Admit it. You want that just as badly. I could see you writing and transposing music there. Plus, the rent is month to month, so we aren't stuck here. We can leave whenever we want."

She sighed, smiling at me. "Rent the house, Dylan. You don't need to keep trying to convince me. I'm more than ready to have a place of our own, again. I mean, staying with your parents has been great and all—."

"Goody. I get it. No need to explain." I loved that she rattled on when she got all nervous or excited about things. And this was definitely making her nervous. Hugging her tighter, I turned to the realtor who was waiting patiently over by her car while we discussed things. "We'll take it," I called to her and she smiled.

"Perfect. I'll get the contracts out and you can sign them right now. I'll process everything tonight and you can have the keys in the morning."

"Come on," I said, loosely draping my arm around Cami's shoulder as we walked over to the agent. "You can't tell me you don't love the house. I know you too well, and I know that you're excited, too."

She smiled and elbowed me slightly in the ribs. "Quit picking on me. I already gave in to your persistent persuading."

"Hey, how are you holding up so far today? Are you feeling okay?" I asked, worried about her. "I don't want this to wear you out. You can sit in the car if you want and I'll bring anything that needs signing to you."

"Dylan, I'm fine," she replied, sounding annoyed. "You don't have to keep asking. I promise I'll tell you immediately if, for some reason, I'm suddenly not fine."

My ringing phone drew my attention away from the transaction. I retrieved it from my pocket, seeing it was Chris on the caller ID. "Hey, Chris. What's up?"

"I'm sorry to bother you. I went by the house, but your mom said you were out taking Cami for a drive."

"We're actually house hunting."

"Really? How's that going for you?"

"It's going great, actually. We're signing the rental papers on a new place right now. I can't wait to show it to you. Maybe Cami and I can host a get together with you and Sheridan, after Cami feels better."

"We'd love to do something with you both. Congratulations. I can't wait to see it."

"So, did you need something?" I asked, curious about why he called.

"Actually, I just had some news, not that it's

any big surprise."

"Okay." I found my shoulders tensing in anticipation of whatever he was going to say.

"We got a ballistics report back on the gun. It was a perfect match for the bullets recovered from the crime scene. Gabby's prints were also on the weapon, too. So you can rest easier about that."

"Did they find out where she got the gun?" I asked and I noticed Cami immediately stiffened in reaction to hearing that word. Reaching out, I began running my hand over her hair and down her back, mouthing the words, "It's all good," so she wouldn't worry. The realtor was still grabbing things out of her car, so I motioned for Cami to walk away from the vehicle with me, not wanting to alarm the woman with our conversation.

"Not yet. They have managed to pull some of the serial numbers off and they're running partial numbers to see if it might match up with one reported lost or stolen. They're still working on it, though. So far everything is looking great and adding up nicely. That's really the only loose end, and it won't make or break the case, anyway. I just thought you'd like to know."

"Well, at least that's something. What about her family? Have we heard anything about them? I can't imagine what it would be like to hear your kid was involved in a crime like this."

"I'm told they didn't have a lot to say. Apparently they've had problems with her for a long time. They'd hoped she'd straightened up after going to jail. They claimed her remains and were given the pertinent details of what happened. Your identities were left out of that, so they haven't been passed on to anyone else."

I grunted. "So, you're saying I don't have to keep looking over my shoulder for angry family members who hold a vendetta anymore?"

He chuckled. "Yeah. Something like that."

"Thanks, Chris. I'm glad we survived all of this. Now I've just got to live through telling mom that Cami and I are moving out."

"Good luck, bro," he replied with a laugh. "I don't want to be in your shoes. I know she's liked having you there where she can cluck over you like a mother hen."

"Yeah, and the clucking is getting to be a little much—not that I don't love and appreciate it."

"You don't have to convince me. I remember when Sheridan and I stayed with them while we were waiting to close on our house. Love them? Yes. Live with them? No. And I mean that in the nicest way possible. Let me know how things go with the house and if you need any help with anything."

"Will do. Thanks, Chris." I ended the call and glanced at Cami. "So, did you get the gist of all that?"

She nodded. "I'm assuming they got the match between the gun and the bullets."

"Yeah. They said the only thing that hasn't come back is a confirmation on the serial number, but that won't affect the case at all. The police just wanted to know where the weapon came from."

"Knowing Gabby, she probably could've picked it up from any of the people she hung out with." She pursed her lips together. "I'm sorry. I shouldn't talk about her like that. I'm just a little . . . bitter."

"You aren't saying anything that'll hurt my feelings. I understand exactly how you feel."

"And yet, you still took the time to ask about her family." She slid her arm around my waist. "That's why I love you so much; you know that, don't you?"

Arching an eyebrow, I glanced at her. "Because I asked about someone's family?"

"No. Because you can be this big tough go-out-and-get-the-bad-guy kind of guy and then turn around and be so compassionate to someone you could possibly lay blame on. It's inspiring."

I sighed. "I just," I stopped, not wanting to upset her.

"What? Tell me?"

"We just lost our child. They lost theirs, too. And whether or not Gabby was a good person, she was still their little girl. You don't just stop loving your kid because they're troubled. My parents taught me that. Now that I'm in that realm of parenthood, I understand; and I sympathize with them."

"How'd I get so lucky to get such a good man?" she asked with a smile.

"I'm the lucky one." I winked at her. "Now let's rent this house."

***

"You're moving out?" I did my best to remain

serious, since I knew she was genuinely upset. "When?"

"Tomorrow."

"Tomorrow? That's impossible. You have no home, no furniture, nothing. You wouldn't even have the clothes on your back if your sister and I hadn't gone shopping for you. You can't just come home and say, 'Mom, I'm moving out.' That's completely unacceptable!"

"Well, Cami and I have already signed the rental papers on a place, and it's furnished. So we won't have to worry about that. You'll love it. It has a great set up for family dinners. I can't wait to host a party." Cami was sitting in the chair behind my mom, shaking her head as she tried not to laugh.

"Does it have double ovens?" my mom asked with interest.

I nodded, hoping to keep her distracted. "Yep, and a built in barbecue in the backyard that will showcase all of dad's great grilling skill."

"What about a bar?" dad asked, his interest piqued as he sat on the couch, sipping a glass of wine.

"Not only a bar, but a man cave. It's in the basement," Cami said. "It has a pool table, popcorn machine, and a theater room filled with leather recliners."

Mom turned back, shaking her finger at me. "Now the truth comes out, *mi hijo*. You want to play with a shiny new toy!"

I laughed, knowing she was partly correct. "Actually, I want a place where Cami and I can spend some alone time—not that we don't appreciate everything you've done. I can't tell you how grateful we are. But, we've been craving some time together ever since the baby—time without doctors, nurses, and well-meaning family. You understand, don't you?"

"Yes; that I understand. And don't worry; we'll give you some time to spend to yourselves, free of interruptions."

"Thanks, Mom. We won't be that far away—even closer then we were before. Then we'll have time to decide if we want to buy or build again."

She gasped. "You aren't going to build on the same property, are you?"

I shook my head. "No. I'm going to have the property cleared and then put the land up for sale." I glanced at Cami. "I don't want any bad memories haunting us. This is a new, fresh start and I intend to make the best we can of it. So, all of you can consider this our "honeymoon" in our new house. Well, so to speak. Maybe honeymoon is a bad word."

"How about "retreat?" Cami suggested.

"That's perfect. A retreat," I agreed. "Tell you what, you give us three days to ourselves, and we'll host our first party next week and invite you over. Deal?"

She sighed. "What about phone calls?"

I laughed. "No phone calls. Three days of complete privacy. That's all I'm asking."

Lifting her hands, she shrugged. "How can I say no to that? You win. Is that what you want to hear?"

Laughing, I hugged her tight. "I want to hear that you'll love me no matter where I live. And that you'll still surprise me with all the good food you make. The guys at the fire station love your visits. It's a good thing we have a gym at work or we'd be a bunch of fat firefighters."

She pushed me away, scoffing. "There isn't an ounce of fat on any of you. Plus, you don't have the genes for it."

"If you say so." I glanced over at Cami. "Do you want to go upstairs and help me pack what clothes we do have? I figured we could take our things over in the morning when we get the keys. Then, if you feel up to it, we'll go grocery shopping. If you don't, I'll take care of it."

"That sounds good to me," she replied, slowly getting up to join me. "I think it'll be fun."

"All right. We have a plan."

My dad raised his wine glass. "Hear, hear!"

CHAPTER TWENTY-NINE
Cami-

"Wait," Dylan said, setting the suitcase down. "I need to carry you over the threshold."

I giggled as he picked me up and stepped inside. "That was so romantic," I said and he set me back on my feet on the other side. Folding my arms, I made a pouty face. "What? You aren't going to carry me to bed like you usually do?"

He laughed. "Of course I will; but let me get the keys out of the door and our suitcase inside." He winked at me and I watched him step out to grab our things. "Besides, it's not very fair of you to tease me about that. Especially when you know I can't follow through with anything, yet."

"Feeling a little lonely, are you?" I bit my lip, smiling at him.

He sighed, shaking his head as he shut the door, locking it. "Yes, and that means no tempting me, either. It's hard enough as it is."

"I bet it is," I replied, grinning as my gaze trailed down his body.

"You are *not* playing nice."

"That makes it more fun." A sudden bout of dizziness caused me to reach for him.

"Whoa," he said as he grabbed me. "What's wrong?"

I shook my head. "Just a little tired, I think. After we packed our things last night, I had trouble going to sleep. I think I'm feeling a little over-stimulated, with the baby's service, moving, and trying to recover. It's catching up with me."

"Well, that's why we're here, so we can have a break and get some rest. Why don't you lie down and take a nap while I run to the store and get a few groceries? I'll pick you up some melatonin too, and we can see if that will help you rest better."

"Can I take that while I'm pregn—," I stopped short, realizing my error. Tears flooded my eyes. "Oh my gosh, Dylan, I'm so sorry. It's been such a habit for me to check everything because of the baby. I just slipped."

"Honey, honey." He held me close and I laid my head against him. "It's a totally natural mistake. You've been pregnant for several months. It's hard to just turn that off all of a sudden. And don't apologize. We lost our baby. That's not something to just sweep under the rug or ignore. You should be able to talk freely about him any time you want. Don't keep it in, okay? You can talk to me about our son no matter where we are or what we're doing."

"The same goes for you. I'm here for you, as well." I hugged him tightly.

"I already knew that."

"How?" I smiled, loving being in his arms and hearing his voice.

"Because you are amazing." Lifting me again, he carried me upstairs to the master bedroom. Laying me gently on the bed, he climbed beside me. "Welcome home, Goody." His lips descended to mine and I placed my arms around his neck. Careful to not lie on my stomach, he deepened the kiss and I sighed, relaxing into him.

"I've missed this," I said, sliding my hands across his shoulders and down his arms to his strong, bulging biceps.

"Remember all those days of kissing, necking, petting and making out we did when we first got together?" His eyes were twinkling.

"Yes," I whispered breathlessly as he lowered his face, kissing across my cheek and down my neck.

"Remember them well, because we're stuck back there again until you get a doctor's clearance."

I sighed in frustration, and he chuckled. "Not so fun being teased when the shoe's on the other foot, is it?"

"No, not at all. But lucky for me, you happen to be an expert at kissing; so I still think I'll have plenty of fun."

He slid his tongue across the front of my neck and kissed up the other side, whispering near my ear. "I think we're going to drive each other crazy."

I laughed, stroking my hand over his thick black hair. "You're most likely right, but with all that anticipation—at some point, it's going to be explosive."

Lifting up, he stared at me, grinning. "Oh, you have no idea how explosive."

"I bet I do."

Grunting, he pushed away from me and got off the bed. "I need to leave before things get too crazy. You rest and I'll be back with food. Anything special you want me to buy?"

I bit my lip, smiling as he readjusted his clothing. "So you got me all riled up, just to leave me?"

Arching an eyebrow at me, he folded his arms. "I think it's pretty evident you aren't the only one riled up. Now answer my question."

I laughed and shrugged. "I'm good with whatever you want. My appetite has been a bit touch and go, lately."

"Understandable. I'll try to find something to tempt you. Be back soon." He headed toward the door. I got off the bed and followed him. "What are you doing?"

"Following you to the door."

"No, you aren't. I just carried you to bed because you were feeling faint. Now lay down. That's an order."

I sighed, knowing better than to argue with him. But it didn't bother me because I was really tired. "I love you. Be careful. Hurry home." He watched as I crawled onto the bed.

"I'll be back before you know it." With a

wink, he disappeared from the room.

**

The sound of the doorbell woke me up and I was briefly confused about where I was. Attempting to shake the fog from my head, I wondered how long I'd been asleep as I crawled from the bed. Quietly, I padded my way to the door and opened it, finding Russ standing on the porch.

"Hey, Russ!" Smiling, I opened the door wider. "Come in."

"I'd love to, but I can't. I'm working tonight. Besides, Dylan told me that I couldn't come by for three days because you're having 'alone time.' No, I don't want to know what that means—though I'm pretty sure I've seen most of the lead up to 'alone time' between the two of you in the past." I couldn't help my laugh as he continued. "I'm just running an errand for the chief." He handed me a large manila envelope. "This is the fire investigators report on your house. Dylan needed it for the insurance claim."

"Thanks. I'll be sure that he gets it. I wish you could stay."

Russ smiled. "So do I. Soon," he promised. "Enjoy your 'alone time'." He turned away and headed toward his pickup.

"Russ," I called after him and he glanced back. "Dylan and I are planning on having a small family get-together this weekend. We'd love it if you'd come."

"I'd like that. Sorry I've got to run. Talk to you later."

"Have a good night. Be careful." He gave a

wave and I shut the door, looking down at the envelope he'd left me. Opening it carefully, I reached inside and pulled the documents out.

Scanning through the first page, I saw it stated things that Dylan had already told me. I flipped to the second page, and the doorbell rang, again.

"Russ?" I called, turning around to open it. But it wasn't Russ on the doorstep.

"Hello, Cami. Do you remember me?" Studying the tall, brown haired guy on the doorstep, I searched my mind. His good-looking features were familiar, but it took me a moment to place him.

"Yes," I said, recognition dawning. "Derek Johnson, from high school, right?"

He smiled and nodded. "Is Hunter . . . uh, I mean Dylan, home?"

"He'll be back shortly." I couldn't figure out why Derek Johnson was standing at my door. "Wait." The memories niggled at me. I remembered he was the guy who Dylan, or in this case Hunter, used to buy his drugs from. "Weren't you arrested in the sting? I thought you were in jail."

He nodded. "I was, but I'm out now. I just wanted to drop by and tell him all he did for me."

"That's sweet. I'll be sure to tell him you stopped by. Do you have a number he can reach you at?" Something wasn't right. No one but Russ and our families had this new address. We hadn't told anyone else about our move.

"Actually, I'd like to tell him in person. Here's

my card." Glancing down, I saw him pull the gun from his waistband. He pointed it at me, leveled at almost the same place I'd been shot before. I started shaking, attempting to slam the door, but he rushed it from the other side and shouldered his way inside. Backing away as he closed the door behind him, I tried to think of someplace I could hide until Dylan got home, but my mind was blank.

"Derek, please." Trying to diffuse the situation, I raised my hands in submission and continued to back away. "I don't know what's going on here, but there has to be a way we can work it out."

"Oh, there is. I'm here to finish what Gabby started, damn girl. If she had followed the plan, she'd still be alive. But no, she was always so impatient to see you suffer."

"You were working with Gabby?" I asked. My heart sank, knowing this was the worst possible thing that could happen. Revenge against us was still in play and Dylan was going to come home and walk into a trap.

"Let's save all the gory details for when your husband gets home, okay?" He waved the gun at me, gesturing toward the stairs. "Come on. Up we go."

Slowly, I turned and did what he said. "Please don't hurt him, Derek." I hated how my voice trembled, showing my weakness. "You still have the power to put an end to this nonsense."

"Nonsense? Is that what you think this is?" he yelled and I jumped, terrified. "If I didn't need you, I'd shoot you right now, just for saying that." As if to prove his point, he shoved the barrel in my back prodding me forward. "Keep moving," he growled.

Doing as he asked, I paused at the top of the stairs, wondering where he wanted me to go.

"Into the bedroom."

I moved in that direction, fear gripping me as I wondered what he intended to do. As we entered, I glanced around, looking for anything that could be used as a weapon. "How did you know where we lived?" I asked, trying to keep him talking, stalling for time to think of something—anything.

"I've been watching you both for a while. Watching and waiting for exactly the right time. Gabby." He sighed and I dared to turn and face him. "She almost ruined everything. Stupid bitch always thought her way was best."

"Then why'd you keep her around?" I didn't know if that was the best thing to ask, but my mind was grasping at straws as I tried to stall him.

"Because—all her faults aside—Gabby was always a great lay."

I swallowed thickly. "So she was your girlfriend?" That didn't bode well for us if he was emotionally tied to her and Dylan had killed her.

He seemed to consider this, before giving me a cold smile. "Partner-in-crime would be more accurate. With benefits." He chuckled. "Now take your clothes off."

"Ex . . . excuse me?"

"Did I stutter?" he snapped. "Take your damn clothes off."

I shook my head, backing away, but he followed. "I can't. I won't."

He shoved the gun in my face. "You'll do it, now," he screamed. "Or I'm going to blow your husband's fuckin' head off the second he steps through the door. Now take your clothes off!" Reaching out, he grabbed the fabric of my blouse, yanking it down and tearing it. Immediately, I set to working on the remaining buttons with my shaking hands, not wanting him to touch me. As soon as I managed to get it open, I shimmied out of it.

"Now the pants," he said, dropping the gun lower and I complied, unbuttoning and unzipping before pushing them off my hips, allowing them to fall to the floor. "That's good. Now lay on the bed, on your stomach."

"Please don't do this, Derek," I said, tears falling down my face. Silently, I called for Dylan, yet I wanted him to stay away, too. "Please."

"Lay on the bed," he ordered again, in a flat tone. Moving, I crawled onto it, lying as instructed. "Put your hands behind your back. Lock your fingers together." Doing as he asked, he quickly straddled me. Grabbing my hands, he bound them with something that felt like twine, but I couldn't figure out where he got it. As soon as he finished with my hands, he moved and tied my feet, before roughly rolling me over so I was face up. It was then that I saw the twine wrapped around his waist, and what appeared to be vials and syringes taped to his chest. I realized, with a sinking feeling, that he had rigged his body to appear normal to anyone who might have been watching, but he was loaded up with supplies. Who knew what he had hidden in the pockets of his cargo pants?

He ran his hand over me, from my neck to the first bandage on my stomach. "Did it hurt? Being shot?" he asked.

"I don't remember much about that night." My voice was shaking.

Grunting, he ripped the bandage off my wound that'd been repaired and stitched closed. Taking his finger, he pressed down, poking the injured area and I screamed out.

"It hurts now, doesn't it?" he asked with a smile as he stabbed at it again and I arched up trying to scoot away.

The gun was suddenly at my temple.

"Don't move." His voice was deadly calm. Sliding the gun across my cheek, he caressed it in a path down my body, pausing at the bandage that covered my C-section incision. "How about this? Does this hurt?" Removing the bandage, he ran his fingers lightly over the damaged skin. "I bet it did, huh? Were you awake when the tore your dead baby out of your body?"

I didn't reply, refusing to give in to the mental torment he was pushing on me. He lifted the gun and slammed the butt of it into my incision.

"Ahhhhh!" My scream echoed off the walls as blinding, white-hot pain pierced my body. I continued screaming; wailing as sobs wracked my whole body.

He started laughing. "There. That's more of

the reaction I was going for." He dragged the gun lower, dipping the barrel between my legs. "You were never my type in high school, but I can see why Dylan might enjoy this ride. Up for a test drive, Cami?"

I shook my head, still reeling from the pain in my body. "D . . . don't. P . . . please," I managed to stutter out and he laughed, again.

"Which is it? Don't or please?" He pressed the gun against me.

"Don't," I choked out between sobs, minor relief passing through me when he removed the gun and sat up.

"Okay. You win—for now. I need to get downstairs. We need to make sure your husband gets his proper invite to this party." Reaching into one of the large pockets on the leg of his pants, he produced a roll of duck tape.

"Dylan!" I screamed hoping he was somewhere close enough to hear.

Derek straddled me and I jerked my head rapidly back and forth in an attempt to keep him from covering my mouth.

"Shut up, bitch!" He slapped me hard across the face and I cried out, momentarily stunned, as I saw stars dancing in my vision. Taking advantage, he slapped the tape against my mouth, followed by a couple others, before rolling me on my side. Jerking my legs up, he used more rope to tie my hands and legs together. "Just a little insurance to make sure you aren't stupid enough to try and get up. He slapped his hand against my stretched belly and my scream tried to force its way out my nose, leaving me struggling to get enough air. "Don't suffocate while I'm gone. I've got big plans for you." Tucking the gun into his pants, he laughed and swaggered from the room.

DYLAN LOVE

CHAPTER THIRTY
Dylan-

Pulling into the garage, I turned the car off and got out, popping the trunk from my key ring. I felt bad for taking longer than I'd intended, but I wanted to make a special dinner for Cami to celebrate our first night in our new place. Plus, I knew we needed a lot of stuff when it came to food, so I'd loaded up on staples, not wanting to leave again during our time together. Grabbing as many bags as I could carry at once, I made my way to the kitchen door, adjusting things so I could turn the knob. Pushing my way inside, I headed to the kitchen.

Grunting as something slammed into the back of my neck, I fell to the floor, groceries scattering everywhere. Shoes appeared in front of me, but then the blackness took over.

***

A groan escaped me, the throbbing in my head intense. *What the hell happened?* I thought.

Blinking, I tried to focus, but the room swam in front of me, the dizziness making me nauseated. I felt like I needed to throw up, but I couldn't move. Something was restraining me. Yanking on my hands, I realized they were tied behind the chair I was sitting in, and my feet were firmly strapped to the legs. Keeping my head lowered, I glanced around the basement, trying to figure out what was going on.

"Ah! Look who's finally coming around," a male voice spoke. It sounded vaguely familiar, but I couldn't remember from where, exactly.

Gingerly, I lifted my head. "Where's Cami?" I asked. Even in my confused state, dread managed to seep through me.

"She's right over here. She and I have been getting reacquainted, haven't we, sweetheart? I have to say, I sure can see why you enjoy worshipping at her altar. I've been itching to give her a try, myself. By the way, it's great to see you again, Dylan, or should I call you Hunter?" Squatting in front of me, he stared me in the face.

Derek Johnson? I cringed, knowing immediately we'd obviously missed a very crucial tie in on our case. There was no way this was a coincidence. He and Gabby were in this together.

"It doesn't matter what you call me," I said, trying to hold a strong posture. "It'll still be these same two hands that kill you."

He laughed; standing and patting me on the shoulder. Even that small touch caused pain in my aching head. "Good to see you still have your spirit, buddy. I'm gonna have fun breaking it."

"Why?" I asked. "We were friends. What would drive you to do this?"

"Friends?" he said calmly. "Is that how you treat your friends—lying to them, then stabbing them in the back?"

"It was my job. Not personal." I said, trying to keep him talking so I could find out what was going on. "I had no intentions of hurting anyone– only helping to make things better."

"Not personal?" He slammed his fist against the pool table. "It was pretty damn personal to me!"

"What are you talking about?" There was a touch of madness in his eyes that worried me.

"Do you know how I got into drug dealing?" he asked, seeming to completely change the subject.

"No." I craned my head to the side, trying to locate Cami's position, my blood running cold when I saw her across the room bound to a kitchen chair, in only her underwear. Her mouth had been duct taped and her bandages were missing. Her eyes were red and swollen and I feared what horror she might've already been put through.

Raged boiled through me, replacing the ice in my veins. *Stay in control of your emotions, Wilcock.* I silently commanded myself. *Rely on your training. You've got to figure a way out of this mess.*

"My dad hooked me up," Derek continued,

bringing my attention back to him.

"Your dad?" I wondered where he was going with all of this.

"I can see the judgment going through your mind right now. What kind of father would pull his kid into something like that? Well, I'll tell you. A desperate one, that's who."

"I have no idea what you're talking about." Slowly, I moved my fingers over the back of the chair, trying to find an edge or something sharp enough that I might be able to cut through the bonds.

"Did you know my little brother had cancer? No?" He continued on, answering his own question, as if I wasn't there. "That's not surprising. Not many people did. You see, my parents didn't have insurance. He needed surgery if he had any hope of surviving. So, our family did the only things we could think of to come up with some fast cash. We got into the drug business."

I could see where this was heading and it was not a good direction.

"Then, one day, this new kid shows up at school. Only he wasn't really a kid, at all. He was an undercover cop!" he yelled, as he got in my face once more. "You're the reason my brother died! Once I was arrested, no one would do business with my dad. We lost everything. *Everything.* Because of you!" Drops of spittle sprayed from his mouth onto my face as he spoke.

I shook my head. "You can't blame me for something I didn't even know about."

He straightened suddenly. "I can. I have. And I do. I came home to a dead brother and a mom who'd lost her mind from the trauma of it all. All of this started with events you set in motion."

I needed more information. "How'd you get messed up with Gabby?"

"Gabby was a stroke of luck. She got out of jail around the same time as me and came looking for a fix. We started hooking up quite a bit and got talking. When we realized we shared a common hatred of you, we started devising a plan."

"Did your plan included for her to end up dead?" I asked, taunting him. He removed his shirt, revealing all sort of strange items taped to his body. Slowly, he started peeling things off as he spoke, setting them on the pool table.

"Gabby was impatient. I kept telling her to watch and wait, that the right time would present itself. But she wanted to force things to move along faster and started doing a lot without my knowledge. We got in fight when I found out you'd both disappeared, but we caught a lucky break when she happened to recognize Cami and you on a news reel about a festival in Eagar."

My heart sank, realizing that was when our plan had fallen apart.

"She went to see if she could find you in the area, which apparently she did, but I guess she decided to take matters into her own hands. Of course, she botched the job and left me with the mess of taking care of you by myself."

"Then you've already gotten your revenge. She killed my son."

"No, that was Gabby's personal vendetta. Her jealousy of Cami consumed her, obviously to the point of stupidity." He shrugged nonchalantly. "I still need to take *my* revenge."

"Then take it—on me—but let Cami go. This is between you and me. She has nothing to do with it."

"She has everything to do with it. You took someone special away from me, so now I get to take someone special away from you. You're going to feel the same trauma my family experienced."

He was going to kill Cami. I was sure of it. Frantic emotions churned inside me, but I tried to remain calm. "Please, Derek. Come on, man. Don't hurt her. You're better than this. Let her go and you and I can figure away to settle this between us."

He shook his head and sighed. "Reduced to begging already, are you? That doesn't bode well for what's to come."

His back was to me now, attention focused on the pool table. I couldn't see what he was doing.

"Besides, someone is going to miss us, eventually," I continued. "They'll come looking for us."

"I doubt that. I overheard your buddy Russ at the door talking about the three days of alone time you asked for. That will be more than enough time for me. Russ almost caught me. That would've ruined everything. Luckily, I managed to duck behind the hedge against the house, so he didn't see me." He glanced over his shoulder. "By the way, he dropped off the arson report on your house. Just wanted to make sure you got the message." Laughing to himself, he continued working at the table.

Glancing around the room, I tried to find anything that could be used as a weapon on the off chance I could get free. Both of my personal weapons had been destroyed in the house fire and my police issued gun had been taken as evidence in the shooting of Gabby.

Turning around, Derek clapped his hands together, rubbing them vigorously. "Okay! Let's get started, shall we?" He cast a smile in my direction before going across the room to where Cami was sitting. I could feel my color draining as my panic skyrocketed. "Okay, Cami. The good news is you no longer have to hide over here in the corner." He grabbed her chair, sliding it across the smooth tile floors. The man cave I'd fallen in love with had become a place I hated. "Let's get you at center stage. You like plays if I remember right. I want you sitting right across from Dylan, so he can see you."

Cami's eyes never left me. They were wide with fear and I was almost certain mine mirrored the same expression. I was terrified and there was nothing I could do to protect her. Continuing to rub the twine that bound my hands on the back of the chair, I didn't know if I was doing any good; but I was losing hope, fast, that we'd come out of this unscathed.

"So, let me fill you in on the rules of the

party real quick." His gaze bounced between the two of us as if he were getting ready to host a game show or something. "I'm going to have a bit of fun with you, Cami, and Dylan is going to see how still and quietly he can sit through it. But for every sound he makes, you'll suffer more. Everybody understand?"

"You're a sick bastard!" I growled, the fear rushing through me was almost more than I could bear.

"No. I'm not. I'm simply allowing you the opportunity to sit by and watch someone you love being destroyed right before your eyes, knowing there's nothing you can do about it." He moved over to the pool table, picking up a couple of items– a syringe and rubber tourniquet. I was going to be sick *now*, and he hadn't even started. "One time, when you and I were hanging out together getting stoned, you asked me if I could get my hands on some meth for you. Well, I'm making good on my promise to get it for you. I also said it would cost you. And it will, but not money."

Kneeling beside Cami, he placed the tourniquet around her arm, tightening it. "Aw, you're shaking already. Don't worry, hun. This stuff will take you on quite the trip. Have you ever shot up before?" He asked in what appeared to be a caring voice and she shook her head. "Well, I'm just going to find a vein and shoot this in. Meth happens to be one of the most addictive drugs there is. Did you know that?"

"Derek, come on. Stop this nonsense. Cami's

a sweet girl. She doesn't deserve any of this." All I had was my words to reach him.

"My brother was undeserving, as well." Cami flinched when he poked her in the arm. "Oh, that's a good flash in that vein. Here goes!" He pushed in the contents of the syringe, then pulled the needle out and stood, looking at me. "I hope I mixed it right and it doesn't kill her right off the bat." He chuckled. "What fun would that be?" He tossed the syringe over to the table.

I couldn't take it. "I swear I'll kill you if you touch her again!"

"Oh, dear. Was that an outburst?" Turning back to Cami, he cocked his arm back and punched her hard in the face, snapping her head backward. Her scream came muffled from the duct tape on her face.

"No!" I hollered frantically. "Don't, please! I swear on my life! I'll do anything you want, just please don't hurt her!"

He shook his head at me. "You aren't following the rules of the game, Dylan. That was another outburst." He punched her hard again, this time causing blood to flow from her nose. She gagged, blood spraying in droplets as she tried to force the air in and out of her compromised airway.

I opened my mouth, intending to beg him to remove the tape at her mouth, but I stopped, afraid he'd hit her again. But I couldn't manage to hold back the anguish sob that escaped my chest as I shuddered with helpless rage.

Derek grinned at me. "Another sound." He

cranked his arm back to beat her again.

CHAPTER THIRTY-ONE
Cami-

The bugs were crawling all over me. Somehow they'd gotten under my skin and I could feel them scurrying around as they ate the flesh inside me, painfully chewing my nerves to raw stumps.

"Get them out! Get them out!" I screamed at Dylan, trying to watch him through my swollen eyes, but he just sat there and did nothing. Quickly, I quieted my screams, glancing around furtively as I looked for the bad guys. They were everywhere now, hiding around every corner and they were coming to get me. I was pretty sure the skeleton in the corner was evil, too. He never took his eyes off me.

Someone loomed in front of me and I yelped. "Please don't hurt me, please," I begged. "I didn't mean to do whatever it was. I'm sorry, I'm sorry." It was so cold. I shivered and tried to reach out to grab the man, but my arms wouldn't move. Nothing was working right.

"Was that another sound, Dylan?" he asked.

I shrieked in pain as the punch landed, this time, on my very sore stomach. Hanging my head, I stared at where I'd been hit, sobbing. Amazed, I watched as my incision came apart and one of the bad guys crawled out of it. They were inside me!

"Dylan! Help me!" I yelled; the sound reverberating off the walls. Yet, he sat in front of me, unmoving and unspeaking.

Glancing back at the bad guy, I stared at him, suddenly wondering if he had bugs under his skin, too.

"What're you looking at?" he asked gruffly.

"Nothing." I continued to watch him, trying to ignore the bugs that were feasting on me. "Are you going to kill me?" I asked, wondering.

"Yes, I am."

"Oh. Okay." Turning back, I watched Dylan. Tilting my head, I tried to make sense of what I could see. He looked like he had blue rivers running out of his eyes. The water was coming fast and if he didn't stop it, it was going to fill the room and drown us all. "Dylan." My words were slurred. "Turn off the water." Glancing around furtively, I saw the shadows of the other bad guys moving around us, again. They were getting closer.

"Hold still," I whispered to him. "They're everywhere. They keep trying to kill me." I could hear them, too; the tile floors were creaking each time they took a step. "Dylan!" I shrieked suddenly. "They're going to kill me! Help me! Help me! I need you!"

His chest heaved, but he didn't move from his chair, simply staring at me with his runny eyes.

"You don't love me, do you?" I asked, my heart hurting. "That's why you won't help, isn't it?" I knew I was right when he didn't answer me.

"Going to play tough guy, are you?" the bad guy said. "Let's see if I can help you out with that." The bad guy grabbed a knife that looked almost as big as he was. Raising it high over Dylan's head, he brought it down swiftly, cutting Dylan's arm completely off, the severed part falling to the floor and flopping around like a fish out of water.

"Ahhhhh!" Dylan cried out, as blood sprayed from him like a machine gun around the room.

"There's that sound I was looking for." The bad guy turned to me, all dressed up in his baseball uniform, now. Lifting his bat, he did a couple of test swings. However, it was too late by the time I realized my head was the ball.

DYLAN LOVE

CHAPTER THIRTY-TWO
Dylan-

I was killing my wife. With every little hiccup, sniff, or sob I couldn't manage to keep in, I watched her move closer and closer to death. And I couldn't do anything, but watch. Any begging or pleading on my part only brought her nearer to her demise. This was hell—pure agony. Derek had delivered his message very effectively, but I didn't think he planned on stopping any time soon.

"Well, damn," he said, stepping backward as he observed Cami's drooping body in the chair. "Looks like I got a little too aggressive that time. I knocked her out."

I was glad, even feeling a moment of relief pass through me. I didn't want her to feel anymore. In fact, I almost wished she would die, just so her suffering would be done. Watching this was eating me alive—I could only imagine what it was doing to her.

"How's that cut on your arm?" Derek asked,

bending to check it with a concerned look. He poked and prodded around it, causing me to grit my teeth. "Ah, it's not too deep. That's good. I can't have you bleeding out too early. There's still the second act to get through." He patted me on the shoulder. "Why don't you take a breather for a moment? All of this aggression has made me hungry. I think I'll go check out the food you bought. Would you like something?"

I'd like to cut your head off and rip your spine out of your neck, I mused, glaring at him. If he thought he was going to get me to say something that easily, then he was stupid.

Laughing heartily when I didn't fall for his trap, he started whistling a little ditty as he made his way upstairs. As soon as I could hear him banging around in the kitchen, I let the emotion lose I'd been trying so desperately to hold back, shuddering violently as I sucked in a breath.

Cami was a mess, beaten terribly. He'd removed the duct tape, thankfully; but the only way I'd even recognize her right now, would be because of her red hair. Some of it was plastered against her scalp, and I noticed a steady stream of blood coming from a cut on her forehead. It ran down a strand of her hair, slowly dripping into her lap. Her face was mottled and swollen, and bruises were evident on her midsection. It appeared that a few of her stitches had popped, as well, and I kept imagining it opening completely and her intestines falling out. I wanted so badly to scoop her up and take her out of here, get her to safety, but I knew that wasn't going to happen any time soon. If only there were some way I could redirect his attention, so he'd take his aggression out on me instead of her. I racked my brain for a plan, coming up empty repeatedly. Anything I said or did would be taken out on her. I couldn't risk that.

Derek reappeared, holding a big sandwich, a bag of chips, and the movies I'd rented. He glanced around the house with a nod. "I've got to say—the two of you have some pretty nice digs. Do you mind if I eat in the theater room?" He was baiting me and I refused to give in. "No? Okay. See you in a bit." Disappearing into the next room, I could hear him rumbling around, trying to get things set up. "You really are whipped, aren't you, Wilder? Wilcock . . . whatever your damn name is! Seriously, romance movies are all you've got? I thought a guy like you would like some action!"

Seeing him standing in the doorway, I tensed up, again. He folded his arms and stared at me. "What shall we do now?" he asked. "Any suggestions?"

The ringing of the doorbell echoed through the house, causing both of us to look toward the stairs. Instantly, he had his gun out of his pants, pointing at Cami's head.

"Make one sound, or call for help, and your girl is dead right now." He threatened, even though he didn't need to. I wouldn't risk her any more. I had no idea who could be here though, since we'd asked the family to stay away.

Whoever it was, I wished them gone, not wanting anyone else to get dragged into this mess. It was only mere seconds later that I heard Russ' voice echo through the house.

"Dylan?" he called. "Cami? I'm not trying to break into the 'alone time'. I just needed to give you another paper that fell out of the folder I brought by earlier." Silently, I was screaming for him to run, hoping he would get out of here; but my hope was short lived when I heard his footsteps on the stairs. I shook my head as he appeared, trying to warn him off, but he just came closer, a puzzled expression crossing his face.

"Hey man, what's going . . . ?" Eyes landing on Derek, he took a step backward. "Shit."

"See that chair over there?" Derek said to him, gesturing to another chair at the table in the corner near the bar. "Get it and bring it over here by Cami."

Hating that I couldn't speak, I watched as he did what Derek told him. "Listen, Derek," Russ said. "I'm not real sure what's going on here, but I know we all used to be friends in high school. Can we go back to that place for a minute and try to sort things out?"

"Grab the rope on that table, sit down, and shut up," Derek ordered. Russ did as he was told, and I felt sick that he'd been dragged into this. "Now start tying your legs to the chair—nice and tight. I'm watching, too, so make sure you do it right. If you don't, I'll shoot Cami."

Russ locked eyes with me and I could see the sympathy in them. "Dude, Dylan, I'm sorry.

Chief overbooked the shift and I got off early. I realized one of those papers fell out of the file I brought earlier. So I came back."

"Shut up!" Derek said, pressing his gun against Cami's temple roughly. Russ quit speaking and finished tying his legs to the chair. "Now, hand me your walkie-talkie, nice and easy." Removing it from the belt clip, Russ held it out. Derek turned it off, tossing it into the corner where it shattered into several pieces. My hopes shattered with it. "Clasp your hands behind you," Derek ordered and Russ complied. Derek moved quickly, tying them up, as well.

Finishing with Russ, he stepped beside me, smiling. "Well, isn't this cozy? Now you have your wife and your best friend here to keep you company. Isn't that great?"

I said nothing.

Dropping his gaze down to me, he folded his arms, frowning slightly. "You know it's rude not to speak when spoken to," he added. "For every time you don't answer me, I'm going to beat Russ over here. And every time you do make a sound, I'll beat Cami. Ready? Let's play." He chuckled; clearly enjoying his devious scheme, knowing there was no way for me to win.

My heart caught in my chest at the change of the game plan, knowing no matter what I did now, someone was going to get hurt. This was so sick—beyond sick. He was completely deranged.

"Don't you dare speak," Russ said to me, nodding his head in the direction of Cami. "She doesn't look like she can take much more."

Tears fell, as I realized my friend was prepared to sacrifice himself for her. I knew he was right, but I hated doing this.

"Who's it going to be?" Derek asked. I said nothing, knowing I was resigning Russ to a horrible fate. "Okay, Russ it is."

Jumping as each punch landed, I watched Russ's head being knocked all over the place, as Derek turned loose on him. I wanted to remind him that he'd only asked me one question, but I was sure that was what he wanted. Then he'd beat on Cami—even though she was unconscious. Trying to keep up with the rules of his supposed game was killing me. I hated being the reason harm was being inflicted on two of the people I loved most in the world.

After what seemed like an hour, Derek paused, taking a step back and catching his breath. Turning, he headed over to the wet bar and got a drink of water, guzzling it.

Russ's head was hanging, blood falling from his split lip. I could already see the swelling and bruising and I wondered what Derek's hands looked like. He had to be pretty bloody knuckled, himself. Cami and Russ both had the appearance of having been in a bad cage match gone horribly wrong.

"Got any whiskey in this bar?" Derek asked. Again I was afraid to answer, or not to.

"The whiskey is reserved for assholes. Sorry, but you're way lower than that," Russ said, licking at some of the blood on his lip.

"Do you really want to start getting smart with me, Weston?" Derek said, glaring at him. "I hardly think now is the time to piss me off."

"Ooooh!" Russ replied in an underwhelmed tone. "What're you gonna do . . . beat me?"

Despite how horrible everything was, it was extremely difficult for me to not give a snort of amusement.

"How about I beat Dylan for every smart-mouthed comment you make?"

"Go ahead." Russ held his gaze eye for eye, despite the rapid swelling there. "But if you beat him, then who's going to be conscious to watch you inflict the rest of your damage? I mean that is what this is all about, isn't it? You trying to show off and teach us what a bad ass you are? Well, I hate to break it to you, but my five-year-old nephew could tie me to a chair and beat me up, too. It's not that difficult. But I understand if you're a little chicken. I wouldn't want to face Dylan man-to-man, either. Have you seen his arms? Hell, no."

I watched Derek carefully to see if he'd take Russ' bait and turn me loose to fight him, hoping he would, knowing I could easily take him. Instead, he left the bar, coming around to stand in between Russ and Cami. "You know what? It's getting awful chatty in here. I think we have one too many players in this game. It's time to start the elimination round."

"Well, I don't know about Cami and Dylan, but I'm definitely voting you off the island," Russ grumbled; only to receive the barrel of the gun smashed up against his temple.

Derek glanced at me. "You get to speak without repercussions. Which one lives and which one dies? The choice is yours. But make it fast, because if you don't choose, they both die. Name the person who dies right now."

Everything inside me stopped—my heart, my breath, my life, as my mind screamed at the injustice of this. How could he do this? How could he make me choose between them? I loved them both!

Moving the gun away from Russ, he pressed it against Cami. Poor Cami, the love of my life, who was so severely beaten she was probably near death anyway. It would be a blessing for her to die at this point. Who knew how many other ways he could torture her? He'd already made lewd comments regarding her. I wouldn't be able to stand seeing her violated in other ways, too. Could I be selfless enough to remove her from this horror—even if death was the only way to do it?

My gaze switched to Russ, my friend who'd been beside me through thick and thin. My friend who'd taken the fall when Clay tried to poison me. My friend who'd made sure Cami was safe when I was dealing with Ripper. He was my brother-in-arms in the fire department. Hell, my brother from another mother.

"Who's it going to be?" Derek shouted, growing angrier by the second. He turned the gun back on Russ. Who was it going to be? Russ stared at me, awake and whole. Cami was oblivious. She'd never know what hit her.

I couldn't do this. "Shoot me!" I hollered, every muscle in my body shaking with rage. "If you want someone so badly, then take me!

That's what you want anyway! So just do it!"

"Make your choice or they both die right now!" Derek screamed, growing even more irate, pushing the gun so hard against Russ' head that he was practically leaning sideways.

A sob caught in my throat as I stared at Russ. He held very still looking straight at me and slightly nodded his head. "Russ!" I cried out, my heart breaking. "I choose Russ!" My vision swam with tears, guilt swamping me.

Derek smiled wickedly. "That's what I thought." He cocked the gun against Russ's head but then whirled it around to point at Cami.

"Wait! What are you doing? I said Cami lives!" Straining against my bonds, I was so fearful I felt like I might actually be able to snap them.

Derek stared at me with a smug look on his face. "I just wanted to know which one you wanted the most." He slowly applied pressure to the trigger and a sob escaped me. "No!" I screamed, rage flooding my system. Unable to stand it I tried lunging at him with the chair still attached to me, succeeding only in tipping myself over.

Bam! The shot echoed through the room and I flinched, vomit rising in my throat as the reality of what had happened hit me full force in the stomach. "Cami!" I hollered as grief wracked my body in the most excruciating form I'd ever felt—worse than any agony I'd ever experienced.

But it was Derek who fell on the floor beside

me, blood spraying rapidly from the gaping wound in his head. Eyes wide, I turned to see Chris standing in the doorway, holding a smoking gun. More officers ran into the room, checking every corner before rushing to our aide.

Panting as if I'd run miles, I stared at him, thinking I'd never seen a more beautiful sight in my life. "How'd you know?" I choked out, my voice raspy.

He moved beside me, crouching to help remove the ties that bound me. "Ballistics came back with a match on the serial number of the gun. It's registered to Derek's father. I knew then that someone else was involved. When Wilson called to say Russ had never come out of the house and the garage door was open, I realized something was going down. I alerted the S.W.A.T. Team and came as fast as I could."

I looked at Russ, tears forming in my eyes. "You lied. You told him you were here alone."

"Well, I sure as hell wasn't dragging Wilson into this. He was our only hope."

Wilson entered the room at that moment, helping to carry a gurney and Russ stared at him.

"Hey, dude. Not to be pissy or anything, but you sure took your damn time. I've been in here getting the crap beat out of me."

Wilson shrugged. "Sorry. I was texting my mom. It took me a while to realize something was wrong when I couldn't reach you on the radio."

Russ rolled his eyes. "Tell your mom she

owes me cake or something."

"Will do, bro."

As soon as I was released, I turned to the medical crew working on securing Cami to a backboard. "He gave her meth, too. And then he beat her. She was tripping pretty badly. I only hope it staved off some of the pain for her." I couldn't stop shaking.

"We'll take good care of her," Wilson said and I relaxed a little, knowing I trusted him with my own life on a daily basis.

Another officer released Russ and I went to him, grabbing him in a giant bear hug. "Russ." I could hardly swallow, as my feelings for him seemed to form a knot in my throat. "I understand if you can't be my friend after this. I don't know how to make this up to you. I'm so sorry." I'd marked him for death. Who could overcome something like that?

"Hey," Russ grabbed me by the shoulders and pushed me back. "Dylan, look at me. Look at me, man." I stared into his eyes seeing no blame there. "In my mind, there was no choice. It was always Cami. You will always choose Cami. And that's the way it should be." He draped an arm loosely around my shoulders. "I don't want you to sweat it, at all. However, have the two of you ever considered moving away from here? You know, to a place where people aren't trying to kill you?"

I knew he was trying to deflect the attention from himself, but I was okay with that. Staring at Cami, who was being attached to all sorts of IVs and tubing—again, I made up my mind right then and there. "As far as I'm concerned, as soon as she's better, the two of us will be on the next plane out of here. There's no way I'm staying."

"Well, if you don't mind, count me in, because I'm getting a little sick of all this, too," Russ said.

"You'd come with us?" I asked surprised, figuring it would be a relief for him.

"Hell, yeah. You and Cami are my family. I do anything for you two." He smiled.

"You've already proved that, Russ." I patted him on the shoulder. "But if you want to help me out right now, you'll have someone check you out. You're looking pretty rough, buddy."

"Shoot, you mean this?" He scoffed. "These are just battle scars. Chicks will dig them."

I shook my head and guided him toward the stairs, signaling for one of the medics. "Take care of him, would you?" I asked before turning back to him. "Treatment now—jokes later, when I know you're okay." I watched as the medic guided him up the stairs before turning back to Cami. She'd been moved to the gurney and was being strapped down so they could take her outside. I was afraid to touch her, worried that I'd hurt her, so I bent down by her ear.

"I love you, Goody," I whispered. "And on my life, I swear, no one will ever touch you, again."

CAMI LOVE

EPILOGUE
Cami-
One year later

Smiling, I laughed as I watched Dylan and Russ tossing a Frisbee between them in the park on the Battery. Never in a million years would I have thought the three of us would end up moving to Charleston, South Carolina—let alone together. I'd never even been to this side of the country in my whole life, but it was turning out to be a good experience for us. I loved all the history and enjoyed learning more about it.

Dylan had gone crazy, buying one of the original southern mansions that faced the water. The house was humongous, but beautiful, even though it was in need of a lot of renovations. I thought it was a good project for all of us and the more we got done, the more excited I became about it.

Russ had pitched in a bit of his own money, not that Dylan wanted him to, but he'd wanted to move in with us. Ever since our ordeal together, Dylan denied him nothing—which I thought was sweet. I loved having Russ around, occupying the third floor and renovating it to be his own place.

I laughed to myself as I continued watching them with our pretty yellow Lab, Sophie, barking energetically as she raced between them. It was obvious they were all having a good time. I was pretty sure Russ and Dylan would be friends forever, seeing that they both still worked in the emergency services together. They were almost always together, cooking up new adventures and things to do. But my favorite moments were still the ones Dylan and I shared alone, together, with only each other. No matter where we lived, or who we were with, there was only one place that I truly called home—and that was in Dylan's arms. Even though we'd all been through lots of therapy to help overcome our ordeal, he was still my safe place.

Lifting my hand, I lightly rubbed the small bump in my nose where Derek had broken it. Thankfully, I didn't remember a whole lot about that day, and I didn't want to. I simply wanted to move on and put the scars of the past behind us. Dwelling on them would only ruin our future.

"Are you sure you don't want to play, Cami?" Dylan called to me.

I shook my head. "No. I'm okay. I'm having fun watching the two of you."

The two of them shared a glance, one that said they weren't falling for it. Dylan held the Frisbee out, allowing Sophie to take it in her mouth. "Take that over to Momma and tell her to come play with us."

Sophie dutifully ran over to me, dropping the disc in my lap, panting and wagging her tail. I pet her, rubbing her head sweetly. "You want me to play?" I asked; and she barked. I laughed. "Not today, okay? Maybe next time."

"What's the matter?" Dylan said, coming up to me, his face a mask of concern. "Are you not feeling good? You've seemed kind of out of it, today."

Glancing up at him, I smiled. "I'm okay. I just found out I'm pregnant."

I laughed as his whoop of glee made everyone in the park turn to look at us. Dragging me to my feet, he twirled me around, spinning me until I was dizzy.

"Dylan, you're making me sick!" He lowered me instantly, staring into my eyes, all the love in the world reflecting back out of them.

"You're sure?" he asked smiling.

"I'm sure."

Pulling me into his arms, he nuzzled his face into my hair. "Cami, I love you. I swear I'm the happiest man on the planet right now."

I laughed. "We still have a problem we need to address."

"What's that?"

"You got me pregnant while I was on birth control . . . again."

He laughed heartily, squeezing me even harder. "Good thing we bought a damn big house, isn't it?"

Coming Soon
The companion to the CRUSH series:
SMOLDER
Russ's Story

About the Author:

Lacey Weatherford is the bestselling author of the popular young adult paranormal romance series, Of Witches and Warlocks, and contemporary series, Chasing Nikki, Crush, and Tell Me Why. She has always had a love of books and wanted to become a writer ever since reading her first Nancy Drew novel at the age of eight.

Lacey resides in the beautiful White Mountains of Arizona. She lives with her wonderful husband and children along with their dog, Talley, and cat, Minx. When she's not out supporting one of her kids at their sporting/music events, she spends her time reading, writing, blogging, and visiting with her readers on her social media accounts.

Visit Lacey's Official Website:
http://www.laceyweatherfordbooks.com
Follow on Twitter:
LMWeatherford
Or Facebook:
Lacey Weatherford

Printed in Great Britain
by Amazon.co.uk, Ltd.,
Marston Gate.